Also by Leonard Schonberg

Deadly Indian Summer

Fish Heads

Legacy

MORGEN'S
WAR

MORGEN'S WAR

A Novel by
Leonard Schonberg

SUNSTONE
PRESS

SANTA FE

Sunstone books may be purchased for educational, business, or sales promotional use. For information please write: Special Markets Department, Sunstone Press, P.O. Box 2321, Santa Fe, New Mexico 87504-2321.

Library of Congress Cataloging-in-Publication Data:

Schonberg, Leonard, 1935-
  Morgen's war / by Leonard Schonberg.
    p. cm.
  ISBN 0-86534-441-8 (pbk.)
  1. Afghanistan--History--Soviet occupation, 1979-1989--Fiction.
  2. Americans--Afghanistan--Fiction. 3. Physicians--Fiction. I. Title.

PS3569.C5258M67 2005
813'.54--dc22

                              2004022448

Published in

WWW.SUNSTONEPRESS.COM

SUNSTONE PRESS / POST OFFICE BOX 2321 / SANTA FE, NM 87504-2321 /USA
(505) 988-4418 / ORDERS ONLY (800) 243-5644 / FAX (505) 988-1025

This novel is dedicated to
International Rescue Committee,
Doctors Without Borders (*Medicins sans Frontieres*),
and to my son, Daniel

The frontiers are not east or west, north or south,
but wherever a man (con)fronts a fact.

—Henry David Thoreau

1

Robert Morgen walked out of the small terminal building in Peshawar, Pakistan into warm, hazy sunshine that seemed to be filtered through sand. He felt like he'd stepped into a sepia-toned world. Dazed by three nights of bad sleep since leaving New York, he set his suitcase and a large cardboard carton down and fished his sunglasses out of his inside jacket pocket. He rubbed his eyes with his knuckles before putting them on.

Pakistanis in *shalwar kameezes*, long shirts and baggy trousers, filed past him to meet waiting relatives. He'd been the only westerner on the PIA flight from Karachi.

"Taxi, mister?" "Best price with me, mister." Taxi drivers surrounded him, jostling each other to get as close as possible to their prospective fare.

Robert forced a smile and shook his head as he scanned the empty street in front of the airport, wondering where his ride was. He'd called from Frankfort about the last-minute change in his flight, but perhaps no one had bothered to relay the information. The passengers he'd disembarked with had already melted away into waiting cars or taxis.

At that moment a Land Cruiser pulled up in front of the terminal and the passenger door sprang open. A tall, bearded figure dressed in a sport shirt and jeans stepped out almost before the vehicle had come to a stop.

"Good to see you again," Sean Cooper said, grinning and pumping Robert's hand. "Sorry we're late. We had a flat. Was your trip okay?"

"Yeah, just long. I'm glad you got the message about the flight change."

"It happens all the time. Let me give you a hand with this, "Sean said, lifting the carton.

The taxi drivers had backed away as soon as Sean stepped out of the Land Cruiser. They huddled together on the lawn in front of the terminal, talking and smoking, watching the two foreigners.

"This is our driver, Zaheer," Sean said, while the Pakistani stowed Robert's luggage in the rear of the vehicle. "Zaheer, Doctor Morgen."

The driver shook Robert's hand. "Good day to you, sir," he said, bowing his head.

"You can sit up front," Sean said, clambering into the rear passenger seat.

They drove past armed Pakistani soldiers at the airport exit who gave a cursory glance at the Land Cruiser with its International Refugee Assistance logo and waved it through.

"Tomorrow is a day off, so you'll have a chance to rest up from your trip."

"Tomorrow's Friday," Robert said, thinking Sean had mixed up his days.

"Muslim Sabbath, so no patients are seen in the clinic. I'll take you to your quarters so you can drop off your bag, then we'll head over to my house. Sam—that's short for Samantha—is taking the afternoon off so we can all have lunch together."

Robert remembered Sean telling him and Alyssa when he visited them in Vermont that he was living with an English woman who worked with Save the Children.

"I can't believe it's been three years since we last saw one another," Robert said. "My son still remembers your dog."

Sean laughed. "Yeah, my mother writes that Kiska is showing his age a little, but otherwise he's fine. How's Davey doing? I didn't recognize him in the photo you sent me. He's gotten so big. I was really sorry to hear about you and Alyssa."

"Yeah, it's been a rough time, especially for Davey."

"I got the feeling when I visited you she wasn't exactly thrilled about having to live in Vermont."

"That's putting it mildly. She's been working in New York for more than a year. Davey lived with me until she asked me to bring him down in January for a short visit. I did and she wouldn't give him back."

Sean shook his head in sympathy.

"So I filed for divorce. It'll be final soon. Anyway, you look the same. The work goes well?"

"Busier than ever. I'll fill you in at lunch."

"Is the hospital near where I'll be staying?"

"Only a two block walk. And it's about that far from my house."

They drove deeper into the city. Peshawar's traffic became a bedlam of cars, garishly decorated trucks, dilapidated buses, and bullock carts.

"You can see why I prefer that Zaheer does the driving. I think you have to be born into this to cope with it."

At a traffic circle three tall men in turbans waited to cross. One of them, his shoulders draped in a brown blanket, held a young boy wearing an intricately embroidered skullcap. Sean, following Robert's gaze, said "They're Afghans, Pathans. Most of Pakistan's refugees are Pathans."

"Good looking people."

"They are. Some people believe they're descended from the ten lost tribes of Israel. They're as tough as they're handsome. They fought off Alexander the Great, Genghis Khan, Tamerlane, and the British. A lot of people think they'll overcome the Russians, too. They have Stinger missiles now. It's making a difference."

Sean hadn't changed at all, Robert thought. The same easy-going, friendly person he'd been when he showed up at their house in Vermont. It was the winter of 1983, less than a year after he and Alyssa had moved to West Roylestown from New York. He remembered their surprise as a pickup truck came down their driveway in the midst of a snowstorm one Saturday afternoon in late February. A malamute, the largest dog the Morgens had ever seen, bounded out of the truck as soon as the driver turned off the ignition.

"Hi, I'm Sean Cooper," he said, a smile spreading between his bushy moustache and full beard. "You must be Robert and Alyssa."

They stood in the doorway with Davey, their son, and stared at the tall stranger, bareheaded, wearing only a bulky sweater in spite of the zero degree temperature. Snowflakes settled on his unkempt mop of red hair.

"Do we know you?" Robert asked.

"Didn't Joe tell you I was coming? He said he would call you."

"Joe who?"

"Joe Ross."

Joe Ross, a urologist, had been one of Robert's best friends when he practiced in Manhattan.

"That's just like Joe," Robert said, laughing. "He never said a word to us."

Sean, looking uncomfortable, reached down to pat the dog.

"Come on in," Robert said. "It's cold out here."

The malamute forced his way past them into the house. Davey, startled, plopped backward into the snow.

"Kiska, out!" commanded Sean.

The dog leaped in the air, caromed off Cooper's chest, fell over on his back and began rolling in the snow.

Robert closed the door behind them. "He'll be okay out there?" he asked Sean.

"He's in his element. Kiska lives for snow."

"I just made some coffee," Alyssa said when they were seated in the living room. "Would you like a cup?"

"I feel foolish barging in on you like this."

"Don't be silly." Alyssa laughed and turned to her husband. "You'll have to call Joe and ask him if he forgot something."

Alyssa disappeared into the kitchen and returned moments later carrying a pot of coffee and cups on a tray. "There's milk and sugar," she said, indicating the pitcher and sugar bowl.

"Black's fine," said Sean. "Thank you."

"Joe probably told you we used to live in the city," Robert said. "He and I go back a long way. But I don't recall meeting you."

"I haven't lived in the city in a long time. Actually, I know Joe in a professional capacity. I see him as a patient."

"What brings you to Vermont in the middle of a snowstorm?" Alyssa asked.

"My brother lives in Burlington. I saw Joe yesterday and told him I was heading up there today. He asked me to drop in and see you. He said he'd call and let you know. Sorry he forgot."

Robert smiled. "Joe's a maniac. I'll have to tell you the story of how we first met."

"You said you hadn't lived in New York in quite a while. Where is home for you now?" Alyssa asked.

"I live in Pakistan."

"Pakistan!" Robert and Alyssa exclaimed simultaneously.

"I've been there for six months. In Peshawar. Are you familiar with it?" The Morgens shook their heads.

"It's near the Afghan border."

"Isn't that dangerous?" Alyssa asked. "With the fighting between the Afghans and the Russians?"

"It makes things interesting, but Peshawar is relatively safe."

"What do you do there?" Robert asked.

"I work for International Refugee Assistance. It's an NGO."

"What's an NGO?"

"Sorry. A non-governmental organization. We're providing assistance to refugee camps in Pakistan and to the Afghan Women's Hospital that just opened in Peshawar."

"Sounds like exciting work," said Robert.

"It's challenging, that's for sure. More than two million Afghans have poured into Pakistan since the Russians invaded."

Davey, fascinated by the bearded stranger, stood next to Sean's chair and stared at him.

"What's your name, little fella?"

"That's Davey," said Alyssa. "I think he likes your beard."

Sean laughed. "Want to touch it?" he said, leaning towards the boy.

Davey put his hands behind his back and stepped backward.

"Looks like he's not having any of it."

"We want to hear more about your work," said Alyssa, "but first things first. When do you have to be in Burlington?"

"I was planning to be there tomorrow morning."

"Wonderful. Then you can have dinner with us and spend the night. You'll be our first houseguest."

"I don't want to put you—"

"Really," Robert said, "we'd love for you to stay. I have a million questions for you about Pakistan and the Afghans."

"Well, thank you. Maybe the snow will have stopped before I head out in the morning."

"What does your brother do in Burlington?" Alyssa asked.

"He teaches biology at the university. Or did until he got sick. That's why I'm in the States. I took leave time so I could see him."

"What's wrong with him?" Robert asked.

"Hodgkin's. He's had it for ten years, but there's nothing more they can do for him. It's tough. He's got two young teenagers."

"That's terrible," said Alyssa.

"Fortunately his wife, Margo, is a strong woman. My mom's having a harder time with it. She wanted to come up with me, but I didn't want to put her through the long drive, especially with snow forecast."

"She lives in the city?" Alyssa asked.

"The Inwood section. She's still in the same apartment where my brother and I grew up."

"That's by the Cloisters, isn't it?"

"She lives two blocks away."

"Aren't you afraid for her? That's not a good neighborhood."

"My mother's a special woman. As the neighborhood changed, she made a point of learning Spanish. Now all the Dominican ladies have adopted her and look out for her. She goes to church with them, baby sits their kids." He laughed. "It's funny to hear little kids call her *abuela* when I'm out walking with her—that's grandma in Spanish."

"She sounds wonderful," said Alyssa.

"Kiska is her dog. As long as I had to go to Burlington, I figured Kiska should have a vacation in the country."

"Are you and your brother her only children?"

He nodded. "Yeah, things have been difficult for her, especially in the past ten years. My father died of a heart attack right around the time Michael was diagnosed with Hodgkin's. And with me being out of the country most of the time . . ." He shrugged.

"So Pakistan isn't the first foreign country you've worked in," Robert said.

"No, my first foreign country was Vietnam. I was drafted as a chaplain during the war. I was a priest then."

"I don't believe it," said Alyssa, looking at him as if she was waiting for him to deliver the punch line.

"It's true. Whenever people hear that they think I quit the priesthood because I fell in love. But that wasn't the case. Indirectly, it was Vietnam that was responsible."

"You mean the things you saw there?" Robert asked.

"There was a young lieutenant I got to know, possibly the bravest man I'd ever met. He won just about every medal the Army gives out. On one occasion he was the only man left in his entire platoon after a VC attack and he single-handedly held them off until reinforcements arrived. Anyway, it all had an effect on him. You can't see so many of your men die without it affecting you, especially when you have responsibility for them. He received a medical discharge and was sent back to Framingham, Mass, his home town, with post-traumatic stress disorder. I'd completed my tour by then and was in Newark working as a parish priest when I heard he'd killed himself. His wife called me. She was hysterical. They were religious folk and the priest up there refused to allow his burial in consecrated ground. She asked me to intercede so I went up to Framingham to talk to the priest, which was like talking to a wall. He was one of these hard-nosed guys—no exceptions to the rule, not even for a guy with a Distinguished Service Cross and two Purple Hearts. I went to see the bishop and that was a disaster. He threw me out of his office. I had to tell the lieutenant's wife there wasn't any more I could do. That was really hard. She was devastated. After I left her, I knew the priesthood was the wrong place for me. I joined the Quakers and went to work for American Friends Service Committee. I spent almost twelve years in Honduras and Zambia. Then I heard about the position in Pakistan and applied."

"I envy you," Robert said. "When I was in med school I dreamed about doing third-world medicine. Schweitzer was my idol. But most of the organizations were church-based, and I have no desire to be a medical missionary."

"International Refugee Assistance has no religious affiliation. All the

OB-GYN's who come to the Afghan Women's Hospital are volunteers. They work with the Afghan staff, training them. The Afghan doctors, all female, of course, are refugees, too. Their education was interrupted by the Russian invasion so our volunteers perform surgery with them, give lectures, and even provide many of the supplies for the hospital. Most of them are American, but we've had some Brits and one New Zealander."

"Hey, don't give him any ideas," Alyssa said with a jocularity that Robert knew was false. "We've been in Vermont for less than a year and I'm trying to adjust to that."

"She knows I've got a wanderlust," Robert said.

"I'm curious about something," Alyssa said, trying to get off the topic of medical volunteers. "When you gave up your religion, how did you replace it? You say you're a Quaker, but you were a Catholic priest. What happened to everything you believed?"

"It's a good question. Belief systems don't die easily. To be honest, I'm still struggling with it. Let's just say it's a work in progress."

"Do you go out with women?" Robert asked.

"Leave it to an OB-GYN to ask that," Alyssa said, giving Robert a disapproving look.

"I live with my girlfriend in Peshawar. She's from England and works with Save the Children. We tell everyone we're married. Muslims think its okay to have four wives, but living with a woman who's not your wife is a no-no."

"Have we asked enough personal questions?" Robert asked, laughing.

"I don't mind. Hey, Davey, should we give Kiska a dog treat? He'd probably like some company."

"Why don't you go, too, Robert. I'll start dinner."

"Don't go out of your way on my account," Sean said.

The dog plowed through the snow, raced up and down in front of the house, and almost knocked Sean off his feet.

"Kiska's a little rambunctious and he's clumsy, Davey," Sean said, laughing. "Better stay close to your dad."

"Bite?" Davey asked, pointing.

"No, he's very gentle. But he doesn't listen very well."

Sean handed Davey a large dog biscuit. "You can hold this out for him."

Kiska skidded to a stop in front of the boy, snow flying. Davey gingerly held out his hand and the biscuit disappeared into the dog's mouth, along with his mitten. Sean grabbed the dog by his collar and extracted the mitten. They all laughed.

"I think he'd get a bellyache if he ate your mitten," Sean said, handing it to Davey. Robert slipped it on his son's hand.

"This is a beautiful place," Sean said, staring at the gray-green hills partially obscured by the falling snow. "It's so quiet and peaceful."

"Too quiet sometimes for my wife. She's still a city girl."

"Big changes take time to get used to."

"Well, let's go in. Davey's getting cold."

"That fire you had going in the fireplace would be a good idea," Sean said.

"What can I get you to drink?" Robert asked when they were back inside. "I have scotch and bourbon."

"Scotch with a little water, thanks."

Alyssa bustled around the kitchen as they sat before the fire nursing their drinks. Davey crawled around the floor with his miniature cars, sometimes holding one up for Sean to see.

"You said you were going to tell me how you first met Joe," Sean said.

"Well," Robert replied, settling back into his chair, "that was about fourteen years ago. I had just started practicing in New York and joined the staff at Lenox Hill hospital." He chuckled. "It still makes me laugh. I was in the doctors' dressing room changing into scrubs for surgery when I noticed a curly-headed guy needing a shave hunched over on the sofa with a newspaper spread open in front of him. He hadn't said a word to me. 'We haven't met,' I said. 'I'm Robert Morgen.' Joe looked up at me and said: 'OB-GYN, right?' 'Right,' I said. He gave me that funny, crooked smile of his and went back to his newspaper, his lips moving as he read. 'Aren't you going to tell me who you are?' I asked, and I swear, this is what he said to me: 'Joe Ross. Urology. Communist.' I laughed out loud and he gave me this dead serious look. 'Something funny?' he said. It was about then that I noticed he was reading *The Daily Worker*. 'Great introduction,' I said. 'You really believe what you're reading in that rag?' 'You believe what you read in *The New York Times*?' he answered. 'Are you serious?' I said, starting to get annoyed. 'You're going to compare the *Times* with that propaganda sheet?' You have to picture this, Sean. Here's this guy with bulging eyes, a nose too large for his face, and a prominent Adam's apple. I've known him for exactly five minutes and he gives me this withering look. 'You need an education, my friend. Like most Americans you're being duped and don't know it. This paper tells the truth.' 'Right,' I said, walking out of the dressing room. I learned pretty quickly that everyone thought he was a good doctor and a great guy, but completely nuts. Don't ask me how it happened, but we became the best of friends. Joe and his wife, Marcy, and Alyssa and I used to get together for dinner quite often. I don't know how well you know him, but there are a lot of inconsistencies and contradictions in Joe's life. He lives in an expensive brownstone in the east Seventies. His wife's passion is shopping. She was a flight attendant on *Finnair* when Joe met her during one of his 'fellow traveler' excursions to Russia. Joe reads *The Daily Worker* and *Soviet Life* while his wife reads *Vogue* and *Harper's Bazaar*."

At that moment Alyssa appeared carrying a tray of stuffed mushrooms and canapés with anchovies. "Would you like some wine with this?" she asked.

"This is fine for now," Sean replied, holding up his glass. "Robert was just filling me in on Joe Ross. Funny guy."

"He is, but he's a sweetheart. Did you tell Sean what Joe's unfulfilled passion is?"

"I hadn't gotten to that yet. Joe hardly ever takes a vacation, and when he does travel it's always to a country with a left-wing government. The only one he hasn't been to and that he yearns to visit is North Korea, and they won't let him in because he's American. It really hurts his feelings. Marcy, on the other hand, still spends a lot of time on planes even though she gave up her job with *Finnair*, but she goes to places like Hawaii and the Caribbean. Her only complaint is that Joe won't go with her."

"Well, I'd better get back to work," Alyssa said, heading for the kitchen. "Yell if you need anything."

"Need any help?" Robert called as she headed out of the room.

"You can set the dining table," she said. "We'll eat in about an hour."

By the time they sat down to dinner, Robert felt he'd known Sean for years. "After what Robert's been telling you," Alyssa said, "you'll probably be too scared to have Joe as your doctor."

Sean laughed. "I have a few wild friends of my own. I'm perfectly comfortable with Joe. I just hope I don't have to see him again in a professional capacity." He raised his wine glass. "To friendship," he said. "And thank you for your hospitality. You're an incredible cook, Alyssa."

"Oh, I just threw it together," Alyssa said. "Next time you come, I'll prepare something special."

Robert wondered if his wife's false modesty was transparent only to him. "It is delicious, Lys."

Davey sat quietly in his highchair, still fascinated enough by their guest to be on his best behavior.

Robert plied Sean with questions about his work during dinner. By the time he uncorked the second bottle of wine, Sean no longer needed any prompting.

"We have schools, clinics, and anti-malarial programs in our camps. We also teach trades. Most of the refugees in the camps are women, children, and old people. The younger men use the camps as bases. They come for a while, just long enough to refurbish their supplies and get their wives pregnant, then slip back across the border to fight the Russians."

"Do you have a family planning program?" Robert asked.

"I wish. Women really get the short end of the stick in Afghan society, no pun intended. They have to wear those hideous *burqas*—robes with a patch of mesh in front of their eyes—or else chadors to veil their faces. No man but their husband can look at them. Even the schools we set up for girls in the camps stir up controversy. Many of the mullahs think women shouldn't be educated. Not that the boys are getting a great education. Most of what they learn revolves around Islam and the Koran. Anyway, as far as birth control is concerned it's a rare Afghan male who'd let his wife use any form of contraception. If a woman begs for help the clinic workers will give an injection of long-acting hormones. It's the only way to keep the husband from finding out. Some of these women have ten, fifteen kids. Their diet's terrible. They're all anemic and totally worn out."

"Tell me about the hospital," Robert said.

"The Afghan physicians, as I mentioned, are all female since males aren't allowed to treat female patients. Since these doctors are only partially trained, we depend on our volunteers to fill in the gaps in their training."

"You bring in male as well as female volunteers?"

"Being a westerner puts you in a different category. Most of the Afghan women don't mind being treated by a western male doctor. Of course, we keep the husbands outside the hospital since they might not appreciate it."

"Is living in Peshawar dangerous?" Alyssa asked.

"It's a frontier town, which puts it in the war zone. There are different *mujahideen* factions—that's what the men fighting the Russians are called. Some are fanatic Muslims, others more western-oriented. They have their own squabbles. Fighting among Afghans is a national sport—Pathans, Uzbeks, Tadjiks, and Hazaras all at one another's throats. The city is crawling with spooks—CIA, KGB, and Afghan Security—all spying on one another. It's not particularly dangerous, but at night you can see the lights of the battles across the border.

"I'll say this for the Afghans—they're tough, courageous, and put up with terrible hardships without complaint. If I had to make a prediction I'd say this war is going to go on for a long, long time. That doesn't make the Pakistanis particularly unhappy—their willingness to accept the refugees makes them look good abroad and it gives their military dictatorship legitimacy. The Pakis need them for labor, too. A lot of Pakistani men work in the Gulf states where the money is better, which means there's a shortage of men to do things, like repairing roads and trucking supplies."

"When do you have to be back in Peshawar?" Alyssa asked.

"I fly back Wednesday. It will give me just enough time to spend two days with my brother and his family, then drive back to New York. I should be back at work by Sunday."

"Let's take our wine and go into the living room," Alyssa said.

Robert, noticing Davey slumped half-asleep in his highchair, picked his son up.

"Looks like someone's had a long day," said Sean.

"I'll put Davey to bed and come join you."

"I've done all the talking," Sean was saying to Alyssa when Robert returned. "Tell me about life in West Roylestown."

"Not much to tell," Alyssa said. "It's not New York." She stood up. "If you'll excuse me, I'll put some coffee on."

"Joe probably told you he thinks we're crazy for moving up here," Robert said after Alyssa left the room.

Sean laughed. "He said something to that effect. My feeling is there's a lot of world outside New York City. I may have grown up there but I'd never live there again. I find it oppressive. New Yorkers always go on and on about their museums, their theatres, their restaurants. And they're all so bloody self-involved. What I can't understand is why so many are working their tails off to make enough money to run away from the city every chance they get to their second homes elsewhere. Does that make sense to you?"

"Don't let Alyssa hear you," said Robert chuckling, pleased to have met someone who thought the same way he did. "It makes no sense to me. I was the one who wanted out."

Alyssa rejoined them and during the next few hours, as the warmth of the fire and the effects of the wine caught up with them, the pauses in their conversation grew longer. They laughed when at one point they all yawned simultaneously.

"Time for me to feed Kiska and let you folks go to bed," said Sean, pushing himself up from his chair. "Thank you for a wonderful evening."

"Robert will show you to your room when you come in," Alyssa said.

Next morning, immediately after breakfast, Sean stowed his bag in the pickup and Kiska, no worse for wear after his night sleeping on the porch, leaped into the truck's passenger seat. The snow had added another foot to the drifts surrounding the house. Sean thanked them profusely, embraced Robert and Alyssa, and lifted Davey in his arms and kissed his cheek. He promised to keep in touch.

Robert felt a sense of loss as the truck drove down the driveway. Sean Cooper had brought not just a breath, but a gust, of fresh air into the Morgen home. It wasn't just the fact that he worked in exotic locales. He was interesting in his own right, a man willing to change the course of his life when circumstances called for it. While Sean seemed to live life the way he wanted to, Robert felt that he himself was only nibbling around the edges. Moving to Vermont had seemed like an adventurous step. It was, he now realized, anything but. He was simply practicing his specialty, as he'd always done, in a rural rather than urban setting. We can't all be Sean Cooper, he told himself. After all, he had Alyssa and Davey to think about.

Alyssa, sensing his perturbation, glanced warily at him.

"Well," he said, putting his arm around her as they watched the truck's exhaust fumes rise into the frigid air, "having Sean as a guest was sure nice, in spite of Joe Ross' turning it into a surprise visit."

She nodded, distracted, and he felt her shiver. "Let's go in. It's cold," she said.

2

"We're coming into our neighborhood now," Sean said. "If you look to the left down the cross-street just ahead, you'll see the hospital. I'll take you over there after lunch to meet the administrator."

Robert, immersed in his memories of three years ago, blinked as if he'd just awakened. So much had changed. His marriage had fallen apart, Davey was now with his mother in New York, and he himself was thousands of miles away from the world he knew. Was he really in Peshawar or just dreaming it?

About fifty yards past the intersection, the driver pulled over to the curb in front of a tan-colored, single-story building.

"Nothing fancy," Sean said, "but it's comfortable." He got out and lowered the tailgate. "The carton has supplies for the hospital? We can leave it in the car and Zaheer will take it over," he said in response to Robert's nod. "Let's put your suitcase in your room.

"We use this building for volunteers and for guests," he said, leading Robert down a veranda lined with closed doors. An inner, grass-covered courtyard ringed with flowers surprised Robert. "There are six rooms in all. Right now you're the only one staying here, so you'll have privacy."

He opened one of the doors and they entered a simple room furnished with a double bed, a dresser, and a sink. In one corner a small refrigerator hummed. "I plugged the fridge in this morning," Sean said. A second door opened into a small bathroom. "This okay?"

"It's fine. Better than I expected. Is there a special place for meals?"

"You'll have your breakfast and dinner with Sam and me. Lunch will be with the hospital staff. And don't worry about having to do anything in the room. Someone will come in to make the bed, change linens, and clean up."

They deposited Robert's bag in the corner and returned to the car. "Now I'll take you to my place. Make a left on the next street," Sean said. "Go up a block, and that's where we live."

Zaheer dropped them in front of a tile-roofed, adobe house, visible only through an ornate, iron filigree gate in the adobe wall surrounding the property. Sean told Zaheer to take the carton to the hospital administrator. He then led Robert toward the gate and greeted the Pakistani who held it open for them.

"Salim is our *chowkidar*," Sean said. "Mainly a watchman, but he's also our gardener and Mister Fixit. We have one chowkidar here during the day, another at night."

The grass of the lawn was covered with a film of brown sand. Flowering shrubs in front of the house stood out in colorful relief against the drabness. At that moment the front door opened and an attractive, blond woman wearing a paisley blouse and skirt greeted them. She was almost as tall as the two men.

"This is Doctor Morgen, Sam."

"Please call me Robert," he said, shaking her outstretched hand.

"You must be exhausted," she said in a British accent. "Come in. Abdul is just setting the table for lunch."

A short dark man in a gray shalwar kameez padded silently between kitchen and dining room, carrying dishes of lamb, rice, salad, and coriander chutney.

"This is a feast," said Robert.

"We usually grab a light lunch," said Sean, "but this is in honor of your arrival."

Samantha whispered to Abdul and he disappeared, returning moments later with a pitcher of juice.

"What were you speaking?" Robert asked.

"Pashto," said Sam. "It's the language of the Pathans. Most of the Afghans in the province are Pathans, as I'm sure Sean's told you."

"Sam's been working here five years with Save the Children. She's got good facility with the language. She even speaks some Dari, which is Afghan Persian."

"I wouldn't use the word good to describe my Pashto," Sam laughed, "but it's better than Abdul's English. He came across the border six months ago with his wife and child. Our previous cook had just moved to Rawalpindi so we were lucky to get Abdul, who'd had his own restaurant in Jalalabad."

"His story is a tragic one," Sean said.

"One of thousands," Sam added.

"A Russian guard up in a tower spotted them just as they neared the border. He fired on them and the bullet caught his wife in the spine. Abdul and his eight-year-old son carried her across, but she's paraplegic."

"Terrible," Robert said, shaking his head.

"You'll be seeing her as a patient next week," Sean said.

Robert looked at him. "But there's nothing I can do for—"

"She wants her tubes tied," Sam said. "Being paralyzed, she's afraid to get pregnant. She wouldn't be able to take care of a baby. It's really to Abdul's credit that he agrees. Most Afghan men would never allow it, even in a case like Abdul's wife. Big families are the norm among Afghans. You'll be seeing women with ten to twenty children when you're in the clinic."

"Where were you working, Sam, before you came to Pakistan?"

"I was doing administrative work for the London office of Save the Children, but when the Afghan war started, there was a sudden vacancy in the Peshawar office and I was fortunate enough to get it."

"Should I tell him why there was a sudden vacancy?" Sean said.

Samantha shrugged her shoulders. "It's not a pleasant story."

"Her predecessor had to be airlifted out to England with a gunshot wound. She and a male friend had stopped by the Pearl Continental Hotel, the one I pointed out to you on the way in from the airport. They were going to have a swim in the pool, then eat lunch. The only Pakistanis who frequent that place are wealthy ones. Some rich playboy type at the hotel took a fancy to Sam's predecessor, even though she was sitting there with a male friend. He was pretty drunk and made a nuisance of himself, insisting that the woman have a drink with him."

"I thought alcohol in hotels is only allowed to be served to non-Muslims," Robert interrupted. "During my night at the hotel in Karachi, I ordered a beer and they made me sign a form stating that I wasn't a Muslim."

"Well," Sean said, "that sort of thing is overlooked when enough money crosses hands. Anyway, the male friend told him to get lost. The Pakistani pulled a gun on them and dragged the woman out to his car in the hotel parking lot. As he tried to force her into the car, she wrestled with him, the gun went off, and she collapsed with a bullet in her abdomen. The Paki tried to escape in his car, but the police had arrived by then and blocked the exit. The woman was taken to a local hospital and after they'd stabilized her, she was put on a military plane and flown to London. We heard she had to undergo three separate surgeries for the internal damage, but she's okay now."

"In fact," Sam added, "she and I have corresponded several times about cases she left behind. Not surprisingly, she has no desire to return to Pakistan."

"What happened to the man who shot her?"

"Nothing. His father happens to be one of the richest men in town and he interceded with the police. I heard that the chief of police called the culprit into his office and had a little chat with him. He told him the next time there was an incident like this, it would be the last time. He'd be shot and his body would be returned to his father."

"Sounds like the old wild west in America," Robert said.

"That was tame compared to the NWFP," Sean said.

"What is that?"

"Shorthand for Northwest Frontier Province. Peshawar is the capital of the province. Our organization is responsible for nine camps in an area southwest of here, about three hours by car. You'll be visiting the camps, too, as a consultant."

"How many refugee camps are there in Pakistan?"

"More than three hundred, most of them in the NWFP. Since I saw you in the States the refugee situation here has gotten worse. There are now four million Afghans in Pakistan and Iran, and that's out of a population of sixteen million in Afghanistan before the war started."

"What makes the NWFP different from other provinces in Pakistan?"

"The province is technically part of Pakistan, but each of the nine tribal areas operates under its own laws. In fact, only the main road between Peshawar and the Khyber Pass is under Pakistani government control. No one can travel in this province without special permission from the government."

"The Pakistani government doesn't mind not having control of the province?"

"There's not much they can do about it even if they did. Just because someone drew a line between Afghanistan and the province a long time ago doesn't mean the Pathans recognize the border. They cross at will. Family members live on both sides. And the Pakistanis know better than to get into a conflict with the Pathans."

3

The Afghan Women's Hospital was a poor man's version of Schuyler Memorial, the forty-bed hospital where Robert first did his deliveries and surgeries in Vermont. It was mud-brick, one level, half the square footage of Robert's old hospital. Parts of the building appeared to be still under construction, with cinder blocks and sacks of cement stored under an open, tin-roofed area.

"They need additional space, but we have to wait for the funding," Sean said. He pointed out some men squatting against the iron fence surrounding the hospital compound. "Those are husbands and relatives of patients inside. They're not allowed to go in."

A *tonga*, a horse-drawn carriage, pulled up as they approached the entrance and three burqa-clad women descended. They looked like colorful ghosts as they floated through the gate in front of Sean and Robert.

"Most women in this society are in purdah," Sean said softly. "They cover up when they're out so no man can look at them. Either they wear those head-to-toe burqas, which can be pretty colorful but must be hell to see out of, or they have chadors, shawls, and veils that they can pull in front of their face."

The chowkidar greeted Sean, whom he recognized. Sean informed him that Robert was an American doctor who would be working at the hospital. The chowkidar smiled and nodded to Robert.

A dozen or so women were in the clinic waiting room as Sean and Robert passed through. They were talking with their faces uncovered and Robert noticed several had tattoos on their foreheads and lips. The women quickly covered their faces.

The administrator's office was down a short, dark corridor. Doctor Mojarri, an obese, pock-marked man, greeted them warmly. He wore a grimy, lavender shalwar kameez that accentuated the pyramidal shape of his body. Mojarri had fled Kabul when the Russians invaded and, like tens of thousands of his compatriots, had arrived in Peshawar. It was Mojarri, a fluent English speaker, who had approached International Refugee Assistance with the idea for a hospital dedicated to the care of Afghan women. "Not the greatest administrator," Sean had confided to Robert on their walk to the hospital, "but he's got some good people working for him."

Robert met one of those good people almost immediately after they followed Mojarri from his office. "This is my assistant, Sahar," Mojarri said, introducing Robert to a sari-clad woman working at a desk in an adjoining office. Sahar stood up and, without hesitation, shook Robert's hand. "Welcome to our hospital," she said in unaccented English. Sahar, who Robert guessed was in her mid-thirties, had the most beautiful eyes he'd ever seen, but her expression, he felt, betrayed a deep-seated pain.

"Sahar is the only Pakistani working full-time at the hospital," Sean whispered to Robert as they accompanied Mojarri to the clinic. "She's excellent—gets things done."

Patients were still being seen in the clinic although it was late in the day. Mojarri introduced Robert to five Afghan women physicians, all dressed in white uniforms. Their hair was hidden under kerchief-like coverings. Only their faces were exposed. They stood at attention, as if Robert were inspecting them.

"We have eight doctors on staff," Mojarri said. "Not all speak English well, but we have English class three times a week. Sahar teaches it. When we have volunteers, they hold classes as well.

"Your English is now much better, isn't it, Afifa?" he said to one of the physicians, a short, round-faced woman who blushed deeply when he addressed her.

"I—I am learning English," she stammered, "but I cannot speak too good."

Mojarri nodded approvingly. "They will ask you to consult on problem cases and examine any patient they think may need surgery," Mojarri said to Robert. "Our morning clinic is from eight to noon, and in the afternoon it is from one to five."

"Who schedules the surgery?" Robert asked.

"Doctor Mathir. She's the senior member of the staff, but she has already left for the day. Her mother is very ill. You will meet her on Sunday." He spoke in Pashto to one of the women, then turned back to Robert. "The other two doctors are with patients in labor."

"Who gives anesthesia at the hospital?"

"We have an arrangement with a Pakistani anesthesiologist. He'll come in whenever there's a surgery scheduled. Except for Cesareans and minor cases, not many gynecological cases are done unless we have a volunteer at the hospital. The Afghan doctors are still reluctant to do cases on their own. That's why it's so important for us to have volunteers like you who can work with them and teach."

Mojarri led them down a corridor lined with patient rooms, each with several beds. In one, a woman was breastfeeding her baby. She pulled the sheet over her face when she saw them.

At that moment they heard cries and muffled voices coming from behind two closed doors along the hall.

"Those are our two delivery rooms," Mojarri said. "Both are in use right now. Come, I will take you to the operating room."

Two nurses, sitting and talking at a desk, stood up immediately as the men entered. Mojarri explained who Robert was and they all moved to the open doorway of the operating room. One of the nurses, a handsome woman named Zaida, spoke fluent English. She told Robert they were looking forward to working with him and she thanked him for the instruments and supplies he had brought from America. "We are sterilizing the instruments now," she said, indicating a small autoclave. Robert was astonished to see rubber gloves and wet laparotomy pads hanging from a clothesline to dry.

"Doctor Mathir did a Cesarean Section this morning," said Zaida.

Robert looked at Sean. "No disposables?"

"None. Too expensive. Everything here is washed, sterilized, and re-used. See how spoiled we are in the States."

A smile flitted across Zaida's face. "Even the disposable gloves you brought we will re-use many times," she said.

Sean and Robert thanked Doctor Mojarri for the tour of the hospital and walked out into the fading sunshine of late afternoon. A corn vendor, whom

Robert hadn't noticed when they arrived at the hospital, stood outside the entrance. Whenever a customer appeared, he removed a cob from sand that he kept heated, cleaned it with a filthy rag, and rubbed it with lemon dipped in a salty chili powder mixture.

"Now you know where to get your snacks," Sean said, an amused expression on his face.

"Zaida strikes me as being very competent," Robert said, as they walked down the block.

"Other OB-GYNs who've worked here tell me she's one of the best OR nurses they've ever worked with. She's from Kabul. Her husband lives in New York. He's trying to get her over. She'll be tough to replace when she goes.

"Let's walk around the neighborhood a bit so you can get your bearings. Then we'll go back to the house for drinks and dinner."

Bearded men with AK-47's jostled them in front of several of the houses they passed. A few, standing guard at entrances, cast unfriendly glances in their direction.

"Some of the Afghan political factions have their offices here. They have no love for foreigners but the reason they're armed is because they don't get along with one another. There are shootouts occasionally. Most of the time when you hear gunfire it means a wedding is in progress and they're celebrating."

"Celebrating with guns?"

"They shoot them into the air. I haven't heard of anyone getting killed, but I'm sure it happens.

"That little grocery," he said, pointing to a shop on the opposite side of the street, "is a good place for things like yogurt, juice, soda. He's got some pretty good fruit and vegetables, too." Sean pointed directly ahead. "If you follow this street you'll come to a big traffic circle. The large building you'll see on the left is the biggest hospital in Peshawar. Our volunteer doctors send patients there if the cases are very complicated. The Afghan doctors send urgent cases there, too, when we don't have a volunteer at the hospital.

"Well, you've seen a little of our neighborhood. I don't think you'll get lost. Let's head back to the house."

"Make yourselves comfortable on the patio," Samantha called from the kitchen when she heard them come in. "I'll join you in a minute."

The patio was walled in and not visible from the street. Robert leaned back in his rattan lounge chair and fought against closing his eyes.

"You'll sleep well tonight," Sean laughed.

"Is Robert nodding off on us?" Samantha said, laughing, as she brought in a tray with glasses and a bottle of scotch.

"I must be getting old," Robert said, stifling a yawn.

"Old!" Sean said. "Are you trying to hurt my feelings? We're the same age, man."

"We are?"

"Forty-eight. I've seen your application."

"Well, I don't know what I'm doing hanging around two old men, so I'd best leave," Samantha said.

"Oh, sit down, Sam," Sean said, "and give this fellow a stiff belt of that Johnny Walker. It'll bring him back to life."

"Where did that come from?" Robert asked, pointing to the bottle.

"It's amazing what comes in by diplomatic pouch," Sean laughed.

"Hope you don't mind leftovers for dinner, Robert," Sam said. "Abdul cooked enough for ten people lunchtime."

"Sounds great."

"Once things are squared away at the hospital," Sean told him during dinner, "I'll take you down to some of our camps in the southwest. We have a base down there, so we'll spend a few days. Maybe we can do it the week after next."

"I feel like I've taken a step back in time, being here. I know this is old hat for both of you, but it's very exciting for me. When I was a kid growing up in Brooklyn, I got hooked on Kipling's books. Is there any chance of my getting to the Khyber Pass while I'm here?"

"The Pakistanis are trying to keep visitors out of the area because of Russian overflights. The MIGs have been crossing the border to hit the refugee camps because the mujahideen use the camps as staging areas before heading into Afghanistan. If things quiet down, I'll see if our friends at USAID can get you there."

After dinner, Sean and Samantha walked outside with Robert. Off to the west the sky was lit up by intermittent flashes and beams of light, accompanied by occasional dull thuds. Bright flares hung in the sky like giant stars.

"Our nightly sound and light show," Sean said. "The Russians are trying to hit mujahideen positions. Now that the mooj have Stinger missiles, the Russians are more cautious with their helicopter gunships during the day. They've lost a bunch of them."

"It's hard to believe that's all going on so close to here. It's so peaceful in—"

Robert's words were interrupted by a short burst of gunfire.

Sean laughed. "You were saying?"

"Where'd that come from?"

"Just some trigger-happy Afghan. Some of them treat their AK-47s like toys. You remember how to get back to your room?"

"I do. Thank you both for everything."

"We thank you for coming to Peshawar. See you around eight for breakfast."

4

Robert stood on the walkway outside his room and stared into the dark courtyard. I'm really here, he thought, his senses still overwhelmed by new sensations. Everything—the sights, the sounds—was different from the world he knew. Pakistan even smelled different. It was as if he was breathing the air of another planet. He stared at the intermittent flashes of light in the sky above Afghanistan. In his excitement, his fatigue abated.

Before going to sleep, Robert sat on the edge of his bed writing letters. His first was to Davey. He conjured up his son's face as he meticulously printed each word. Until Davey's fifth birthday he and Robert had never been apart. Robert frowned as he thought of the trap he'd walked into, the trap that had cost him his son.

"I got a job offer," Alyssa had told him. Robert remembered the day well. It was shortly after they'd returned home from spending Thanksgiving in New York with the Farbers, Alyssa's parents.

"That's great," Robert said, surprised and relieved. Alyssa, who'd been a psychiatric social worker for the public schools when they'd lived in New York, had been unable to find work in Vermont. Her fruitless quest had led to increasing friction between them, culminating in an evening shouting match on their lawn earlier in the autumn.

"What'll you be doing?"

"Exactly what I was doing when we lived in Manhattan. It sounds perfect and the money is good. They'll pay fifty-five a year."

"Wow, that's great," Robert said, glad that the source of their stress was about to disappear. "I knew it would happen if you kept looking. So where is it?"

Alyssa hesitated. "Westchester."

"You applied for a job in New York?"

"I saw the ad in *The Times* and did it for a lark, just to see what would happen. I never thought they'd call me. I'd be involved with schools in Scarsdale, Eastchester, and New Rochelle."

"But how can you do it? You can't drive ten hours a day."

"I'll have an apartment down there during the week."

An image flashed through Robert's mind: Alyssa and her mother whispering in the kitchen on Thanksgiving Day. She must have known even then. Now he understood.

"How long have you known this?"

"They called me just before Thanksgiving. I told them I'd let them know by the end of this week."

"When were you planning to tell me? Or were you just going to drive away and call us from down there?"

"I wanted to tell you sooner, but didn't know how."

"You didn't know how? The same way you told me today, that's how."

"See, I knew you'd be upset. I knew you'd never understand what I was feeling."

"That's not true. I do understand how much this means to you. I just don't know how it can be done."

"I don't want to put the burden on you. I can take Davey down with me and put him in a pre-school."

Robert shook his head. "No, I can keep Davey up here."

"But how? You can be called out at all hours for deliveries. You can't leave him alone and you can't take him over to Lucy Potter's in the middle of the night."

"You know I've been thinking about giving up OB. I'll bring it up at the next staff meeting."

"But that's a big part of your practice. You'd lose a lot of income. We can't afford that."

"I can't go on being on call twenty-four hours a day, seven days a week.

I feel guilty every time I ask Todd Jones for coverage, and my patients get upset when they have to drive to Brookville to see him."

"I warned you, didn't I? You knew that Schuyler was a family practice hospital. All they cared about was getting rid of their OB patients. You were the sucker they were waiting for."

"Well, it's time to change that. If I give up OB it means Jones would only have to cover me for GYN patients, which is no big deal. And it also means we can get away, take real vacations."

"It's not vacations I want right now," Alyssa said. "It's work."

"It won't be cheap to live down there."

"A small apartment won't set me back too much, even if I have to furnish it. I know this is a lot to ask of you, but I tell myself that maybe it will lead to something else, something a lot closer to here. When we left Manhattan I quit my job without having anything else to go to. This time, I'd be able to begin looking while still working. I'd really like to try it, at least for a year."

Robert's mind was going in many different directions. He'd never known anyone in a commuter marriage, but he knew they existed. It can't be good for the relationship, he thought, but then again, having one spouse miserable all the time wasn't good either. Above all, he wanted to avoid a repeat of their battle on the lawn back in September. And then there was his practice to consider. Alyssa's working would help to make up for the drop in his income from giving up obstetrics, but then again, would it really? Much of it would go toward supporting her in Westchester. Several times in the past few months he'd told Alyssa he would like to give up the obstetrical part of his practice. Alyssa had been ambivalent about the idea. She knew his always being on call was wearing him down, but she worried about the loss of income. That, and his concern about the hospital's response to his taking such an action, had kept him from going through with it. Now his hand would be forced, and he had to admit that he wasn't sorry.

"How would we get to see one another?" he asked. "How would Davey see you?"

"I'd drive up Fridays after work, then head back Sunday."

"That's a long drive to do every weekend, Lys."

"I wouldn't mind. Try to understand, Robert. I came up here with you to try a different kind of life. I've given it more than a year and it hasn't worked for me. All I'm asking is for you to let me try this job for a year to see where it leads. You know me. When I'm happy working, everything else becomes easy. That's why I know I wouldn't mind the drive. It would give me something to look forward to, spending the weekend with you and Davey without being miserable because I have nothing to do."

"Can I ask you to hold off going until after the first of the year? I'll need time to make the changes in my practice."

"You mean referring your OB patients?"

He nodded.

"What do you think the hospital will say when they learn about it?"

He shrugged. "I'll find out on Wednesday morning at the medical staff meeting."

Three long tables were placed end to end in the conference room. The hospital administrator, Henry Pelham, and three physicians were already seated, their full breakfast plates in front of them. The rest of the doctors were lined up in front of an assortment of juices, toast, and hot trays filled with waffles, scrambled eggs, bacon and sausage.

"Hey, Henry," called one of the doctors, "why don't you feed us like this every day?"

Pelham, a short, stocky man threatening to burst the seams of his sport jacket, laughed like he'd heard a good joke. He was moonfaced, his cheeks pink and smooth-shaven. A crewcut masked his tendency to baldness.

He waved when he spotted Robert coming into the room.

I'm the golden goose keeping his OB beds filled, Robert thought. His stomach had been in a knot since he got up and he couldn't bring himself to look at the food trays. Instead, he filled his Styrofoam cup with coffee and sat down next to Jeff Trumbull. Trumbull was a fifth generation Vermonter who prided himself on never having been out of the state except for occasional conferences at Mary Hitchcock Hospital in Hanover, New Hampshire.

"Are you on a diet?" he asked Robert.

"No wonder you're so thin," Wally Nugent said. Nugent was the first physician Robert had met at Schuyler Memorial. He had the largest ears Robert had ever seen, spiky black hair, and one bushy eyebrow running continuously across his forehead. Robert had never heard him talk about anything but hunting.

"Just not very hungry," Robert replied.

During the initial part of the meeting, Robert sat in silence. He listened with half an ear to Pelham's report for the last quarter. Admissions were up, major surgery cases were up, deliveries were up, emergency room visits were up. "So we're in good shape, gentlemen," he concluded, a big smile on his face. "Keep up the good work."

It wasn't until Archie Meagher, the general surgeon who chaired the meeting, asked if there was any new business, that Robert raised his hand.

"Doctor Morgen?" Meagher said. Meagher was a prim, unsmiling man in his fifties and a stickler for formality.

Robert licked his dry lips and stood up.

"I've had a change in my circumstances," he said, "and as of January first, I'll no longer be doing obstetrics or taking emergency room call."

Eleven general practitioners, two general surgeons, and Pelham, the administrator, stared at him. The only sound in the room was the electric coffee pot humming.

Pelham was the first to find his voice. "What are you talking about?" he said flatly.

"My wife has accepted a job in New York, so she'll only be in Vermont on weekends. Our son is staying with me, which means there's no way I can continue doing obstetrics or taking ER call. I can't leave him alone at night."

"Why can't your son be in New York with your wife?" Frank Epps, one of the GP's, asked.

"Because this is the way we've set things up."

"Well, I say this is bullshit," Wally Nugent said. "The hospital brought you up here to do obstetrics and you knew before you came that everyone has to take ER call."

"Things change," said Robert. "I won't be the first OB-GYN to give up the obstetrical part of his practice. And I've learned that the American College of Obstetrics and Gynecology doesn't permit its fellows to see male patients. I should never have been put on the ER call roster."

"This is not what we agreed on," Pelham said. "We backed you and guaranteed your income because you were coming here to do OB."

"Yes, you did that," said Robert, "but I never had to take a cent from Schuyler. I was busy from the time I arrived. And I intend to continue doing major surgery, so it's not like I won't be bringing in income for the hospital."

"The major surgery isn't the issue," Archie Meagher said icily. "We were getting along fine with surgery before you came. Obstetrics is the issue. Every family practitioner willingly referred his obstetrical patients to you."

"Yes, they did. Very willingly. What I didn't know, however, was how much of a problem it was going to be to get coverage. Todd Jones in Brookville has been gracious about it, but it's an imposition on him and on my patients. He has his coverage worked out with the Montpelier OBs, so there's no way I can repay him. And my patients have to go to Brookville to deliver when he covers me. He won't come here."

"Why don't you take in an associate?" Pelham said.

"There's not enough work for two OB's. And even if there was, finding someone to relocate to Catamount, Vermont, wouldn't be easy."

"*You* came here," said Pelham.

"Well, I've learned a few things since I came. We might as well put all our cards on the table. Sure, another OB would resolve the coverage problem, if there was enough obstetrics for two of us, which there isn't. But no OB would put up with being required to take ER call, and I doubt any OB-GYN would come here when he learned that the general surgeons refused to refer their GYN cases. Just because I was a fool doesn't mean you'll find another one."

Archie Meagher glowered at him.

"What about getting a locum tenens when you want to be away?" Epps said.

"That wouldn't solve anything. I can't leave my son alone at night."

"I'd like to remind you that you have a contract," Henry Pelham said.

"A one year contract," Robert said, "and I've been here for more than a year."

"But the contract specifies that you would do obstetrics."

"Goddamn right it does," Wally Nugent said. "I reviewed that contract."

"Like I said, I can't leave my son alone at night. He's not even four."

"Maybe you and your wife should have thought of that before she took a job in New York," Nugent snapped.

"What my wife and I do is none of your business."

"But it is our business," Archie Meagher said. "Your actions affect all of us."

"Look," Henry Pelham said, standing up, "this isn't getting us anywhere. I think we need to talk to the hospital's lawyer. And Doctor Morgen, you might want to see yours as well.

"I'll schedule a special meeting for next week. You'll all be advised of the date."

5

Robert hadn't seen Alyssa so happy since their days in Manhattan. She was so elated that she removed Davey from Lucy Potter's daycare so that he could spend the month before her departure with her at home.

"Was Lucy upset?" Robert asked.

"No. With the holidays coming, it's an abbreviated month for her anyway. I told her Davey would be back with her in January."

"Did you tell her you were leaving?"

"I mentioned it."

"Did she say anything?"

Alyssa hesitated. "No. What did you think she'd say?"

"Nothing. Just asking."

Now that Alyssa's job in Westchester was certain, she enlisted her parents' help in finding an apartment. She—or rather they—had decided it would be best to find an apartment in Scarsdale. When they located something they felt was appropriate, Alyssa would drive down to see it. In the meantime, she busied herself thumbing through catalogs, looking ahead to furnishing whatever place she (and they) decided on. "You know how I love to shop," she laughed. "And think of all the goodies I'll be bringing up from the city on weekends. We'll have some real feasts."

Robert, who constantly discovered rotting food in the refrigerator and surreptitiously emptied their freezer to make room for the vacuum-packaged steaks, salmon, and chicken Alyssa bought, said nothing. Lionel, a local teenager who helped them with getting in their wood and tending their garden, also contributed to the food glut by bringing venison steaks and roasts. "Don't you eat venison?" Robert asked the boy. "Sure," he said, "but we can't fit any more in our freezer." Robert was no hunter but he knew the quantities of meat brought by Lionel didn't come from only one whitetail buck, which was what each hunter was allowed.

During the last days before Alyssa's departure for New York, Robert had far more than food on his mind. The follow-up medical staff meeting had been a disaster. The entire medical staff was in attendance and, true to his word, Henry Pelham had the hospital's lawyer present. Robert, believing it wasn't necessary, hadn't sought legal representation.

"The contract guarantee was for one year," Robert insisted.

"It was," Lawrence Kilpatrick, Schuyler Memorial's lawyer, said, "but doing obstetrics was a condition of your staff privileges."

"You mean to tell me," Robert argued, "that I can't exercise my free will? If I decide I'm not going to do obstetrics, I can't have privileges?"

"That's what's written in the contract," said Kilpatrick. "If you have a problem with it, better have your lawyer review it."

"So if you're serious about giving up OB," Pelham said, "your privileges won't be renewed in February."

Robert's heart skipped a beat. He'd thought of this possibility before the staff meeting, but refused to believe they'd go that far. Now he knew he'd been right to worry. He looked purposefully at each physician in the room to see if anyone would support him. No one uttered a sound.

"In that case," Robert said, "I resign. I have privileges at Brookville and I'll be taking all my patients there. Schuyler's going to lose a lot of GYN surgery and the people in Catamount aren't going to be very happy when they learn what's going on."

"We'll survive it," Pelham said stone-faced.

Son of a bitch, Robert fumed, as he left Pelham's office. What did he think I was going to do, beg him to keep me on the staff? Bastards. He knew he had to think carefully now and not do anything rash, but his hands were trembling when he reached his office. Before seeing his first patient, he called Todd Jones and asked if he could meet him in Brookville after office hours.

"Come on up," said Todd, "I'll buy you a drink. Meet me at the office. Is five-thirty okay?"

Robert called Alyssa and told her he'd be home late. She was so preoccupied with her move that she never asked him what had transpired at his staff meeting.

Todd Jones drove them to a new Radisson Inn that had opened on the outskirts of Brookville. They chose a table at the rear of the dimly-lit bar and Todd ordered their drinks. The waitress placed their beers and some peanuts on the table.

"So why the serious face?" Jones asked, when the waitress moved away.

"I'm leaving Schuyler Memorial."

Todd's eyebrows went up. "You're leaving Vermont?"

"No, just Schuyler, which is why I wanted to talk to you."

Robert related the events that had occurred that morning, Jones listening attentively.

"Well," he said, when Robert had finished, "I guess that made you feel like a turd in a punchbowl."

"No, actually it made me feel like a diamond in a cesspool."

Jones laughed. "Well put. And now, I want to tell you something I haven't been able to tell you before this. Did you ever wonder why I never got privileges at Schuyler?"

"I thought you wanted to keep your practice at one hospital."

"That's true, of course, but there's more to it. I wouldn't touch Schuyler with a ten-foot pole. If you'd come to me before you made your agreement with them, I would have warned you away. The general practitioners run that place and they're a nasty bunch. All they were interested in when you showed up was in getting rid of their OB patients."

"My wife said the same thing, but I guess I put on blinders. I wanted so much to get out of the rat race in New York and move to our Vermont house that I refused to see what should have been obvious."

Todd nodded. "Not even the two surgeons stuck up for you, huh?"

"Nope. Those two guys are still doing GYN surgery."

Jones snorted. "Those two call themselves general surgeons but they're not even board-certified. No one on that staff is except for you. I couldn't believe it when you told me they were making you take emergency room call. The American College of OB-GYN says its members can't treat male patients. If the general surgeons in my hospital had told me they'd be doing GYN surgery instead of referring the cases to me, I never would have come here. That was a mistake on your part."

"One of many apparently. I was so anxious to move to Vermont I never thought of all the ramifications."

"Yeah, well, that's understandable. You're not the first one who found himself in that predicament. Other docs have had to leave because their wives found it too quiet, too remote. I was lucky, I guess. My wife is from the Northeast Kingdom so this area is like heaven for her. Being close to Montpelier is a big advantage."

"I just want you to know how much I appreciate your giving me coverage when there was no way for me to pay you back. And I want to reassure you that I have no intention of competing with you. I plan to do only GYN, no OB, at Brookville. I need to find a new office, someplace closer to Brookville, and hope that I can retain most of my Catamount patients. I'll have to educate them to use Brookville's hospital instead of Schuyler's."

"If they like you, they'll be willing. And if I were you, I'd make sure the reasons for your departure get into the newspapers. The folks in Catamount might as well know what they're dealing with in that hospital. All I can say is welcome aboard. You're fortunate to get out of that rat's nest. Would you be interested in assisting me on my surgery patients? I've been using the general surgeons, but it would be far better to have an OB-GYN. It would boost your income a bit, too."

"That would be great. I'd appreciate it."

"And if you need coverage, just call. Without OB patients, it'll be a breeze."

The two men shook hands and Todd drove him back to his car. Even while he berated himself for his stupidity in his dealings with Schuyler, Robert felt better after his talk with Todd. What Todd had told him about Schuyler's medical staff was what he himself had been feeling for some time. It was nice to have it confirmed.

For the next two weeks Robert felt like he was on a treadmill. He left his resignation letter with Pelham's secretary, found a new office ten miles from Catamount but closer to Brookville, and advised his patients of the move. He also made it known that he was giving up obstetrics and would be doing no deliveries after December thirty-first.

Alyssa's response to his resignation from Schuyler and his move to a new office was not what he'd expected. He received a sympathy that bordered on indifference. It was as if her own path back to New York was now marked out for her, so what happened in Vermont no longer concerned her. "You'll do fine in the new office," she said. "Guess what. My parents found an apartment for me in Scarsdale. They say it's perfect, not too small, with one bedroom and a nice kitchen. It's right near a park and the rent is very affordable."

"Will they hold it for you till you can get down there to see it?"

"I trust my parents' judgment. They already put a deposit on it for me. And they'll be there Monday when the futon and love seat I ordered arrive."

"I still find it strange that you're setting up a new place to live."

"You can think of it as our *pied a terre* near the city. We won't have to stay with my parents when you come to New York."

6

Afew days before Christmas Robert arrived home and found Alyssa dancing around the living room with Davey in her arms. At that moment, Robert had a vision of her as he'd first seen her, the day she had walked into his Manhattan office. She was accompanying a high school girl, one of her clients who was in an abusive home relationship, for her first gynecologic examination.

"Don't you worry," Alyssa had said, comforting the terrified girl, stroking her hair as she sat on the examination table. "Doctor Morgen will be very gentle, won't you, Doctor?"

"I will," Robert said, "and I won't touch you without telling you first."

He'd admired Alyssa's interaction with the girl—no condescension, just calm reassurance. He also was taken with her beauty. She was slender, with shoulder length black hair, enormous brown eyes framed by long lashes, and lips he wanted to kiss the very first time she smiled at him. They spoke in private after the examination and by the time she left the office, he'd asked her out to dinner.

Robert met Alyssa at the Café Geiger, a sedate German restaurant in Yorkville.

"It's nice to see you again," Robert said after the maitre d' had seated them.

"This is a charming place," Alyssa said. "It's like being in Vienna."

"I have a confession to make," Robert said. "I come here sometimes for the Black Forest cake. It's irresistible."

Alyssa laughed. "Chocolate is a vice we share."

For the next two hours Alyssa talked about herself and her family. She was thirty-four, seven years younger than he. She'd been born, raised, and educated in New York. After graduating from NYU, she had moved to Boston, where she earned her master's degree. She spoke enthusiastically about her work with troubled youngsters in New York's public school system. "I really feel I'm making a difference," she told him. "So many of these kids have real potential, but their home situations are deplorable."

Alyssa spoke so softly at times that Robert had to lean forward to hear what she was saying. It was as if he had become the only person she could confide in, as if no one else mattered. The elderly diners at neighboring tables and the soft hum of their spoken German ceased to exist. Robert's gaze was fixed on Alyssa. He watched her sipping wine and found himself envying the rim of the wineglass. She was the most beautiful woman he had ever known. Their eyes met frequently and what they expressed required no words.

"This will sound funny," Alyssa said as she paused in mid-sentence, "but, are you married?"

He laughed and shook his head.

"You've never been married?"

"No. I came close once, but we decided it would never work. And you?"

"I was married briefly for a year while I was in my master's program."

"Why did it end?" Robert asked.

Alyssa shrugged. "We barely knew one another when we decided to get married. It was impulsive and, maybe for that reason, exciting. But we both sat down one day and looked at one another, and that was it. It was as if we were asking ourselves the same question. What am I doing here with this person? 'We made a mistake,' he said. 'I know,' I answered. So we got it annulled, shook hands, and went our separate ways."

"Was it really that simple?"

"It really was. Even now, all these years later, I can't believe I did something so rash and so foolish. God, I was immature. Have you ever done anything that made you feel like that?"

"My guess is probably more than once, but nothing so dramatic comes to mind. Do you like opera?"

"Now there's a segue," Alyssa laughed. "Yes, I do."

"I have two tickets for the final performance of *Boheme* at the Met a week from next Wednesday."

"Is that an invitation?"

"It certainly is."

"I'd love to go with you."

"Have you ever been to the Ninety-second Street Y?"

"For opera?" she said straight-faced, then laughed.

"Isaac Bashevis Singer will be reading this coming Saturday."

"Really? He's one of my favorite authors."

"So we have a date?"

Alyssa looked down for a moment at her plate, her food barely touched and growing cold.

"I have to tell you something," she said, looking directly into his eyes.

Robert smiled in anticipation.

"I'm living with someone."

Robert's smile disappeared.

Seeing his pained expression, Alyssa reached out to him, her fingers touching his hand.

"I wish I had known," Robert said.

"We've been together for six months, but it's not working," Alyssa said. "I'm going to be moving out."

"Does he know?"

"He will after I get home tonight."

"Are you sure that's what you want to do?"

She placed her hand on top of his. "I'm sure. Can I call you and let you know about Saturday?"

"Of course."

Robert paid the waiter, while Alyssa complimented him on the fine service.

The old man bowed. "*Danke, fraulein.* I hope to see you again."

"You made his day," Robert said as he accompanied her to her car. They walked slowly in spite of the early fall chill. "I'm sorry this evening has to end," he said.

"I feel the same way," she said as they stood next to her car.

She wrapped her arms around him and pressed her lips to his.

True to her word, Alyssa moved into a sublet studio apartment in Kips Bay before the end of the week. During the next two weeks, they saw one another as often as possible. It was during intermission while they were at the opera that Alyssa suggested a trip to Vermont for the following weekend. "It's the perfect time to go," she said. "The foliage should be peaking. And I'll do the driving."

"I've been looking forward to this ever since you suggested it," Robert said on the drive up. I feel like a kid whose mother has promised to take him to the circus."

"You'll love it. It's so beautiful, especially this time of year."

"You've been there before, I take it."

"A few times. But now it's special."

"Why is that?"

"Because you're with me."

Robert leaned over to kiss her cheek.

They drove to an inn between Bennington and Shaftsbury in the southwestern corner of the state. If Robert had been asked to conjure up an image of Vermont before going there, the inn and its surroundings would have come to mind. He breathed deeply as he stepped out of the car. The crisp air made his nose tingle. It was already past eleven and the only sound in the October night was the distant hooting of an owl. A small light burned above the entrance door.

"I'm afraid we'll be waking them up," Robert said.

"They know we're coming. I told them we'd be here late."

Old photographs lined the dimly lit hallway of the inn. Their footsteps were muffled by the thick braided wool runner that led them to the registration desk, illuminated by a single lamp. An envelope with their names on it rested on the counter under a room key.

Welcome to the Green Mountain Inn, read the enclosed note. *Please take room eight, one flight up. I will see you in the morning. Enjoy your stay. Your host, Benjamin Aldridge.*

They slept together for the first time that evening and it seemed the most natural thing in the world. "I'm in love with you," were the last words Robert said before falling asleep.

"I love you," Alyssa whispered, curling up next to him.

They awoke to a perfect Vermont morning: the sky a crystalline blue, the smell of woodsmoke in the air, the trees burnished in gold, flaming in hues ranging from red to violet.

"Let's never leave here," Robert said, pressing her to him.

"I have an idea," Alyssa said. "Since I have to be out of my sublet by the end of November, why don't we look for an apartment together."

"You mean live together?"

"Don't get nervous," she laughed. "If it makes you more comfortable, we can get a two-bedroom. I just thought—"

"I think it's a great idea. But one bedroom is fine."

A year later Alyssa called him at work and suggested they have dinner out that evening at *Minetta's* in the Village.

"I haven't been here in a long time," Robert said to her after the waiter took their orders. "Here's to us," he said, raising his wine glass and leaning across the table to kiss her.

Alyssa touched her glass to his. She smiled uncertainly and touched her lip with her finger.

"Is something wrong?" Robert asked.

"I've been thinking, Robert. I am so happy with you."

"I feel the same way. This has been the best year of my life. But why do you look so serious?"

"I hope this won't scare you, but I want to marry you."

"That doesn't scare me. But are you sure we won't ruin what we have?"

"That's impossible. We're too much in love."

There was no doubt in Robert's mind that they were deeply in love. Their first year together seemed like a prolonged honeymoon in spite of their work schedules. Candlelit dinners, frequent lovemaking, trips to Europe—it was an idyll that Robert thought would never end.

They celebrated their wedding by purchasing a vacation home in

Vermont, an older home with enough acreage for a horse. Alyssa had told him before they began their search that she'd like to learn to ride.

"You know what," Robert said after they'd been married a few months. "I love you just as much now as before we got married."

"That's nice to know," said Alyssa, "because I have something to tell you. You'd better sit down. I'm pregnant."

"What? How can that be? You're on the pill."

"I started one pack a few days late. I'm sorry. Please don't be angry with me."

"I'm not angry. Just surprised. I think it's great news. Are you excited?"

"My parents will be thrilled."

"Yes, but what about you? How do you feel about being a mother?"

"Well, I never really thought about it, but—sure, I'm glad."

"You know what I think? You forgot those pills accidentally on purpose."

"Robert, how can you say that!"

He laughed and embraced her. "And I'm glad you did."

Alyssa paused in her dancing with Davey and watched him. "What are you thinking?" she said, putting Davey down. "You look like you're someplace far away."

"I was just thinking how much I love you, how much I'm going to miss you."

"That's sweet, Robert. But I'll be here three days a week.

"Go play, honey," she said to Davey. "I'll call you when dinner is ready."

"What should we do about Davey's birthday in two weeks?" Robert asked. "It's on a weekday and you'll be in New York."

"We'll have his party when I come up on the weekend. At four, he won't know the difference."

"Did you talk to him about your going?"

"What do you think? I'm just trying not to make a big deal out of it. I told him mommy will be working weekdays in New York and will be here on weekends."

"I'm not saying you should make a big deal out of it. I just think if Davey had any say in the matter, he'd rather have you here all the time."

"Robert, really. Don't try to make me feel guilty. Davey will survive just fine. If we act like it's a perfectly normal thing, he'll think of it that way. I'll talk to him on the phone, see him every weekend. He'll know I'm not deserting him."

"What did Davey say when you spoke to him about working in New York?"

"Nothing. Why? Did he say something to you?"

"No," Robert lied. When he'd talked to Davey earlier in the week, his son had wanted to know why his mother didn't want to live with them. Robert reassured him that that wasn't the case and he'd see her every weekend. "Will I still be able to go to Lucy's?" Davey asked. "Of course," Robert told him. Retaining two of the three mainstays in his life seemed to alleviate whatever anxiety Davey felt about his mother leaving.

On New Year's Eve, Robert sat with Alyssa in front of the fire as dusk fell and they toasted one another with champagne.

"I hope it's a good new year for you, Lys," he said, "and that your new job works out."

She sat down on his lap and kissed him. "Everything will be fine, you'll see."

They made an effort to keep the mood light during dinner although Alyssa's bags and boxes, sitting in the hallway ready for loading into the car in the morning, were a constant reminder of her impending departure. She instigated lovemaking that night, acting more passionate than she had in a long time. Immediately afterward she fell asleep. Robert, on the other hand, tossed and turned, finally slipping out of bed to stand at the window. He looked out at the uniform whiteness of their pasture, bathed in the light of the moon. He had no idea how this separation would affect them, but he suspected that their life would change. Shivering from standing in the cold room, he slipped under the covers and finally fell asleep.

Breakfast the following morning was a subdued affair. Davey sat with his elbow on the table, leaning his head on his hand.

"Aren't you hungry this morning?" Robert asked.

He shook his head.

"You feel okay? No bellyache."

"I feel okay. Daddy, will you make a snowman with me today?"

"I will, right after Mommy leaves."

The boy's eyes darted toward his mother, then looked away.

"Leave the dishes," Robert said to Alyssa, "I'll do them later." He stood up and carried an armload of boxes out to the car.

Alyssa put on her coat and knelt down to hug Davey. "I'll see you in just a few days, sweetheart. You be a good boy with daddy. Mommy will bring you something from the city."

Robert turned as Alyssa came up behind him with her suitcase.

"Aren't you cold?" she said, stamping her feet to keep them warm as Robert made room in the BMW's trunk for her bag. "You're only wearing a sweater."

"It's not bad today. Where's Davey?"

"I kissed him goodbye and told him I'd see him Friday night. He's a little mopey. I wouldn't worry."

"Well," said Robert, standing in front of her.

She smiled at him and opened her arms. "I'll see you soon."

7

With Alyssa gone, Robert found his daily routine little changed from what it had been. He drove Davey to Lucy Potter's in the morning and picked him up on the way home from work. Preparing their dinner every evening posed no problem for him. He had lived alone for enough years to be a better than average cook. After they ate, Davey occupied himself with Lego or his miniature cars while Robert did the dishes. Their television received only one station and they never turned it on. In the evening Robert read to his son or played card games or checkers with him until bedtime.

The night before Alyssa was due to arrive home, Davey asked him to read *Make Way for Ducklings*. Robert had performed two difficult surgeries that morning and seen patients in his office all afternoon. He was tired. Thinking his son wouldn't notice, he took shortcuts in his reading, skipping sentences.

"No, Daddy," Davey said, "read what it says. You missed some."

Robert guessed Davey had the story memorized since he'd heard it so often. "What did I miss?"

Davey leaned over and placed his finger on the sentences Robert hadn't read. Can he really read? Robert wondered. Davey had known the alphabet for a long time and Robert had taught him the sounds of letters and some simple words, but he never suspected his son could actually read. A thought occurred to him. The last time he and Alyssa were in the city together, they'd bought copies of *Black Beauty*, *Treasure Island*, and *Lad, a Dog*, planning to save them until Davey was old enough to read them.

"I'll be right back," he said, heading for the bedroom and rummaging on the top shelf of the closet where he thought Alyssa had stored the books. He returned to the living room with *Lad, a Dog,* showed Davey the cover, and opened the book to the first page.

"This may be too hard for you," Robert said. "Daddy will read it to you if it is."

Davey placed the book in his lap and almost effortlessly, began to read. Robert felt the same surge of pride and wonder he'd experienced when his son took his first steps across the room. It seemed so long ago.

"That's wonderful, Davey," he said. "You're a good reader. So how come you ask daddy to read to you?"

Davey shrugged his shoulders and smiled. "Because I like it when you read."

"I have an idea," Robert said. "Let's go the library in Brookville Saturday and we'll get you a library card. Then you can take out whatever books you like."

"Can't I read this one, Daddy?"

"It's not too hard for you?"

Davey shook his head forcefully.

Alyssa called him on Friday morning to tell him she'd decided to leave the city early Saturday morning. "I have so much to do in the apartment and so little time to do it. And I've got to go shopping tonight. I should be in Vermont by lunchtime. I've got so much to tell you," she said excitedly.

On Saturday morning, Robert took Davey with him to Brookville when he made hospital rounds. They stopped in the public library after leaving the hospital and Davey's eyes opened wide when he saw the shelves lined with books. Robert walked him to the children's section and although Davey was still reading *Lad, a Dog,* carrying it with him to Lucy Potter's, he insisted on taking out more books.

They'd been back at the house only five minutes when Alyssa drove up. She came through the door like a whirlwind, her arms filled with grocery bags. Pausing to give them each a kiss, she dashed back out to the car. Robert followed to help her with the unloading.

Nothing gave Alyssa more pleasure than stuffing her purchases into the refrigerator and freezer or stacking them on pantry shelves. Fortunately, the previous evening Robert had thrown out everything in the refrigerator that had gone bad, leaving room for her new supply.

"I guess you're going to have to eat all this," Robert said to Davey, winking at him.

Davey watched his mother racing around the kitchen, then picked up his library books from the table.

"Davey," Alyssa called, "look what I brought for you. Here's some little cars that I don't think you have. And here's a game called ring toss. I'll show you how to play it."

"We have that at Lucy's," Davey said.

"Well, you could still say thank you."

"Thank you," he said and headed off to his room, leaving his mother's gifts on the table.

"You must be hungry," Robert said. "Can I make you a sandwich?"

"Look what I brought for lunch," she said, opening bags of bagels and bialys. "And smoked salmon," she added. "I picked this up after work yesterday."

"That's great. I'll make a tuna sandwich for Davey. You can make ours."

"So how have you and Davey been, good?" she said, while Robert prepared his son's sandwich.

Before he could answer, she was telling him about her new apartment, the purchases she'd made for it, her neighborhood in Scarsdale, her job, and her co-workers. She continued talking non-stop through lunch and afterward, while Robert washed the dishes. He missed half of what she was saying with the water running.

"Daddy, can you pull me on the sled," Davey said, interrupting his mother.

"Davey, you're interrupting me," said Alyssa. "Doesn't Daddy teach you manners?"

Davey ignored her and looked imploringly at his father.

"Sure, you get your clothes on and go get the sled. I'll be out in a few minutes."

"It's freezing out there," Alyssa said.

"He doesn't feel it. He's used to it."

"Now I forget what I was talking about," Alyssa said. "Well, I'll remember it later. How's your new office."

"Fine. Everything's easier without OB. No interruptions, no patients complaining about cancellations or long waits."

"Good."

"The drive up was okay?"

"Easy. And I bought a bunch of new tapes to listen to. Did you invite anyone for dinner?"

"I didn't know you wanted me to."

"It's just as well you didn't this weekend. Next time I'll leave right from work on Friday. I'll invite friends. Would you mind company next weekend? I'll cook something delicious."

"Daddy, I have my sled," Davey called from the hallway.

"See you in a little while," Robert said.

An hour later, he and Davey returned, their faces reddened from the cold.

It was only four o'clock, but Alyssa was going full speed ahead with dinner preparations.

"You must both be frozen," she said.

"It's not so bad, but a cup of hot tea would hit the spot. Hot chocolate for you, Davey?"

The boy nodded and headed off to his room, returning with *Lad, a Dog*. He sat at the table reading while Robert made his hot chocolate.

"You'll have a delicious dinner tonight," Alyssa said. Busily paring and chopping vegetables, she glanced at Davey. "What's that big book?" she said.

"*Lad, a Dog.*"

"The one we picked up in New York?" she said, looking at Robert.

"Yep."

She laughed. "I didn't know it had pictures."

"It doesn't," Davey said. "Just the one on the cover."

"Since when does he pretend to read?" she asked Robert.

"He's not pretending."

"I don't believe it."

"Show her, Davey."

Alyssa stood behind him while he pointed to the first paragraph on the page and began to read.

"Amazing!" she squealed, leaning over to give him a hug and a kiss. "Wait until I tell Grandma and Grandpa. They won't believe it."

"I have a library card, too."

"You do? You're getting to be such a big boy." She turned to Robert. "How did this happen? I left Monday and come back Saturday and he's reading."

"I was as surprised as you," Robert said.

"Did you contact any of our friends in the city? Mike and Lynn?" Robert asked while they had dinner.

"Not yet, but I will. I'd love to invite Mike and Lynn to Vermont, but Lynn's probably busy with the baby and with her illustrating.

"Between the job and the apartment, I've been going non-stop this week. By ten o'clock I'm ready for bed."

"You can't kid me. You love it."

"You're right," she said. "It feels so good to be working again. But I miss you both," she said, almost as an afterthought.

It was strange having Alyssa in bed next to him again. Her presence felt almost like an intrusion. He'd grown accustomed to being by himself, the pillows propped up behind him as he read. Alyssa, accustomed now to going to sleep early, must have felt the same way. She turned off her light as soon as she slipped under the covers, although it wasn't even ten. "The week's catching up with me," she said. "Let me give you a kiss goodnight."

Moments later she was asleep.

In future weeks, as the novelty of her move wore off, the weekends took on a rhythm of their own. Alyssa spent her days cooking and reading through mail, mainly catalogs that had arrived while she was in New York. Robert pressed her to join him and Davey for short walks or sled rides, but she declined. Winter outings had never appealed to her.

One weekend Robert invited Ted and Charlotte Anderson and Jay and Amy Dumont for dinner. The Andersons and Dumonts were their only friends in Vermont. Charlotte and Amy were patients of Robert. Alyssa had met them while working in Robert's office during his first year of practice in Catamount.

During dinner, Alyssa regaled them with tales of her life in New York.

They listened politely and asked appropriate questions, but it was apparent to Robert that none of them could understand the Morgens' long-distance relationship. Alyssa, busy talking, never noticed the exchange of glances between Charlotte and her husband or between Amy and hers, but Robert did. He also didn't tell his wife about the conversation he had had with Amy the last time he had seen her as a patient in his office.

"How can she just leave Davey?" Amy said. "Jennifer is only seven months old and I couldn't bear the thought of leaving her even for a day. I don't mean to be hard on Alyssa, it's—it's just incomprehensible to me."

Amy taught at the Catamount elementary school and had been on leave of absence since she had her daughter. Although they lived in Catamount, her husband, Jay, ran the classified department at the *Brookville Herald,* that town's newspaper.

"She's here every weekend, Amy."

Amy responded with silence. When she next spoke, it was not about Alyssa. "I'm sorry you had to move your office out of Catamount, but I know why."

"You do?"

"Jay hears things at the newspaper. He says the doctors in Catamount are a bunch of shits, pardon my language. Everyone in Brookville thinks that, you know. They say you were the only good doctor on Schuyler's staff."

Robert thanked her for her words of support.

As the routine of Alyssa's weekend visits continued, she and Robert no longer felt like strangers when they were in bed together. Their sex life had resumed, even though it seemed rather perfunctory. Robert was aware, too, that he now felt like the West Roylestown house was *his* house—his and Davey's—while Alyssa's home was in New York.

Robert did not miss doing obstetrics, but more and more the tedium of his work made him feel like he had in New York. It was as if he'd simply picked up his Manhattan office and set it down off Route 89 in Vermont. The patients were different, certainly—no celebrities here—but the work he was doing was identical and didn't give him the satisfaction he craved. Life in Vermont with his son had definite advantages over New York—no worries over crime, traffic, pollution, or the frenetic pace of life. Those were the reasons he gave himself for having left the city, but now he wondered if it was more than that, if it was the private practice of medicine itself that prompted his discontent. Most of the time he felt like a small-business man. Maybe that's what medicine has evolved into for most physicians, he thought, but it was not a fraternity he enjoyed being a part of. He was now closer to fifty than forty and he felt that life was passing him by. Was this the mid-life crisis women's' magazines prattle on about, usually in articles warning their readers to keep an eye on their husbands when they're in their horny forties? All he knew was that he needed more, but what?

He wondered if the recent letter he and Alyssa had received from Sean Cooper had anything to do with his restlessness. More than a year had gone by since Sean's visit and they hadn't expected to hear from him again.

My brother, Michael, died, Sean wrote, *a month after I left the States. It hit me much harder than I thought it would. I saw how sick he was while I was in Burlington and knew the end was near, but no matter how prepared you think you are, when it happens it's still devastating. My heart ached for his wife and children. Whenever I ask if there's anything I can do to help them, Margo writes to tell me everything is under control, no help needed. She's an amazing woman. In spite of her own grief, she's made several trips to New York with her children to make sure my mother was okay. My mother took Michael's death very badly. I could tell from her letters how terribly depressed she was. Now that a year has gone by, she sounds better, both in her letters and when I speak to her on the phone, so maybe she's finally coming to terms with it.*

Work was my salvation, work and Sam's understanding of what I was going through. The Afghan refugee population has grown exponentially since I saw you. The fighting in Afghanistan is fiercer than ever, but I'm not so sure the Russians still have the upper hand. The Red Crescent clinics and hospitals in Peshawar are flooded with wounded mujahideen, those strong enough to have survived the rigors of crossing the mountains to get to Pakistan. The majority of the wounded become amputees.

The Afghan Women's Hospital is also inundated with patients from the refugee camps. Some women travel for hours by bus or walk miles to get treatment. We have eight Afghan physicians at the hospital now, none of them adequately trained, at least not by American standards. Equipment, medications, supplies, textbooks, nursing staff—all are in short supply. In spite of that, whenever volunteer doctors arrive we get a fresh infusion of what we need and we're able to do much more surgery. When there are no volunteers, the only procedures the Afghan doctors feel comfortable doing are Cesareans and minor surgeries.

Robert had read and reread the letter, wondering if Sean was making a silent appeal to him to volunteer his services. It was tempting, but given his situation in Vermont, it was also impossible. Someday, he told himself, wanting more than anything to believe it.

Enclosed with the letter was a photograph of Kiska. *I took this at my mother's house before heading back to Pakistan,* Sean wrote. *I thought Davey might like it. Ask him if he remembers the big dog. I still have fond memories of my stay with you in Vermont and hope that someday we'll meet again. I'm not the greatest correspondent but I love getting mail. Send me a photo of the three of you.*

"Look what I have, Robert said, carrying the photo into Davey's room that same evening. "Do you remember who this is?"

Davey looked at the photo and immediately smiled. "That's big dog—Kiska."

When Alyssa came up for the weekend, he showed her the letter.

"Well," she said, "it's nice to know he hasn't forgotten us."

By the time he remembered to tell her about Davey's response to seeing the photograph, Alyssa had hauled the vacuum cleaner out of the closet. The appliance roared to life as Robert stepped into the room. He watched for a few moments as Alyssa dragged the vacuum around, then decided to go outdoors with Davey.

8

Twice during the summer, Robert and Davey drove down to New York to spend long weekends with Alyssa. Davey had no memory of apartment living and was fascinated by the elevator that carried them up to her apartment on the eighth floor. Riding up and down in the lift would have kept him occupied for hours had Robert and Alyssa permitted it. Her living room, with its view to the east, overlooked a strip of park adjoining a wide stream. Davey pointed down at the geese feeding on the grass and asked Robert to take him down to the birds. Alyssa crumbled up some bread into a paper bag and they strolled with their son, following the course of the stream, while Davey fed the geese.

"How do you like the apartment?" Alyssa asked.

"It's very nice. I like the way you furnished it. The things you bought will look good in the Vermont house, too."

Alyssa gave him a sideways glance but said nothing.

It was obvious to Robert that his wife was completely at home in her apartment, more so than she had been in the Vermont house. The carpets were spotless, each item of furniture was tastefully chosen, houseplants either lined the windowsills or hung suspended from hooks, and paintings and prints he'd never seen before were on the walls. It was easier for her to keep the place clean without a child, he rationalized. Nevertheless, something about the apartment troubled him. It was as if her time spent in West Roylestown had simply been an interlude. Inwardly, he wondered if she would ever be able to make the transition to Vermont or if, for that matter, she had any intention of trying. For him, the few days he spent in her apartment during each visit only reinforced what he was already certain of—it would be impossible for him to return to an urban lifestyle. After two and a half years in his own home in Vermont, the concept of apartment living had become as foreign to him as the idea of living in a Mongolian yurt. Given the choice, he would have chosen the latter since the doors of the other apartments lining the hallway from the elevator gave him a claustrophobic feeling.

Another thing he noticed were the clothes Alyssa had accumulated in little more than half a year. Her bedroom closet was crammed with dresses and suits that she had purchased since moving to Westchester. A shoeholder suspended from the rear of the door held at least twenty pairs of shoes, mostly pumps, while boots, running shoes, and sandals were jumbled on the floor. It was true that Alyssa had been a clothes horse when they lived together in the city. He rationalized that her bursting closets were to be expected now that she had a new job. And yet, he couldn't entirely dismiss the fact that Alyssa had never asked him how finances were in Vermont. She knew his practice income was nowhere near what it had been while he was doing obstetrics. Their unspoken arrangement seemed to be that he paid his way and Davey's, she paid hers. It was as if they were no longer a married couple.

When Robert asked her about their friends in the city, the Finkels and Rosses especially, Alyssa told him she'd telephoned several times without reaching any of them. "It's summer," she said, "and they're probably all away. I'm sure we'll make contact at some point."

On the day before Thanksgiving, Robert and Davey drove down to New York for the holiday. They stopped at Alyssa's apartment just long enough to transfer their suitcase to her car, then headed out to Rego Park, where Alyssa's parents lived. It was late afternoon when they arrived. Evelyn Farber, standing in the doorway, stretched out her arms to receive her grandson. The ruddy flush on her face indicated that she'd already started on the martinis she loved. Alyssa bore no resemblance to her mother, for which Robert had always been thankful. Evelyn was at least four inches shorter than Alyssa, and even wearing a girdle she couldn't mask the barrel-like shape of her waist and buttocks.

"How's my precious little Davey?" she said, enveloping him in her arms and covering his face with kisses. "Let's go say hello to grandpa."

They followed Evelyn into the living room where Arnold Farber sat reading the newspaper. The house was so quiet it didn't feel like a holiday, a marked contrast to the previous year when the Morgens had arrived from Vermont on Thanksgiving Day. Then they'd walked into a house filled with Alyssa's relatives and before the night was over, he and Alyssa weren't speaking to one another. The whole scene flashed through Robert's mind as he watched Arnold poring over his *Wall Street Journal*, oblivious to their presence. It was during that last Thanksgiving at the Farbers, Robert recalled, that Alyssa had confided in her parents about her decision to move back to New York. Robert, of course, was outside the loop.

"Everyone's here," Evelyn Farber had called over her shoulder to Robert as he followed her in. Alyssa had already headed off to the kitchen. 'Everyone' was an assortment of uncles, aunts, cousins, and the distinguished Myron Kleinberg, a 'brilliant' sociology professor at Columbia University, and his wife, Esther, who as far as Robert could determine was a 'brilliant' housewife. The Kleinbergs, distant relations of Evelyn, never stayed more than a half-hour, just long enough to bestow their brilliance upon the gathering while having a drink. Robert had learned long ago that 'brilliant' was the most overused word in his mother-in-law's vocabulary. Every relative, friend, and acquaintance of the Farbers was 'brilliant.'

Alyssa's father, Arnold, a psychologist, was pontificating to other members of the Farber clan when Robert joined them. Arnold had immediately beckoned to him.

"I hope I'm not interrupting anything," Robert said, hoping he wasn't about to be bored by a deluge of psychobabble.

"No, not at all. Joe and Myra were just talking about horses," Arnold said. Joe and Myra Feld, Alyssa's cousins, sat next to him.

"Horses?"

"Yes, Joe's niece lives in the boonies somewhere in New Jersey—"

"Lake Hopatcong," Joe said.

"Right. Well, her mother just got her a horse." Arnold sipped his vodka tonic and dabbed at his fleshy lips with a napkin. His bullet-shaped head was bald except for a gray tonsure and his prominent eyes were made even larger by the thick glasses he wore. How the Farbers had managed to produce his beautiful Alyssa was a mystery.

"And Arnold was telling us," giggled Myra, "that horses have such a long—you know what—that men have to hold it to guide it into the mare while they're breeding. Otherwise they can't do it."

Robert looked at his father-in-law, waiting for the punch line, but it never came. Arnold sat there sagely nodding.

"Yes, it's true," he said, confirming it for Robert.

"That's preposterous," Robert said, laughing and expecting Arnold to join him.

"No, it's a fact. I have it on good authority."

"Really," Robert said. "How many penis-holders do they have to hire out west for the herds of wild horses? If it wasn't for them the herds would die out."

Arnold stared at him, his mouth silently opening and closing.

"Anyone want their drink freshened?" Robert said, standing up before his father-in-law could regain his voice.

He excused himself and headed for the kitchen.

Alyssa was standing at the center island preparing salads. She gave him a look that was half-questioning, half-accusatory. For him to reappear after being with her father for only five minutes didn't bode well.

"Everything all right?" Alyssa asked.

"Fine. Just came in to pour myself a drink."

Evelyn, holding Davey in her arms, was standing at the stove with Melinda, the black cook brought in by the Farbers for special occasions. Robert's mother-in-law, already on her second martini, was slightly tipsy, sufficiently unsteady on her feet to worry Robert that she might fall while holding Davey.

Melinda bent over the oven and arranged yams on a rack for baking. She paid no attention to the instructions Evelyn was giving her. She turned to look at Robert as he approached them and a big smile transformed her stern face.

"Here's my boyfriend," she said in her slow Alabama drawl, giving him a hug.

"Hi, Melinda, how are you?"

"I'm fine, Doctor Robert. That's quite a boy you have. He's sure grown since I last saw him."

"Let me take him, Evelyn," Robert said. "He's no lightweight."

"Well then, I'll go see how everyone is doing. Dinner should be ready in about an hour. Is there anything you need, Alyssa? Melinda?"

"No, we're fine, Mrs. Farber," Melinda said, rolling her eyes when her employer turned away.

"You go ahead, Mother. Melinda and I can take care of everything in here."

Robert put Davey down as soon as Evelyn was out of the room. He tickled him, making his son squirm and giggle. "Three years old and you make your grandma stand there holding you? You're almost big enough to hold her."

"Go in the living room and bother everyone in there," Robert said.

"Robert, that's not nice," scolded Alyssa while Melinda chuckled. She looked at him while she sliced tomatoes. "It's awfully quiet in there. Are you sure everything is all right?"

"You been giving Mr. Farber a hard time?" Melinda laughed, looking at him over her shoulder.

Robert smiled. "No more than usual."

"What went on in there?" Alyssa asked, not willing to let him off the hook.

"Your father has come by a startling piece of information. He insists that horses' dongs are so long that people have to hold them and aim them at their target so they can impregnate a mare."

"Lord, that's the dumbest thing I ever heard," Melinda said. Seeing Alyssa's glare, she turned back to the stove.

"I'm sure you disabused him of that idea," Alyssa said.

"I just wondered out loud how many people the government had to hire to make sure the wild horse herds didn't die out."

Melinda's shoulders shook with silent laughter. She kept her back to Robert and Alyssa, but he saw her lift her apron to wipe the tears from her eyes.

"I don't appreciate this, Robert," Alyssa said, her teeth clenched.

"Oh, come on, Lys. I was just having fun."

"Yeah, at someone else's expense."

"Daddy," Davey said as he came back into the kitchen, "can I have a carrot?"

"Sure," Robert said, glad for his son's interruption. "Keep eating those vegetables and you'll be as strong as Popeye."

"Popeye eats spinach," Davey said.

"That's right, but it's a vegetable."

"You ought to go back in and smooth things over," Alyssa said, not willing to let him off the hook.

"All right, but first I'd better make sure Popeye here is dry." He caught Melinda's eye as he left the room and winked.

Alyssa was all smiles during dinner and no one would have guessed there was still tension between them. It would have remained that way if Alyssa hadn't interrupted the inane discussion between her father and Joe Feld about foreign and domestic cars.

"Robert had his car broken into at the hospital this week," she said.

From the cries of dismay someone would have thought a terrible tragedy had befallen the Morgens.

"That's why no one can live in the city," Myra Feld said. She looked around to make certain Melinda was not in the room. "Those *schwarzes* make life impossible for everyone."

"We live in the city," Robert said, "and this is the first time anything like this has happened. Besides, drug addicts are like Lifesavers candy. They're everywhere and they come in assorted colors."

"Well," Myra said, flushing, "I only meant—"

"Statistically, of course," Arnold interjected, "Myra is right. You can't deny that drug use and crime are more prevalent among the underprivileged, and their ranks, as you well know, are made up mainly of people of color."

Robert, annoyed, ignored Alyssa's warning look.

"Well, let's just say there were no pigment traces in my car. Anyway, a missing radio and a broken window aren't exactly the end of the world."

They slept over at the Farbers that night, Alyssa still angry and keeping her distance.

"You'll fall out of bed," Robert said, "if you get any closer to the edge."

She swung around to face him. "I wish you'd make more of an effort with my family," she said. "Sometimes I think you take pleasure in provoking them. Why do you hate my father?"

"I don't hate him. Please, Lys. I don't want them to hear us arguing."

"You should have thought of that before you started this. Always so superior."

"Me? I'm the one who's so superior? What about your father, that pompous prick?"

"That's what you think of him?"

"Lys, I'm sorry," he said, fearing things were getting out of hand. "That was uncalled for and I apologize. I'm just tired. Let's forget it."

She turned her back to him, her silence louder than any words.

It was now a year later and Robert hoped this Thanksgiving would be less tempestuous.

"Arnold, put down your paper," Evelyn said. "Look who just arrived."

"Well, here's the good doctor," Arnold said, rising from his chair.

"You don't have to get up," Robert said, shaking his hand.

Alyssa gave her father a peck on the cheek. Evelyn held Davey out toward him. "Give grandpa a kiss," she said.

That evening, after a light dinner, Alyssa and her mother prepared for the next day's feast. Watching Alyssa race around the kitchen, Robert asked about Melinda. "Doesn't she usually come on Wednesday to help?"

"She wanted to spend the holiday with her family," Evelyn said in an exasperated voice.

The mood that Thanksgiving was different. Robert had hoped for a calmer family gathering, but the atmosphere was distinctly subdued. Alyssa's relatives greeted him and made small talk, but he might just as well not have been there. He felt excluded and didn't know why. Are they still upset about last year's holiday? Or do they blame me for Alyssa's moving by herself to Westchester? he wondered. Alyssa chatted animatedly with them about her job and apartment, but no one asked him about his practice or about Vermont. Am I just being overly sensitive? he asked himself.

Later that evening, when he and Alyssa were in bed, he asked her if she'd picked up on any strange vibrations from her family. "You're imagining things," she said.

He put his arm around her and she shifted her hips, increasing the distance between them.

"You tired?" he asked.

"Exhausted. It was a lot of work without Melinda."

9

In the past Robert and Alyssa had looked forward to having sex in her parents' home. It had the air of the forbidden about it, making it even more enjoyable. He thought of trying to arouse her, but she had turned her back to him and moved away. Was he imagining that, too?

Robert had noticed in recent weeks that whenever Alyssa came to Vermont, she seemed more and more distant. Sex between them was infrequent, and when it did occur he never felt her heart was in it. It was as if their relationship had sprung a leak and the intimacy it once held was slowly dripping away. Was he imagining that, too?

Lying there in Alyssa's parents' guest room, Robert realized it had been just about a year since his wife first told him about her having applied for the job in Westchester. January would be a year since she moved down to Scarsdale. What was it she'd said to him? That it might lead to something closer to Vermont? That she'd like to try it for at least a year? Well, that year was almost up. They'd have to talk about it at some point. And soon, Robert thought.

At the beginning of Christmas week Alyssa called to ask him if he'd bring Davey down on Christmas Day. "We can take him to see the tree in Rockefeller Center," she said. "The city is so wonderful this time of year. And Robert—" She hesitated momentarily. "My parents would like to spend a week with him during New Year's and his birthday."

"I thought you were coming up here for New Year's and Davey's birthday."

"My parents specifically asked. I can't expect them to make the drive up to Vermont in the winter. Please, Robert, bring him down Saturday. And pack plenty of his clothes. It's cold down here, too."

Robert was troubled by Alyssa's request. Several times during the next few days he was on the verge of calling her to tell her he wouldn't be coming down. He knew it would lead to a row, but it wasn't his fear of confrontation that gave him pause. It was the brittleness he sensed in their relationship in recent months. He didn't want to do anything to push their marriage over the edge, especially since he intended to talk to her about moving back to Vermont. Besides, he rationalized, Alyssa had been making the drive between New York and Vermont almost every weekend. Perhaps he owed this to her. And her parents only saw Davey a few times a year, usually on Passover and Thanksgiving. But, he thought, even when he and Alyssa lived in Manhattan, her parents, in spite of frequently attending shows and concerts in the city, made no effort to visit them. It was always he and Alyssa who brought Davey to them. Why did they suddenly need him for a week? he asked himself.

Christmas Eve was still a special time for Robert. His mother, in spite of having no religious leanings, always set up a tree in their living room before Christmas. It was a holdover, he was sure, from her own childhood. She always made a festive occasion out of it as she and Robert hung the decorations and lights, and draped the tinsel. Robert's father, who never celebrated any holidays, even the Jewish ones he must have known as a child, always insisted that he be the one to plug in the lights. His face lit up with childish pleasure when the small bulbs sparkled to life. Each of them placed their presents to one another under the tree and Robert was always the first one up on Christmas Day.

On the day before Christmas, Davey picked out a small tree in the woods and Robert cut it down. They set it up and decorated it together. Since they planned to leave early the following morning to drive to New York, Robert gave Davey his presents that afternoon. Robert roasted a small chicken for dinner while Davey sat on the floor constructing cabins with the set of Lincoln Logs Robert had given him. The tree's flame-shaped lights twinkled, a fire blazed in the fireplace, the aroma of food filled the house, Christmas carols played on the radio, and Robert and his son were content to be together. Before putting Davey to bed that night, the two of them stood at the window, staring through the ice patterns on the glass at the fields blanketed with snow. In the distance, tree limbs bowed under their white cover, and the December moon seemed far, far away.

After leaving Davey with the Farbers, Robert and Alyssa had spent a subdued New Year's Eve at her apartment, finding they had little to say to one another. Robert had a sense of foreboding, and on the morning of New Year's Day was inclined to drive back to the Farbers to pick up Davey. He knew, however, that he and Alyssa would have a major fight if he did. Well, it's only one week, he told himself.

At times, during the drive back to West Roylestown, he'd turn his head to say something, forgetting that Davey wasn't in the back seat. By the time he exited the highway, the sky was leaden. More snow was coming. He rolled slowly down his driveway, the tires crunching on the snow and gravel, toward a house that now looked forlorn in a world of black and white.

Ordinarily during the workweek, Robert would pick Davey up from Lucy Potter's on his way home from the office and listen to his son's chatter about the day's activities. When their house hove into view, he was sure Davey felt the same way he did, that they were approaching a sanctuary promising warmth and a quiet serenity. Within minutes after entering he'd have a fire going, and while Davey hauled out his Tinkertoys or Legos, he'd pour himself a glass of wine and contemplate making dinner. Today, there was no such anticipation. Without Davey, the house was mired in gloom. Its rooms appeared unlived in, the ashes in the fireplace as cold as if they'd been there for years. Robert started a fire with newspaper and kindling, but the fire provided no warmth. He stood there in the empty house and listened to the silence. In the middle of the living room floor he spotted two colored Lego pieces Davey had overlooked. Robert picked them up and looked at them as they lay in the palm of his hand. He felt like crying. Angry with himself, he cleared his throat, went into the kitchen, and poured himself a scotch. He opened the refrigerator and stared at the food on the shelves. Unable to make up his mind what to cook, he closed the door and returned to the living room. He stood at the window, morosely watching the falling snow. If Davey were there, he'd be asking if they could go outside after dinner to build a snowman. But without his son, the snow was a white shroud on a bleak world.

Robert was glad when the first gray light came through his bedroom window. Working would take his mind off Davey's absence.

With the holidays over, it was business as usual. His waiting room was filled. But as the day drew to a close, he dreaded returning to a house sucked dry of life. His reluctance to go home puzzled him. He'd never had a problem in the past with being alone. Before marrying Alyssa, he had, in fact, welcomed the quiet evenings by himself after work. Even now, it wasn't Alyssa's absence that bothered him. He missed his son. No wonder people talk about the empty nest syndrome, he thought. If after five years with Davey Robert felt his absence so acutely, what would it be like when he was eighteen and went off to college?

That evening Robert drove to Brookville and had dinner by himself at the High Country Inn. A fire blazed in the large stone fireplace and Robert relaxed in the room's warm ambience. There were few diners and he prolonged the intervals between courses, sipping his merlot and taking comfort in the soft conversations of the people around him.

By the time he drove home, Robert was laughing at himself. His son would be back in less than a week. Instead of bemoaning his absence, he should be taking advantage of the time alone, catching up on his reading.

On the sixth of January, Davey's fifth birthday, Robert called Alyssa. No one answered. He called the Farbers and Arnold answered. Alyssa was at work, but they'd be having Davey's party that evening. His father-in-law called Davey to the phone. Robert's spirits lifted as soon as he heard his son's voice.

Davey hated to talk on the phone for long, and this day was no exception. "Daddy, I'm building a big cabin with my logs. I have to go now."

Robert laughed, wished him a happy birthday, and said he'd see him soon.

On Friday evening, he called Alyssa to tell her he'd be down the next day.

"We can spend the day in the city if you like and have dinner out before picking up Davey at your folks. I don't have to start the drive back with Davey until Sunday afternoon, so we can enjoy a slow, lazy morning."

She was strangely silent on the phone after he'd said that.

"Is something wrong?" he asked.

"I'd like to keep Davey down here," she said.

"What do you mean?"

"You've had him for a year. Now I'd like to have him here with me. I've already enrolled him in pre-school."

"What the hell are you talking about? That wasn't what we agreed on. You were supposed to give it a year to see if it would lead to a job closer to our home and Davey was supposed to live with me."

"Robert, you know damned well there's nothing for me in Vermont. Don't be selfish. Davey should spend time with his mother, too, you know."

"Look, Alyssa, it wasn't my idea for you to go to New York. You can't just kidnap Davey because he was down there with you and your parents for the week."

"Kidnap? He's my son."

"Goddammit, Alyssa, this is wrong and you know it."

"Look, why don't you come down tomorrow like you planned and we can discuss it like two rational human beings. I'm going out to my parents in the morning to pick Davey up, but I don't want him to hear us fighting. Let's just have a nice day together and talk about it after he's gone to bed."

"What is there to talk about? You're going back on your word."

"I didn't promise you anything. I only said maybe it would lead to something. We didn't put any definite time limit on it. And we never really talked about Davey except for the first year."

"You're really something, Alyssa. You put your own spin on everything, don't you."

"Robert, don't be angry. Come down and we'll talk. I'll expect you tomorrow."

Robert stared at the phone in his hand after she'd hung up. "Bitch!" he yelled, slamming the phone down.

10

"Hi, Daddy," Davey said, as Robert entered Alyssa's apartment. He sat on the floor playing listlessly with his miniature cars. It was not the exuberant welcome Robert had expected. He knows what's going on, Robert thought.

"I'm going to make some sandwiches for lunch," Alyssa said. "Would you like one?"

As hungry as he was, Robert shook his head. "Do you have any coffee made?"

"I'll warm it up."

If the air between them had been any colder, icicles would have formed. Robert felt as if he were talking to a total stranger, a hostile one at that. He sat at the table with them while they ate.

"Have you been feeding the geese?" Robert asked.

Davey shook his head. "I was at Grandma and Grandpa's."

"Oh, that's right. Would you like to feed them this afternoon?"

Davey shrugged and pushed his plate away.

"You hardly ate any of your sandwich," Robert said.

"I'm not hungry."

"Try eating a little more and drink your milk, then I'll take you out to the park."

Alyssa ate in silence, saying nothing until Robert and Davey were putting their coats on to go out.

"I'm not invited, I suppose?"

"I didn't say that."

"Then I'll join you. Do you want some bread for the geese, Davey?"

He nodded and Alyssa crumbled bread into a paper bag.

"I don't think people are very happy to see you feeding the geese, Davey," she said. "And you know why."

Davey cracked a smile, his first since Robert had arrived.

"Why is that, Davey?" he asked.

"Geese poop all over the grass in the park and people step in it."

Robert laughed.

Davey ran ahead of them tossing chunks of stale bread to the fearless geese. They cackled as he approached, then moved reluctantly out of his way.

"Look, I know you're angry," Alyssa said, "but let's try to work this out."

"And how do you suggest we do that?"

"You've had Davey for a year. And I've driven up to Vermont almost every weekend, haven't I?"

"What has that got to do with your trying to kidnap him? It was your choice to move to New York and do the commute."

"Don't you think it's only fair that he gets to live with me now? I'm his mother. We can work something out on the commuting."

"You're missing the point. Davey lives with me. I don't care if he spends time with you or with your parents. I think that's very nice. But he lives in Vermont and he enjoys being at Lucy's while I'm at work. Didn't I bring him down when you said your parents wanted to spend his birthday with him?"

"Robert, I want to spend more time with him. And he'll enjoy the preschool here in Scarsdale as much as he enjoys Lucy's."

"If you want to spend more time with him, move back to Vermont."

"I can't. Don't you understand?"

"And I refuse to live in New York. All anyone cares about here is money and appearances. I'm not exactly a stranger here, don't forget. I grew up in the city and worked here for years. I find living in this environment intolerable."

She shook her head. "Robert, Robert. How are we going to resolve this?"

"Look, I'd be the first to admit that Vermont has some drawbacks. I'd hoped we'd have more friends, but we've been there less than three years. I still believe our social life will improve if we give it time. Our so-called friends in

New York haven't been tripping over themselves to come see us, have they? The winters in Vermont are long, but they're long in New York, too. And the pace of life in Vermont, especially now that I've given up OB and don't have emergency room call, is certainly better than it was here. The practice is going well enough, even without OB."

"You could practice in New York without doing OB. It doesn't have to be in the city. You can open an office in Westchester. That would take away a lot of the stress."

"We're going in circles, Lys. I don't want to live and work in New York."

"And I don't want to live in Vermont, and I sure as hell can't work there. Davey will start kindergarten in the fall. What am I supposed to do in Vermont— sit around twiddling my thumbs during the day while he's in school?"

"Couldn't you work at something other than psychiatric social work?"

"What do you suggest? Waitressing? Maid in a ski lodge? Very rewarding. How would you like it if I told you you could work at something other than being a physician?"

"I might welcome the chance if I thought I could afford it."

"Fine. Move here, give up medicine, and I'll support us."

"This is getting us nowhere."

Davey emptied the last crumbs from his paper bag and watched Robert and Alyssa with an anxious expression on his face.

"Does Davey know what's going on?"

"I've told him I'd like him to stay here with me."

"What did he say?"

"What do you suppose he said? He said he wants to live with both of us."

"You really got us into a fix by moving here."

"And what about you and Vermont? You knew I had reservations about moving there."

"You barely gave it a chance. I thought you had more gumption, more willingness to try something new. What is it really, Lys? Your parents? You're so tied in to them you can't leave them? Or is it the work? Do you value yourself only through your job?"

"Go to hell, Robert. I've tried to reason with you but it's hopeless. Davey is staying with me."

"Davey lives with me."

"What are you going to do? Make a big scene? Should I call the police? Is that what you want your son to see?"

"I never thought you could be such a bitch."

"I want to resolve this, you don't."

"How can we if neither one of us will budge? I have my practice in Vermont and we have our home there."

"You had a practice in New York and left it. And we had a nice apartment in the city before we moved to Vermont."

"Your getting Davey down here under false pretenses sure as hell didn't solve anything."

They stood glaring at one another. Davey turned his back on them and walked listlessly along the stream's edge. He knows we're arguing, Robert thought, and can't bear to watch. Poor kid.

"When are you going back?" Alyssa asked.

"I was going to take Davey back tomorrow. I have surgery scheduled Monday morning."

She shook her head. "He's staying here, Robert."

They headed back to the apartment in silence.

"Do you want to play some card games, Davey?" Robert asked.

He shook his head and went into his mother's bedroom.

"Can't you see what you're doing to him?" Robert asked softly, trying to contain his anger. "You're taking him away from his home. He doesn't even have a room for himself here."

"He'll adjust, just like he adjusted to Vermont. A two-bedroom apartment on the sixth floor will be available the end of next month. We'll move there."

"You've got it all planned out, don't you, and it looks like your plans don't include me."

"I never said that."

"Well, I'm going to say it for you," he said. "I'm divorcing you, Alyssa."

"Oh, Robert, don't be melodramatic."

He turned his back on her and headed for the bedroom, where he found Davey lying prone on Alyssa's bed with a book open in front of him.

"What are you reading?" he asked.

"*Aesop's Fables.* Grandma bought it for me."

"That's very nice. Davey, listen, I'll be leaving now."

"Where are you going?"

"I'll probably go see Grandma and Grandpa Morgen and spend the night there."

"Will you come back to see me?"

"You know I will. Things are a little difficult right now, Davey. Do you know what's going on?"

"Mommy wants me to live here and you want me to live in Vermont."

"What do you want?"

"I want to live with both of you."

"I know. But what if Mommy and Daddy can't agree on where to live?"

"Then I want to go back to Vermont."

He sat up and threw his arms around Robert's neck.

Robert bit his lip to hold back his own tears. "Listen," he whispered, "Daddy doesn't want to get in a big fight with Mommy. It will only make you feel bad. Why don't you tell Mommy that you want to come back to Vermont. If you keep telling her, maybe she'll change her mind. In the meantime, I'll come here to see you."

"When?" Davey asked, his eyes welling with tears.

"I'll work that out with Mommy when we both calm down."

He kissed his son and walked back to the kitchen, pausing when he heard Alyssa on the phone. "He says he's divorcing me." Robert knew without asking that she was on the phone with her parents. She caught sight of him in the doorway. "I'll call you back," she said.

"I'm leaving. I'll be talking to you on the phone."

"You're welcome to stay here for the night. You don't want to drive back now, do you?"

She stood near the phone, perfectly composed. "Really, Robert, stay for dinner and have a good night's sleep. It will make Davey feel better and you can spend the morning with him before heading back."

"I didn't know making Davey feel better was one of your priorities." The voice of reason, he thought, and all he wanted to do was strangle her. How could I ever have loved this woman? he wondered.

He picked up his jacket and headed for the door. She was right. He didn't want to drive back now. He also didn't want to spend the night at his parents' house. They were old people and he didn't want to lay this mess on them. But he couldn't stay in Alyssa's apartment. He was seething and the last thing he wanted was to expose Davey to a loud, hostile argument. He closed the door behind him and headed for the elevator.

As he walked to his car he thought about calling Mike and Lynn Finkel, maybe go see the new baby, but then he'd have to lie and say he was in the city by himself while Alyssa was in Vermont. They'd guess something was wrong. Too soon for that, he thought.

What are you going to do? he kept asking himself on the long drive back to Vermont. The only thing he knew for certain was that he'd follow through on what he'd told Alyssa. He was going to file for divorce. The thought of living with her again, of touching her, was now repulsive. "She's a viper," he said aloud. The one unknown was how the situation with Davey would play out. Can a father get custody in court? he wondered. The only divorced person he knew was Joe Ross. Marcy was his second wife. But Joe had no children with his first wife. "It was no big deal," he'd told Robert during one of their conversations years earlier. "We split up the money, said goodbye and good luck, and that was it."

Robert knew nothing about the intricacies of divorce and child custody, but he did know Alyssa, which meant he had a battle on his hands. Poor Davey, he thought, why'd he have to get caught in the middle of this? The thought of his son suffering brought tears to his eyes, blurring the oncoming headlights.

11

Robert stared at the letter he'd printed to Davey. Ten lines eked out with effort. Strange, he thought. It was so easy to talk to his son when they were together, but writing a letter to a five-year-old was another matter. He opened his suitcase and removed the pouch that held his passport and traveler's checks. It also contained a photo of Davey that he'd taken a year ago in Vermont, his son sitting on top of their woodpile holding a log above his head.

"Then I want to go back to Vermont," Davey had said, throwing his arms around Robert's neck. The clarity of that moment caused Robert to catch his breath. For a moment, he could actually smell the vanilla aroma of Davey's skin. The memory was almost too difficult to bear.

Robert closed his eyes and conjured up the image of Roland Sverdrup, his lawyer in Vermont. He was sitting in Sverdrup's Brookville office, his eyes roving over the wood-paneled walls and diplomas while the lawyer, who had the face of a bloodhound and the hands of a stevedore, scribbled notes on a legal pad. Roland Sverdrup was the only attorney Robert knew in Vermont since it was Sverdrup whom he'd consulted when he and Alyssa bought the West Roylestown house.

"It's sad," the lawyer said, "but your situation isn't uncommon. I get at least a half-dozen clients a year who move to Vermont in pursuit of a dream, only to find that their spouse can't adjust to rural life. What we have to do now is try to make the divorce as painless as possible. I'll need a list of the assets so we can divide everything equitably."

"All that's secondary," said Robert. "Davey—my son—is what matters to me."

"I'm sure your wife will agree to joint custody."

"Yeah, but I want him back here in Vermont to live with me. She's insisting he stay in New York with her."

"I've been at this for a lot of years, Doctor Morgen, and I can count the number of fathers who've been awarded custody on the fingers of one hand. And in almost every case it was because the mother didn't want the child or disappeared. Judges tend to favor mothers. Those are the facts. If your son were still living in Vermont with you and you could prove desertion by the mother, you might have a case, but as things now stand—"

"But he was living with me. She got Davey under false pretenses. She asked me to leave him with her for a week so her parents could celebrate his birthday with him. When I went down to bring him back she wouldn't give him to me."

"Why didn't you simply put him in your car and drive away?"

"You don't understand. How could I do that to him? Was I supposed to pull him by one arm while she pulled at the other, the two of us screaming at one another? How would I have felt if the police had come? The memory of that scene would always have remained with Davey."

"I know you have the boy's best interests at heart and I can understand your frustration. But she is his mother and the fact remains that he's now with her in New York. That means you'd have to pursue any custody battle in a New York court, which complicates matters for you even more. Is your wife an alcoholic or a drug addict? Does she abuse the child? Does she bring men home and have sex in front of the child? Does she leave him alone and go out for the night? If the answers to those questions are no, you won't have a prayer in a courtroom."

"In spite of her deceit?"

"In spite of her deceit. I think your best bet is joint custody. Let her have primary domicile, work out visitation you can both agree on, like alternating weekends and dividing the summer, and agree on child support that's reasonable."

"Davey's told me that if he can't live with both of us he wants to be in Vermont with me."

"He's a five-year-old. Judges don't give much credence to what a five-year-old says."

"This stinks," Robert said angrily.

"Believe me, I know how you feel. I'm just telling you the facts. If you're convinced you want to go through with this, I suggest we serve her with papers and wait to see what her lawyer's response will be. Do you know what lawyer she'll choose?"

"Probably someone her father chooses for her."

"Let me get the papers drawn up, then I'll call you."

Robert walked dejectedly back to his car. If Sverdrup was right, he had no chance of getting Davey, unless he dropped his divorce petition and moved down to New York to live with Alyssa. And that he wouldn't do. He simply couldn't live a life of pretense, not even for Davey. But was Sverdrup right? He was, after all, just a small-town lawyer with a general practice. If a patient in a small town was told by her GP to undergo a major surgical procedure, wouldn't it make sense for her to get a second opinion from a specialist? Well, this was no different, he decided, and it was what he would do.

Robert drove to his office. It was Wednesday afternoon and the staff was off. He sat down at his desk and dialed Joe Ross in New York.

"You're still alive?" Ross said. "I thought by now the bears had eaten you."

"Listen, Joe, the reason I'm calling is that Alyssa and I are divorcing."

"Schmuck, I told you not to move to Vermont. You take a Jewish girl out of New York, it's like taking a fish out of water. They can't survive. No Bloomingdale's? No Saks Fifth Avenue? No MOMA? Life is over."

"Yeah, but it's not funny. She's been living in Scarsdale the past year and Davey was living with me in Vermont."

"She left him behind? That's weird."

"She took a job in Westchester. The same work she was doing when we lived in the city. She said she'd try it for a year and see if it would lead to something closer to Vermont. Then in December she tells me to bring Davey down for a week so her parents can celebrate his birthday with him. Like an idiot, I did it. When I went down to pick him up she wouldn't let him come back to Vermont with me. She wants him to live with her."

"So move back to New York. It's where your roots are and then you can have your son back."

"It's not that easy. After what she did, I could never live with her again."

"You're just angry. If a kid wasn't involved, you could say adios and not look back. But that's not the case."

"Joe, if someone fucked you over, you'd feel just like I do."

"I remember when you and Alyssa came back from France after you got married. I'd never seen you so animated. You were happy."

"We'd been on our honeymoon, for Christ's sake. What's that got to do with what's happening now?"

"What I'm saying is get out of West Bumfuck or wherever the hell you are and come back home. Wait a minute, did you sign a non-compete clause when you sold your practice?"

"Sure. That's standard, right?"

"It's standard, but if they make it far enough away, you can't practice any closer than Perth Amboy."

"It's irrelevant. I'm not coming back to practice in New York."

"So what are you going to do?"

"The lawyer here says I don't have a prayer of getting custody of Davey. Not custody, actually. I'm willing to do joint custody, but I want him to live with me. My lawyer says no court will do it. Maybe he's right, I don't know. I need a referral to a lawyer in New York, someone good who deals only with these types of cases. Do you know anyone like that?"

"As a matter of fact, I do. He's a patient of mine. Hold on, I'll give you his name and number.

"Here it is. Philip Abramowitz. He's got an office in the Empire State Building. Here's his number. Tell him I told you to call. If you're going to be in the city to see him, let's get together."

"Thanks, Joe. I'll call you when I'm in the city. Give my best to Marcy."

Abramowitz's office on the fortieth floor was larger than Robert's and Sverdrup's combined. He sat behind a massive desk and peered at Robert through small wire-rimmed glasses. A thin, wiry man, wearing a suit and tie that cost more than Robert's entire wardrobe, he was dwarfed by his surroundings, yet seemed totally at ease in them. He was framed by a picture window behind him. The east side of Manhattan spread out before Robert all the way to the East River. Beyond that sprawled the borough of Queens.

Abramowitz listened in silence as Robert explained his predicament, then stood up and paced behind his desk.

He stopped abruptly and turned to Robert. "I'm not going to bullshit you," he said. "Your lawyer in Vermont was telling you the truth. It's tough. Damned tough. The only thing you have going for you is the fact that she left him behind for a year. But she'll say she came up every weekend to see him, which shows how much she loves him. Her getting your son down to New York under false pretenses? She'll put a spin on that favorable to her—like what she told you, you had him for a year, now I want him. I'd be willing to take the case, provided you understand it would be very expensive and I can't give you any guarantees as to the outcome. My hourly rate is two hundred fifty dollars. By the time this is over, you'll be out twenty or thirty grand, maybe more. And if you lose you'll probably get hit with her legal fees."

"So what you're telling me is that it's a lost cause."

"Lost?" he shrugged. "Let's say miracles happen, just not too often. If your son was older, maybe ten or twelve, and told the judge he wanted to be with you, then you'd have a better chance. But even then, who knows. Let me put this into perspective for you. Do you want to hear about the judges you might draw for this case? One is a former Jesuit. Another still lives with his mother. Another is a devout Catholic with eight children. Do you get my drift?"

Robert felt a lot worse after departing from Abramowitz's office than he had when he entered. He told Abramowitz that he'd call if he wanted to pursue the custody battle. Knowing that the game was over before it had even started, he felt like crawling into a hole where he could lick his wounds in solitude. He stopped at a phone booth in the lobby and called Joe Ross' office, leaving word with the receptionist that he wouldn't be able to meet with Joe. "Tell him I'm heading back to Vermont," he said.

Everything happened the way Sverdrup had predicted, from division of assets to joint custody, with Davey's primary home being with his mother in Scarsdale. Alyssa agreed to Robert's getting the Vermont house as his residence, but if he sold it, they'd divide the proceeds. Child support was set at eight hundred a month. Robert's visitation with Davey was every other weekend and four weeks in the summer; they'd alternate major holidays. Prior to being served the divorce papers, Alyssa had remained outwardly friendly, the voice of reason on the phone, but once she was served, that changed. No pretence now. She glared at him when he came for Davey; and they spoke only when necessary, acid dripping from every word.

On the surface, Davey appeared to have adjusted to his new life. Alyssa had moved into the larger apartment, so he now had his own room. He told Robert he liked the pre-school, but not as much as Lucy Potter's. And Alyssa had gotten him a library card in Scarsdale, which pleased him.

Rather than inflict the long ride to Vermont on Davey, Robert usually stayed with his parents in Massapequa during his weekend visits. Harry and Emily Morgen had been at a loss for words when he'd told them about the divorce. "Pity, pity," Harry murmured. "I'm sorry," his mother said, knowing how badly he was taking the separation from Davey.

The older Morgens were pleased to have their son and grandson staying with them when Robert came down from Vermont, and Robert, too, was glad that Davey was finally getting to know his grandparents better.

One Sunday afternoon in early spring as Robert drove Davey back to Scarsdale after their weekend with the Morgens, Davey surprised him by saying, "I keep telling mommy I want to move back to Vermont, but she says no."

"Does she tell you why?"

"Mommy says I lived with you in Vermont and she missed me a lot. Now she wants me to be with her."

Robert lapsed into silence, trying to think of what to say.

"Daddy," said Davey, "can't you tell her to let me go to Vermont with you?"

"Davey, I can tell her what you want and what I want, but Mommy only knows what she wants. I'm sorry."

12

Vermont had now lost its luster and Robert no longer took pleasure in his surroundings. Two months earlier he would have been delighted by the sun reflecting off ice-encrusted branches; the smell of wood smoke at night as he gazed at the star-filled sky; a solitary whitetail bounding across his meadows; or flocks of waxwings descending to the birch outside his bedroom window. Now he was entirely introspective, oblivious to the beauty around him. He might as well have been living in New Jersey.

His practice, too, no longer served as a distraction. He sat in his office and stared at the photos of Davey on his bookshelves and desk. He had removed the photographs with Alyssa in them and stashed them in the bottom drawer of the desk.

In the evening, Robert drove home slowly, dreading his arrival at his darkened, joyless house. He was seldom in the mood to cook and knew he was losing weight. During the year that Davey lived with him, he had begun writing children's stories, reading them to his son and asking Davey how he should tell the story. The boy was a good critic and Robert credited Davey for sparking the urge to write, and for his success in having two of his stories accepted for publication. Of course, Lynn Finkel's showing the drafts to her editor had been the real reason he was published. And her willingness to do the illustrations for the books and jackets hadn't hurt either. Now when Robert sat at the kitchen table and tried to write, it was hopeless. Davey was gone and so was his creative urge. He lived only in anticipation of the weekend when he'd see his son.

You can't go on like this, he told himself, but when he tried to set a course of action, a plan for the future, his thoughts flew off in all directions like colliding atoms, leaving behind a black hole of despair.

He needed to get away to think clearly. One Wednesday afternoon when his office was closed, he stopped at the town's travel agency and picked up a handful of travel brochures. Pictures of smiling couples walking hand in hand on beaches lined with palm trees, or toasting each other with champagne on cruise ships, made him even more aware of how alone he was. He tossed them in the trash as soon as he got home. That evening, clearing old shopping lists and bills off the kitchen counter, he came across the letter from Sean Cooper that had lain buried there for months.

Robert removed the letter from its envelope and read it through. Maybe volunteering as a physician, working with Sean in Pakistan, was the answer. Hadn't he always wanted to emulate Albert Schweitzer and serve in under-privileged countries? That was what he had told Sean Cooper. Now he had the chance to follow up on his words.

When Sean had visited them in Vermont, he'd told Robert that the International Refugee Assistance main office was in New York City. They recruited volunteers and staff for their Asia and Africa projects in New York. Robert called information and jotted down the number.

He telephoned the next morning. The medical placement office advised him that there was a desperate need for an OB-GYN at the Afghan Women's Hospital in Peshawar for the month of May and half of June. "I'll do it," Robert told the recruiter. "Send me an application."

For the first time since Davey had gone to live with his mother, Robert felt alive again. Instead of indulging in self-pity, he had a purpose. He eagerly awaited the arrival of the application. When it came, he closed his office door and immediately filled it out, volunteering for six weeks. He sent it off the next day. Confirmation of his appointment, along with his flight information and tickets, arrived two weeks later. At the bottom of the appointment letter, the recruiter had appended a handwritten note. *Sean Cooper says he's looking forward to your arrival.*

Robert immediately called Todd Jones, who covered for him during his absences, and explained the situation.

"I envy you," Jones told him. "I've always wanted to do something like that." He readily agreed to cover Robert's practice for the six weeks he'd be gone.

During his next weekend trip to Westchester, Robert told Alyssa.

"I'll be leaving in two weeks, on April twenty-ninth. I'll be back the third week in June."

"You always wanted to run off, didn't you?" she said, scorn in her voice.

"You're the one who knows all about running off," he replied. "I don't consider working as a medical volunteer for six weeks running off."

"And after that?"

"What do you mean?"

"I was just wondering what you're going to do when you get back."

Good question, Robert thought, but he said nothing.

Robert had planned to take Davey to the Bronx Zoo that Saturday but a cold spring rain was falling in the city. He opted for the Museum of Natural History instead. Davey was now in his dinosaur phase and enjoyed rattling off the names of the prehistoric beasts. Driving into Manhattan, Robert told Davey about his forthcoming trip to Pakistan. Davey listened solemnly, his face so serious Robert thought he was about to cry.

"I'll only be gone for six weeks," he said, patting his son's leg. "And I'll see you again before I go."

Davey nodded and turned away to look out the window.

13

Robert sealed the envelope for Davey's letter and started on one to his parents.

Dear Mom and Dad, he wrote, pausing then to consider how long it had been since he'd written a letter to his parents. It has to be more than twenty-five years, he thought, when I was doing my Fulbright in France. He tried to visualize his parents in those days, but it was difficult. He saw them only as they were now.

His father, Harry, was eighty. He'd undergone a gradual shrinking process during the past few years. His pants were two sizes too large and would have fallen off were it not for the suspenders he wore. Brown age marks blotched his face and bald scalp. One of them had turned black recently and bled if he scratched it.

"You should get that removed," Robert told him every time he visited.

"I'll do it when I turn a hundred," Harry said. His stock answer.

Robert's mother, Emily, had not aged as dramatically. The wrinkles on her face and the bags under her eyes were more noticeable, but she still carried herself erect and was as trim as he always remembered. Her hair, now totally white, was cut short, giving her face a boyish quality.

Alyssa had always thought they were an odd couple. Robert recalled a discussion they'd had when they were driving to the Farbers for a Passover seder. Davey, who was two at the time, was sleeping in his car seat. Alyssa, frustrated by the traffic heading to Queens, accelerated abruptly to prevent the car on her left from cutting in front of her, then hit the brake.

"Hey, take it easy," said Robert. "Don't wake Davey up."

"How does he look?" she asked.

"He's still flushed. Did you take his temperature before we left the house?"

"It was down to a hundred. He'll be all right. He hasn't been on the antibiotic for twenty-four hours yet."

"You could have told your parents he was too sick for us to come."

"Not go to their Passover seder? Are you out of your mind? You know them."

Yeah, Robert knew them. At that time he'd known them for four years. Alyssa had dragged him to her parents' home after their second date. "I want them to meet the man I love," she said when he tried to demur. He still believed the purpose of that first visit was to have him vetted.

"What if one of us was really sick? What if I died of a heart attack? Would they still expect you to come to their seder?"

She smiled, leaning over to kiss him. "They'd ask to see a death certificate."

He laughed. "Seriously, Lys, look at this mess. We're not moving at all. I've never seen traffic this bad."

"You say that every Passover."

The blast of a car horn startled them. A hundred feet ahead two men had gotten out of their cars and were yelling at one another. Whatever they were saying was drowned out by the cacophony of car horns.

"Better put your window up," Robert said. "All we need now is for Davey to start kvetching."

Alyssa laughed.

"What's so funny?"

"I can't help laughing when I hear you using Yiddish words. It's so out of character. What would your waspy mother say?"

"She married my father, didn't she? You think she's an anti-Semite?"

"I didn't say that. It's just that I never think of you as Jewish."

"I don't think of myself as any religion. Neither do my parents."

"They're an unlikely pair."

"Who?"

"Your parents."

"Why, because my dad's Jewish and my mother is Protestant? You think that's so rare?"

"No, it's just that I can't understand what attracted them to each other. They don't have much in common."

"Neither one practiced any religion."

"I know, but your father's an immigrant and your mother was born here. He's quiet and serious, she's outgoing and—and completely different."

"He's probably a wild man in the sack. Their orgasmic cries kept me awake my entire childhood."

Alyssa laughed. "Idiot," she said, giving him a poke in the ribs.

Yes, they were different, Robert thought, his pen poised above his note pad. Different certainly than Alyssa's parents with their pretentious lifestyle and their big home in Kew Gardens. What you saw with the elder Morgens was what you got. Their Massapequa home was a forerunner of those built in Levittown after the Second World War, constructed in the thirties without giving a thought to aesthetics. Their move to Long Island had surprised Robert for many reasons. They'd lived in a two-bedroom apartment in Brooklyn since their marriage, the apartment where Robert grew up. More preoccupied with their work than with their surroundings, they never hinted at wanting a home of their own. His father was in his fifties and Robert was in his final year of college when they bought the house.

"Won't you miss Brooklyn?" he'd asked them when they told him about their plans over dinner one evening. Robert was still living at home with them while attending Brooklyn College, but had already received his acceptance letter from University of Pennsylvania College of Medicine.

"I already miss Brooklyn," his father said, "but Brooklyn the way it was when your mother and I first came here. Not like now."

"What about your job?"

"Pharmacists are always in demand. Brooklyn, Long Island, what's the difference? Same pills, same prescriptions."

He looked at his mother. "So you don't care about leaving Brooklyn either? What about all your students? They're not going to travel to Long Island for their piano lessons."

"As long as people keep having children, they'll want them to take piano lessons. I'm sure I'll have a whole new group of students in a very short time.

"And you?" she said. "You'll be leaving, too. Will you miss it?"

"I guess I'll be too busy to think about it."

"Your father and I are proud of you, you know."

"Just to get into that school with a name like yours is a miracle," his father chimed in. "They must have known from the spelling—"

"Dad, times have changed," he interrupted. "These aren't the bad old days."

"Well, some things never change. Let me show you something." He stood up and left the room, returning moments later with a large manila envelope. Pushing aside the dinner dishes, he removed a document from the envelope and spread it out on the table. "I never showed you this," he said, holding down the edges with his hands.

Robert leaned over his father and looked at the German script. He saw the name Herschel Morgenstern and the date, March 24, 1906.

"That's your birth certificate?"

"Yeah, that's me."

"You changed your name?" He knew his father had come to America from Germany when he was six years old, but he hadn't known about the name change.

Harry laughed and looked at Robert's mother, who was sitting opposite him. "Emily, he wants to know if I changed my name."

His mother smiled. "Yes, dear, he did change it. At the time I couldn't conceive of Emily Rawlings becoming Emily Morgenstern. I was young and foolish and it was too foreign-sounding for this waspy lady. Now, it wouldn't bother me."

Years later, when Robert told them he and Alyssa were moving to Vermont, his mother reacted with surprise. "What about your practice?"

"Remember what you both told me when you decided to move to Long Island? Dad said there'll always be a need for pharmacists and you said children will always need piano lessons. Well, women will always be having babies and gynecologic problems."

"How does Alyssa feel about this?" his mother asked.

Robert hesitated. "She has some doubts about the move, but she's willing to go along with it."

"Is it because of her parents?"

It was what Robert expected his mother to focus on. Alyssa's parents and his saw one another seldom. They had little in common and Robert knew his mother had contempt for the Farbers' style of living.

"It's not only that," Robert said. "It's her job, her friends, the city—life in New York doesn't seem to affect her the way it does me. She worries that I might be giving up everything for a future that's uncertain."

"Since when can't a doctor make a good living anywhere he goes?" Harry asked.

"I think she'll adjust to the change. It may take a while." He looked across the table at Davey, who was gorging himself on Emily's apple pie. "Now that young man should love living in the country. Better take it easy on that pie. We're having company for dinner and your mother will get upset if you don't want to eat."

Emily snorted. "Alyssa would only get upset if her company didn't want to eat," she said.

Her remark surprised Robert, but he couldn't argue with it.

Well, Robert thought, as he began writing his letter, his mother had certainly had Alyssa's number. He only wished he'd been able to see Alyssa as clearly back then. He wrote quickly, reassuring them that he was well and that he had comfortable accommodations. He sealed the envelope and placed it next to the one to Davey. He glanced at his watch. It wasn't too late to write the third and final letter, but it was one he didn't want to rush through. He needed time to think about what he wanted to say to Lynn.

Robert put his notebook aside, peeled off his clothes, and stepped into the shower. The dust of Peshawar ran off him, discoloring the water around his feet.

14

Robert awoke in darkness. The chanting sound that had become part of his dream persisted. He eased himself up onto his elbows, then slid out of bed. He padded barefoot across the room to the window and pushed the shutters open, admitting the muezzins' calls to prayer from mosques in different parts of the city. Off to the east, a faint slash of light cut across the dark sky. He breathed deeply of the smell of dust, the smell of Pakistan.

After breakfasting with Sean and Samantha, Robert spent his free day roaming around Peshawar, winding his way through the narrow streets of the old city. It's like the Arabian Nights, he thought, as he walked among men in turbans, embroidered skullcaps, and brown woolen Chitrali hats. Most of the men wore the Pathan version of the shalwar kameez, a *pirahan*, or long, loose-fitting shirt, and *tombon,* baggy pants. Some wore long, dusty robes or embroidered waistcoats. There were hardly any women on the streets. When he did see them, they flitted by in groups of two or three, colorful apparitions of pastel blue, lemony yellow, and pale green. Some, veiled in black from head to toe, resembled spectral phantoms. Noise assaulted Robert's ears as cars and trucks threaded their way past sheep, goats, and donkey carts.

He followed two men into a dark alleyway, emerging onto Andar Shehr, a street lined by jewelry shops. "Sir, sir, come see, sir, good price," the sales clerks beckoned to him from doorways. Gold and silver jewelry sparkled under bare incandescent light bulbs. He passed a mosque crowded with worshipers and paused to look into its courtyard. Two Pakistanis glared at him as they removed their sandals and Robert moved on.

He came to a large square where a black-bearded man harangued a small crowd gathered around him. Sean had warned him to avoid political demonstrations and Robert skirted the square, entering a bazaar thronged with shoppers. On Sethi Street he stared admiringly at tall, ancient buildings of wood and brick, their wooden facades intricately carved. Two-storey homes with overhanging balconies surrounded central courtyards. Robert caught glimpses of their interiors whenever someone opened one of the beautifully carved wooden doors.

In the Meena Bazaar, which sold fabrics, lace, and beads, throngs of burqa-clad women filed past him. It was as if the men of Peshawar had conceded this street to them. On Qissa Khwani, the Street of the Storytellers, Robert was dazzled by a profusion of brass and copperware. Whenever he passed a shop or stall, the proprietor would dash out and clutch at his sleeve. "Come look, sir, just look. Have some tea with us." Robert's patience with their hardsell tactics was wearing thin as he began to feel the heat. Wiping the perspiration from his forehead with the back of his hand, he entered a *chaikhana*, a Pakistani tea house, and found an empty table. A waiter wearing a filthy shalwar kameez looked at him inquiringly.

"Chai," Robert said. He pointed at the cups on the neighboring table. The waiter brought a cracked Isfahan blue bowl of green tea flavored with bits of cardamom and lemon that floated to the rim each time he took a sip. It was delicious and he ordered a second cup. Only then did he remember that he hadn't changed money at the airport.

Robert fished in his pocket and pulled out two dollar bills. The waiter took both of them.

Then, fatigued from the heat and jet lag, Robert made his way back to his lodging on foot. He stopped at the grocery Sean had shown him and bought a half-dozen containers of yogurt and a few cans of soda. As soon as he entered his room, Robert turned on the overhead fan to move the stale, dusty air. He considered taking a nap, but feared it would foul up his inner clock as he struggled to adjust to Pakistan time. Instead, he ate some yogurt, opened his door, and stepped out onto the veranda. Seeing it was in shade, he decided to sit outside until it was time to head over to Sean and Samantha's for dinner.

Shadows lengthened on the lawn as dusk approached. Lulled by the singing of birds and the droning of bees in the courtyard, Robert closed his eyes.

Neither asleep nor awake, Robert thought he heard Davey's laughter, first close by, then more distant. He heard Lynn calling his name. Where are you? she said.

He woke up as he slid from the chair, one arm stretched out to break his fall. Laughing at himself, he went back inside and called Sean.

"I think I'll pass on dinner," Robert said. "I just fell asleep sitting in the chair and had to pick myself off the ground."

Sean laughed. "Get some sleep. We'll see you for breakfast."

On Robert's first day of work, he met Doctor Mathir, the most senior of the Afghan physicians. Mathir was a serious, coarse-featured woman with pock-marked skin. Robert guessed her to be older than the other physicians he'd met, in her mid-thirties or closer to forty, and in contrast with the others she was not intimidated by the Western doctor.

"We will ask you to consult on any patient we think needs surgery," she advised him. "Also, if we have any questions about how to manage a particular patient we will ask your advice."

"Who will schedule the surgery?"

"I will. And I will arrange anesthesia."

"What kind of routine do you follow pre-operatively?"

"I examine every patient and order a blood count."

"Is blood available if we need it?"

Robert thought he saw a fleeting smile. "It can be obtained but it's best if we don't need it."

For the rest of that morning, Robert was called into each of the four examining rooms by the young Afghan physicians. Dr. Mathir, who sat in the hallway with him, always accompanied him, interpreting if necessary. Since there were more physicians than rooms, two of the doctors made rounds on hospitalized patients, while the remaining one covered the delivery room.

The Afghan patients instinctively covered their faces when Robert entered the examining room. Reassured by Doctor Mathir that he was a Westerner, they promptly pushed their veils aside. Robert was surprised by the colorful garb and jewelry of lapis and gold worn by the Pathan women beneath their burqas. He tried not to stare at their tribal tattoos, geometric lines of blue dots on cheeks or lips.

Lunchtime, the entire staff of the hospital—doctors, nurses, even Doctor Mojarri, the administrator—met in the dining room. Dishes of chicken, rice, and salad were passed around the table. Teapots were placed within everyone's reach. They were all curious about Robert. Their first questions concerned his family—how many children he had, why he'd had only one, did his parents live in the same compound. Doctor Mojarri translated for those who didn't speak English. Robert felt it best to omit the fact that he was divorced. In turn, he asked them about their lives in Afghanistan before coming to Peshawar.

"Most of us were still in medical school in Kabul or doing our training at the hospital when the Russians came," Doctor Mathir said. "I myself was in the laboratory when the planes came over. When the bombs began to fall, I crawled under one of the tables."

"I ran away from the hospital when the Russian soldiers came," Doctor Ahmad, a young women with striking green eyes, said. Her English was good but she spoke so softly that Robert had to lean forward and listen intently to hear. "My husband and my mother were at home with my little girl and I wanted to make sure they were safe. When I got there my mother and my daughter were crying. The Russian soldiers had come to the house and taken my husband away."

"Why did they take him?" Robert asked.

"Because he refused to serve in the army. He told them he wouldn't kill other Afghans."

"What happened to him?"

"I never saw him again. When I asked government officials where he was, they said they had no record of him."

"So you and your daughter left the country?"

"Yes. My mother came with us. We crossed the mountains in the winter. It was difficult. Very cold with deep snow. My mother was so weak by the time we reached Pakistan. She died two weeks later."

"I'm very sorry," Robert said.

A short, dark woman with a face so somber it could have been chiseled from stone was sitting next to Doctor Ahmad. She lowered her gaze as Robert looked at her and said nothing until Doctor Mathir addressed her.

"This is Doctor Shah," Mathir said. "She has only been with us for three weeks and speaks no English. She was visiting her husband's family in Mazar-i-Sharif when the invasion came. It was very difficult for her to get out. She has a ten-year-old son with spina bifida and her husband had to carry him across the mountains on his back."

Doctor Shah spoke for several minutes to Doctor Mathir. None of them ate as they listened to her.

"It is still very hard for her here in Peshawar. Her husband was an engineer in Kabul but here he works as a waiter. A neighbor must watch her son when she and her husband work. He can only crawl, so he doesn't attend school. She and her husband try to teach him at home."

Every story Robert heard was more poignant than the previous one. By the time lunch was over, he was filled with admiration for the courage and endurance of these Afghan doctors and nurses. They had all suffered and been uprooted from their country, but they'd gotten on with their lives. More than that, they were helping other Afghan women, refugees like themselves.

In the clinic that afternoon, Robert saw that finding surgical cases to train the Afghan physicians was no problem. So many women were in need of surgery, the dilemma was how to fit them in on the operating room schedule when each day promised to bring even more cases. Many women came to the clinic with their uterus falling, in some cases so severe that the uterus protruded from the vagina. With six children on average, this wasn't surprising. Large fibroid tumors of the uterus were also common. What surprised Robert were the cases of severe pelvic inflammatory disease and infertility, something he didn't expect in a society where the women were practically confined to their homes and monogamy was the norm, for women at least. When he asked Dr. Mathir about it, her discomfort was apparent.

"It is the men," she said finally. "They often find bad women or engage in other acts I can't talk about. They bring disease to their wives."

One young woman had been trying to conceive for three years without success. She brushed tears from her eyes when she talked to Mathir.

"She says her husband is going to get another wife because she can't give him a son."

"Her exam was normal. The problem might be her husband. You should do a sperm count."

When Mathir repeated that to the woman, her face betrayed a mixture of astonishment and fear.

"She says her husband would beat her if she told him that. Pathan men always believe the fault is the woman's."

Robert was shocked when Dr. Mathir did the blood counts for women who were scheduled for surgery. Every Afghan woman was anemic. The great number of pregnancies and inadequate diet obviously had taken their toll. In some cases the anemia was so severe, Robert would have recommended hospitalization if he were in the States.

"We can't operate on women who are so anemic," he said. "I don't understand how some of them have the strength to stay on their feet. Surgery would be too dangerous. Do you have iron in your pharmacy? You can treat them for a few months, then repeat the count."

Mathir shook her head. "We have no iron tablets."

"Can these women buy it in a pharmacy in town?"

"They are too poor."

In the end, Robert was forced into a compromise, one he wouldn't have accepted back home.

"Look, we'll operate if the hemoglobin is greater than nine," he told Mathir. "I'm not comfortable with anything less than that, especially if no blood is available."

"It will mean turning many women away."

"I can't help that. They can't tolerate any blood loss during surgery. Turning them away is better than having them die in the operating room. I'll talk to Sean Cooper. Maybe there's some way we can get iron for these women. If not, I'll send you a regular supply of iron when I get back to the States. You can build up their blood and operate on them later."

He knew that in Mathir's eyes he was perceived as strict and dogmatic. Inwardly, however, Robert ached with compassion for the Afghan women. They'd already suffered enough for many lifetimes.

At the end of that first day, in spite of denying surgery to the most anemic women, Mathir had scheduled sixteen cases. At that rate, Robert thought, it would take only six days in the clinic to fill his surgery schedule for six weeks.

During dinner that evening with Sean and Samantha, Robert spoke animatedly about his first day at the hospital.

"I'll see what I can do about getting the funds to purchase iron," Sean said. "Just don't forget, these women are the fortunate ones. They managed to reach Peshawar and their husbands permitted them to come to the hospital. That's the exception rather than the rule here."

"In Pakistan there's a saying," said Samantha. "*Chador, chardiwari.* It means behind the veil and behind four walls."

Robert shook his head. "It's medieval."

"The women and children suffer the most in this war," Samantha said. "You'll hear no end of stories about the terrible injuries suffered by the mujahideen in the fighting, and you'll see lots of amputees in Peshawar. Still, it's the families of these men, their wives, children, female members of the family, who bear the brunt of the war. When you see the fighters missing limbs from land-mine explosions, think of all the Afghan children who have their hands blown off by the colorful little bombs they pick up on the roads and in the fields. Those children don't make it to Peshawar. You'll hear a lot about aid money and food pouring into this country for the refugees. Don't be taken in by figures. Corruption is terrible in Pakistan and much of the aid never reaches the refugees. Malnutrition is rife among women and children. You saw that today in the hospital. In male-dominated Pathan society, the men eat first. What's left, assuming there's anything left, goes to the women and children."

Samantha's face was flushed with anger.

"Don't let Sam discourage you, Robert," Sean said. "The plight of the refugees is terrible, but in some ways they live better in the camps than they did in Afghanistan, or at least the rural people do. Many of them do get more food and if their husbands let them go to the clinics in the camps, they receive medicines they might need. Some girls even get to attend school, a rarity in rural Afghanistan. Only two percent of rural women can read. We just do what we can to help as many as we can. We have to think that way to prevent ourselves from going off the deep end."

15

Robert paced the floor of his room. Sleep was out of the question. He thought of the patients he had seen in the clinic that day, and he thought of his confrontation with Doctor Mathir about performing surgery on women with severe anemia. He knew he was right. No physician in America would perform elective surgery on a woman with a hemoglobin of six. The problem was, he was not in America. There was always the chance that the condition of the anemic Afghan women he saw would worsen, that fibroid tumors of the uterus would cause hemorrhaging that would aggravate the anemia. Or that abscesses of the tubes and ovaries would rupture, putting the patient at graver risk. It was a nightmarish predicament, a case of damned if you do, damned if you don't. Iron tablets cost pennies and yet there weren't any. But there was no shortage of AK-47s and landmines. It made no sense.

His conversation with Sean and Samantha didn't make him feel any better. Sean's words were "we just do what we can to help as many as we can," but Robert felt it wasn't enough. It was the equivalent of applying Band-Aids to a body bleeding from everywhere. Many of the problems were cultural. It would have taken a blind person not to see that. How could he fault Sean or any other foreigner trying to help? There was so much to learn about the Pathans, a people who until now he'd only read about in brief news items in America's newspapers.

Robert sat down heavily on the edge of his bed. He felt the need to get his impressions down on paper. He decided he would do that in a letter to Lynn. He couldn't understand his hesitation about writing to her, especially in view of the experiences they'd shared. Perhaps it was those experiences and what they implied that gave him pause. On the other hand, if there was anyone who would understand what he was trying to come to grips with in his work at the Afghan Women's Hospital, it was Lynn.

He picked up his notebook, propped pillows against the wall at the head of his bed, and visualized Lynn as he wrote the words *Dearest Lynn*.

Alyssa always referred to the Finkels, Lynn and Mike, as her dearest friends. Robert intuitively knew the term only applied to Mike Finkel. Like Alyssa's father, he was a psychologist, and had even studied under Arnold Farber. He dressed like Arnold, right down to the bowties, and Robert swore that he aped some of Arnold's mannerisms and speech patterns. Mike had known Alyssa much longer than Lynn had, longer, in fact, than Robert had, and he and Alyssa always seemed to have a lot to talk about. The two couples saw one another often while Robert and Alyssa were living in Manhattan. Lynn's attempts at conversation were lost in Alyssa and Mike's dominating interest in their work. Robert lost patience sometimes listening to their excitement over the latest trends in popular psychology.

Alyssa had invited them for dinner shortly after she and Robert had decided on the move to Vermont.

"My God, Robert," Mike said, "do you really want to isolate yourself like that? I was a camp counselor in upstate New York when I was a kid and I know what these rural communities are like. You won't fit."

Mike was about Robert's age, but looked older. His hairline was receding, his complexion was sallow, and his overbite gave him a chronically fretful expression.

"Are you speaking for me or for you?" Robert said.

"I think Alyssa's concerns are justified," Mike persisted. "You'd be giving up too much. You have a wonderful practice here, a nice apartment, and all the advantages of Manhattan. Sure, Vermont is beautiful, but I can't see you two being happy up there. Not in the long run. The Vermont house is your summer place. Why not keep it that way?

"Look," he said, less forcefully, "maybe I'm coming on too strong. That's not my intention. We're good friends and I feel we can speak honestly to one another. You and Alyssa have to make up your own minds. I'm just throwing out some things to consider because I care about you both."

Robert shrugged. "Well, I appreciate your concern but we're still going to give it a try."

"The poached salmon is delicious," said Lynn, obviously trying to steer the conversation away from Vermont. "And how did you prepare the broccoli? I can taste ginger."

"Oh, just some ginger and garlic, a little fish sauce. Nothing very complicated."

She didn't fool Robert with her false humility, and he was sure she didn't fool Lynn. Alyssa couldn't get enough of praise for her cooking. After telling Lynn the recipe for her broccoli, she turned to Mike. "Did you see Michaelson's study of diet as a factor in childhood autism? What do you think about that?"

Davey sat quietly in his high chair, picking sleepily at a slice of American cheese Alyssa had put on his tray. Robert had taken his son to see his grandparents in Massapequa earlier that day and the long trip had exhausted him.

"I'm terrible, aren't I, to talk shop?" Alyssa smiled at Lynn. She stood up and went to the refrigerator. "I'll make dessert while you put on the coffee, Robert."

"Oh, no!" Robert heard her say moments later.

"What's wrong?"

"There's mold in this box of blueberries. I should have known better than to buy them in a supermarket. Robert, be a sweetheart and go to D'Ambrosio's. He usually has beautiful berries. I'll get the coffee going."

"Let me just get Davey to bed first. He's pooped."

Robert lifted Davey out of his high chair, his son's sneaker catching on the edge of the tray, without waking him. Lynn jumped up from her chair to help but Robert, holding Davey with one arm, freed his foot before she could get to them. Davey went limp in Robert's arms, his head resting on his father's shoulder. Lynn reached over and stroked the boy's head.

"He's a sleepy little guy, all right," she said.

Robert carried his son to the bedroom, returning moments later with a smile on his face.

"He was fast asleep before I put him in his bed. How many boxes of blueberries do you want?"

"Get two. When I was in there the other day they were beautiful."

"I need a few things, too," Lynn said. "Do you mind if I go with you?"

"I can get whatever you need if you'd rather stay," Robert said.

"No, I'd like to go."

As they walked out of the apartment building, he was aware that Lynn was watching him. He glanced at her and smiled. "You haven't said much tonight. Do you think we're making a mistake moving to Vermont?"

"No," she said. "I'm actually glad you're going."

Robert was surprised. "You're the first person who's said that," he told her. "I take it you think it's right for us?"

"I don't know, but I'm still glad you and Alyssa are going."

"Do you dislike us that much?" he teased.

The lights of D'Ambrosio's were visible a block ahead of them. Lynn touched his arm. "Robert, do you mind stopping for a minute so we can talk?" She guided him to the window of a bookstore, its books illuminated by a fluorescent bulb although the store was closed.

Robert, surprised, looked directly at her as he waited to hear what she had to say. Her eyes, gray with a violet tinge, were her most striking feature. Lynn had a small, oval-shaped face and curly brown hair. Shadows played across her face, partially obscuring the sprinkling of freckles across the bridge of her nose and cheeks. Robert had never thought of her as beautiful, but in the four years he'd known her he'd come to think of her as attractive.

"You know that Mike is in love with Alyssa, don't you?"

"Because they're always talking about psychology?" he said, thinking she was joking.

"They used to go together, before you knew Alyssa and before I met Mike."

"I know they've been friends for a long time, but that doesn't mean—"

"More than friends, Robert. They were lovers. Mike told me."

Robert, annoyed, turned away. "That must have been long ago. Alyssa was living with someone else when I met her."

"It was about six years ago. They had a fight. Mike didn't tell me about what, but they broke up over it. It was about that time that I met him."

"Okay," said Robert, "but that doesn't mean he loves her now."

"But he does. You just don't want to see it. And Alyssa—"

"Alyssa what?" he said testily.

"Alyssa is obviously still fond of him. Anyway, that's why I'm glad you and Alyssa are moving to Vermont. I think it's better if they don't see much of one another. I will miss *you*, Robert, but I want to save my marriage."

"Lynn, you can't be serious about this."

"I am." She paused, her mouth open as if she were about to say something else. "Robert, you know Mike and I are unable to have children."

"Alyssa mentioned that there's a problem. I didn't know you'd actually been trying."

"We've tried for three years. Mike tells everyone there's an infertility problem, hinting that I'm the one with the problem. The truth is he has oligospermia. I'm sure you know what that is."

Robert nodded.

"He had mumps as an adolescent. Apparently that's the cause. He acts like he doesn't care if we have children, but I know he desperately wants a child. He envies you and Alyssa for having Davey."

"How do you know that?"

"In an unguarded moment one night, after we had dinner at your house and he'd had too much wine, he looked so morose I asked him what was wrong. 'So goddamn easy for them to have a baby,' he said. 'It's not fair.' Who? I asked him, but I knew the answer and he wouldn't say anything else."

"Have you thought of adopting?"

"I suggested it to him. He won't have it. 'I don't want to raise someone else's kid,' he says. He wants to believe all the doctors are wrong and that if we keep trying, it'll happen. But it won't, Robert. His urologist told me."

"I'm sorry, Lynn."

"Robert, I don't know how to say this. I've always thought you're a great guy and I don't want you to think badly of me."

"What are you talking about?"

"I want you to give me a baby."

Robert was speechless.

"I'm very regular, Robert, and always know when I'm ovulating. You're not leaving until the end of July, so we'd have three months to try. It's the only way and you're the only person I'd ask."

"Lynn, you don't know what you're saying. You're asking me to commit adultery. How could I do something like that?"

"I'm asking you to help me save my marriage. You're the only person I trust. Please don't make me beg."

"Just for the sake of argument, what if it didn't work? What if we tried during those three months and you still didn't get pregnant?"

"Then at least I'd know I had done everything possible. I'd have to accept it and hope that Mike would somehow come to terms with it."

"And if you did get pregnant? Don't you think Mike would know that it wasn't his? What if it didn't look at all like him?"

"Mike's biggest sin is pride. He'd never suspect it wasn't his, no matter who the baby looked like."

"What about Alyssa? She'd see the baby someday and she'd know right away. Women are more perceptive about things like that."

"Robert," she said, shaking her head, "you're deluding yourself if you think Alyssa would notice anything. I hope you won't take this the wrong way. Just think of it as coming from a woman who considers herself your friend. Whatever Alyssa's good qualities are, being a mother isn't one of them. I'm not blind. Don't you think I see how you're the one who does everything with Davey? Alyssa likes being the center of attention, she likes compliments, she doesn't like competing with a baby. I'm no psychologist, but I see other things, too. Don't you notice the resemblance between Mike and Alyssa's father? It's not that they look alike, it's that Mike imitates him and Alyssa loves it. And I think she loves Mike, even if it's not on a conscious level."

"I'm not a psychologist either and I've always thought that Alyssa has some issues with her father, but that's not what we're talking about, is it?"

"No." She smiled sadly. "We're talking about my having a baby."

"And what if having a baby didn't save your marriage? What then? Would you expect me to admit to being the father?"

"The baby would be Mike's, not yours. How could you even think that?"

"I don't know what to think, Lynn."

"I'd call you at your office when I know I'm ovulating. And I'd arrange a hotel room near your office, so you wouldn't have to take much time away from patients. It would be like a house call."

"God, Lynn."

"Thank you, Robert. Now we better get those berries before Alyssa wonders what happened to us."

Alyssa and Mike were deep in conversation when they returned. Robert knew she had no idea how long they'd been gone.

"Coffee's all made," she said, standing up and taking the blueberries from him. "I'll get dessert."

As the days passed, Robert stopped thinking about his conversation with Lynn. She was just upset that night, he told himself. She was being impulsive. She's a rational woman and she'd never go through with it. Two weeks had passed when his receptionist told him a Mrs. Finkel was calling and that it was urgent.

Robert's hand trembled as he reached for the phone on his desk. He waited until the receptionist left before speaking.

"Robert, are you there?"

"I'm here."

"I've booked a reservation at the Hampstead House. It's a short walk from your office. Can you meet me at noon?"

16

Are you really going to do this? he asked himself as he walked up Madison Avenue. You've been married for only three years, have a two-year-old son, and now you're going to sleep with the wife of Alyssa's best friend. It didn't really matter if Lynn was right and Alyssa and Mike had once been lovers. That was in the past, long before he met Alyssa. But this was now. Aside from the guilt he would feel if he went through with it, it was stupid. What if Lynn got pregnant? What if Mike wasn't as obtuse as Lynn thought and realized the baby wasn't his? Blood testing would show he wasn't the father. There's time to back out, he thought. No harm done. But as he entered the lobby of the Hampstead House, he visualized Lynn's face and heard her words "please don't make me beg."

"Miss Finkel," he said to the desk clerk, wondering why Lynn hadn't registered under an assumed name.

The clerk asked for his name and buzzed the room number.

"You can go right up, sir. Room thirty-four. That's third floor and the elevator is behind you to the left."

He knocked softly and Lynn, wearing a white turtleneck and navy blue slacks, opened the door.

"Hi, Robert. Come in."

Once inside the room, they just stared at one another. She looked as terrified as he felt, so young and vulnerable that he felt guilty being in the room with her.

She smiled weakly. "My heart's beating so fast, I feel like I'll faint if I don't sit down." She sat down on the edge of the bed and looked up at him.

"What do we do now?" Robert asked.

"How much time do you have?"

"I don't have patients until two-thirty."

"Come sit by me," she said.

"So how are you?" Robert asked, feeling stupid even as he said it. "What have you been up to?"

"I'm fine. Illustrating a children's book, the usual."

"It's nice that you can work at home, isn't it? Set your own hours?"

"That part's good. I could use more commissions, but when they do come the work is fun."

Lynn stood up and reached for his hands. "Please, Robert. Just pretend you're making a house call." Leaning over him, she loosened his tie and began unbuttoning his shirt.

Robert got to his feet and fumbled clumsily with the buttons of her blouse. She turned her back to him so that he could unfasten her bra and remained with her back to him while she slipped off her panties. Robert, too, turned away in embarrassment as he took off his pants and underwear. They turned to face one another.

"You're beautiful, Lynn," Robert said, getting aroused in spite of his embarrassment.

"Thank you, Robert. You're very handsome."

Robert laughed. "Do you feel as strange as I do? The two of us standing here stark naked, not knowing what to say to one another?"

She stepped closer. "It is strange, but I feel very comfortable at the same time." She held her hand out to him. "Let's get into bed."

They slid under the topsheet. Once he had Lynn in his arms, her soft, slender body pressed to his, he wanted her as much as he'd ever wanted any woman. They kissed tentatively, then deeply. Robert's hands roamed over Lynn's breasts and buttocks. Lynn eased him on top of her and spread her legs. Robert was so aroused he feared coming too soon. He tried to think of something that would take his mind off what they were doing, but Lynn had taken him in her hand and was guiding him into her.

"Oh, Robert, oh, Robert," she said, hoisting her knees up and pulling him in deeper.

"I can't hold it much longer."

"Just come whenever. It feels so good."

She began to moan softly and he felt a shudder go through her body. She repeated his name over and over and Robert, unable to prolong his release any longer, let himself go with a cry he was unable to muffle. He collapsed on top of her, then began to draw himself up with his weight on his arms.

"No, don't move," she said. "Stay inside." She embraced his shoulders and pulled him down."

"I'm crushing you."

"I love it."

"I want you to know I never made a house call like this before."

Lynn stroked his back. "I just know your treatment is going to be successful, doctor. I feel it."

After a few minutes, Robert eased himself off. Lynn lay there with her knees drawn up. "I don't want to waste a precious drop," she said.

"That was really nice, Lynn."

She laughed.

"What's funny?"

"Lying here like this, I suddenly thought of my stodgy parents up in Laconia. Don't ask me why. I pictured them, so prim and proper, so set in their Lutheran ways, and wondered what they would say if they could see me now."

"Never mind parents. What would Alyssa and Mike say?"

"They'll never know."

Robert got up and picked up his shorts.

"Don't go," Lynn said. "You have time."

He crawled back into bed and propped up his pillow. Lynn looked over at him.

"I know this wasn't easy for you, Robert."

He took her hand in his. "Thinking about it beforehand was the difficult part. But I have to be honest. I really like being here with you and it was wonderful. Will this be the last time we meet like this?"

She looked into his eyes and nodded. "It will have to be. I don't think I'm imagining it, but I've always felt we were attracted to one another. Still, we don't want things to get complicated. I'm going to miss you."

"You won't visit when we're in Vermont?"

"Mike will want to, I'm sure. I just think it would be better for everyone if the visits were few and far between, or none at all. You understand."

She freed her hand from his and slid it down his abdomen until she held him. He surprised himself by getting hard immediately.

"If this is the last time," she said, "we better make the most of it."

Lynn straddled him, rocking back and forth with her eyes closed. "Tell me when you're ready," she murmured softly. "I want you to be on top."

17

Robert sat up abruptly when his pager beeped. He looked at his watch. "Jesus!"

"What's the matter?" Lynn asked sleepily.

"We dozed off. It's almost three. That's probably my office. I'll have to call."

He rang the office, told the receptionist he'd been delayed at an appointment, but would be there in fifteen or twenty minutes.

Springing out of bed, he dressed hurriedly. "I wish I didn't have to go," he said, as he tied his shoes.

"That makes two of us."

Lynn embraced him at the door, her naked body again arousing him.

"You'll let me know what happens?"

"Of course. The worst thing that can happen is we have to do a repeat performance. It's been fun, Robert." She kissed him and pushed him out the door.

Robert played catch-up with patients that afternoon, his thoughts far from his work. Every now and then he caught the faint fragrance of Lynn's perfume wafting off his skin. He knew it would be best if she conceived on the first go-around. Being together again would only intensify the attraction between them and, like Lynn said, would complicate things. He might even regret the move to Vermont. He daydreamed about telling Alyssa he'd changed his mind, that he preferred to stay in New York. She'd be happy, but what would it lead to? He pushed it from his thoughts.

He arrived home at the same time as Alyssa and Davey. Davey, seeing him entering the lobby, ran and jumped into his arms. Robert held him as they waited for the elevator.

"Busy day?" he asked his wife.

"Busy," said Davey.

"You were busy, too?" he laughed.

"I picked up some Chinese takeout for tonight," Alyssa said. "I'm too bushed to cook."

"That's fine."

Alyssa was strangely silent during dinner and Robert worried. Was it possible she suspected something? Had she caught a whiff of Lynn's perfume?

"Something wrong?" he said.

She shook her head. "No, just a big backlog of cases to clear up. I gave my notice today and told the schools I wouldn't be back next semester. There's so much to do, sometimes I feel overwhelmed. I was thinking today that we'll have to move our stuff up to Vermont a week or two before August first so I can get the house ready. How are you going to live here in an empty apartment?"

"All I need is a cot. I'll survive. Our lease expires the end of July, so the timing is perfect. I'll let the landlord know in a couple of weeks."

After dinner, Robert read to Davey, then tucked him into bed. Alyssa came into the bedroom and leaned over to kiss Davey. She took Robert's hand as they left the room and sat down next to him on the sofa.

"I've been a bit of a pill the past week or two, haven't I?" she said. She rested her head on his shoulder. For a moment he was afraid she'd pick up the aroma of Lynn's perfume.

"No, you're just tired." So tired, he thought, that every night he found her already asleep when he got into bed.

"Have you missed me?" she said, resting her hand on his crotch.

I don't believe this, Robert thought. No sex for two weeks, then twice today with Lynn, and now she's interested.

"What do you think?"

"Why don't we make an early night of it?"

"That sounds good to me. Let me take a fast shower."

"You're clean."

"The smell of antiseptic soap from my office can't be much of a turn-on. I'll only be a minute."

Women, Robert thought, as he stepped into the shower stall. Would he ever understand them? Being a gynecologist had brought him no closer to how they think. He took a final deep inhale from the skin on his shoulders, hoping to capture the last traces of Lynn's perfume before stepping under the shower's warm spray. He lathered himself with extra care and hoped he was up to what Alyssa expected of him.

The first day back after the Memorial Day weekend, Robert checked the appointment book when he arrived in the office and was surprised to find Lynn Finkel's name down for the ten o'clock slot. About a month had passed since their tryst and he hadn't heard a word from her. He expected Alyssa to announce that she and Mike were coming for dinner, as they did at least once a month, but she hadn't mentioned them and he was reluctant to ask. During the past week, he'd wondered whether she had had second thoughts about another meeting, or, on the other hand, whether that first time had been successful. It looked like he'd get his answer today.

At ten o'clock the nurse came into the consultation room. "Mrs. Finkel brought a urine for a pregnancy test. Should I run it before I bring her in?"

Robert nodded. Lynn hadn't been to him before as a patient. He sat at his desk with her blank chart open in front of him, staring at the patient information sheet. Lynn's birth date was April twenty-seventh. He checked his calendar. That was the same day he'd been with her at the Hampstead House. It had been her birthday and he hadn't known it, but perhaps he'd given her the present she most wanted. He noticed the year she was born: 1948. She was three years younger than Alyssa.

The nurse ushered Lynn in and placed the slip with the pregnancy test result in front of Robert. He smiled at Lynn but said nothing until the nurse was out of the room. As soon as the door shut Lynn leaped from her seat and threw her arms around him almost tipping over his chair.

"You know already?"

"It is, isn't it?"

"It is."

She laughed. "I've been queasy every morning and did my own test a few days ago. I just had to make sure."

"Does Mike know?"

"Not yet. I'll tell him tonight."

"Happy?"

"Ecstatic."

"You're sure he'll believe you?"

"There's not a doubt in my mind. I can hear him now ragging on doctors and how stupid they are. He'll be so full of himself, he'll be unbearable." Suddenly she turned serious. "Thank you, Robert, thank you. You're a good friend—the best."

"It really was my pleasure."

"And mine, too. I'm almost sorry we can't make another try."

"What do you want to do about your prenatal care?"

"Can you suggest anyone?"

"The two doctors who purchased my practice are very good. I worked with them often during their residency. You'd like them."

"Then I'll see them."

"Do you want me to start a chart on you and do an exam today, or do you want to wait for—"

"I'll wait for your successors." She smiled. "I'd feel a little awkward being on the table as a patient."

"Incidentally, do you know your blood type?"

"I'm Rh positive."

"Good. Then I won't order any labwork today. That can wait until you see Doctor Cheroff or Doctor Lovett."

"Alyssa called me yesterday."

"She did? She didn't say anything to me. I wanted to ask her if you and Mike were coming over, but didn't want to arouse—"

"She was a little miffed that I hadn't called her, so I gave her the song and dance about how busy I was with the artwork for the book. She's planning a farewell party for the Fourth of July and wanted to make sure Mike and I would be there."

"That's news to me, too."

"You guys should communicate better."

"Will you come?"

"I'll see. Even if I don't, Mike will be there. At least knowing he's going to be a father will prevent him from going into mourning over Alyssa's leaving."

"It'll look funny if you don't come."

"Alyssa will know I'm pregnant so I can make a plausible excuse. To tell you the truth, Robert, I'd rather say goodbye to you in private—today—than at your home. I don't want to make a spectacle of myself by bawling."

"Will I see you again before I leave for Vermont?"

She shook her head. "It really is better if we say our goodbyes now." She stood up and embraced him, kissing him tenderly on the lips. "I'll send you a birth announcement. And a photo." She was out the door before he could say anything else.

That evening the telephone rang as Robert was reading to Davey. Alyssa picked it up in the kitchen and he heard her squeal. He knew it had to be Mike calling.

"He did?" Alyssa said loudly. "He never said a word to me. Oh, Mike, that's wonderful. Put Alyssa on so I can congratulate her."

"Moon," said Davey.

"What?" said Robert, still listening to the conversation.

"Moon," Davey said, pointing at the picture in the book. "Goodnight, moon."

Alyssa poked her head in the door. "Mike wants to talk to you. You could have told me."

He wagged his finger at her. "You know better," he said. "Besides, I knew they'd call you."

"Hey, Mike, congratulations," he said.

He listened patiently as Mike expounded on how he always knew the urologists didn't know what they were talking about.

"Well, you sure proved them wrong. I think that's great news."

Mike proceeded to tell him how sorry he was that they were moving away. "It would have been great for my kid and yours to play together."

"I'm sure they will. Some day."

"How could the doctors have been so wrong?" Alyssa asked him after he hung up. "Mike told me he'd been to three different urologists and they'd all told him the same thing, that it was impossible for Lynn to get pregnant because his sperm count was so low. He didn't believe it, he says, but I don't understand."

"Hey, doctors aren't infallible, you know. Present company excluded, of course."

"You," she said, making a dismissive motion with her hand. "I'm happy for them. Mike's wanted this for a long time."

He studied her face and thought about what Lynn had told him. Turnabout is fair play, he thought, then admonished himself for having entertained the thought.

The chanting of the muezzin roused him from his reverie. It was followed by a short fusillade of gunshots, which he didn't give a second thought to. He was getting used to Peshawar. He glanced at his watch. Two hours had gone by since he entered the room and. The only words he'd written were *Dearest Lynn*. He set the note pad aside and got ready for bed.

18

Taxis and horse-drawn carts pulled up daily in front of the Afghan Women's Hospital depositing their burqa-clad women. The waiting room was always crowded with women who reflexively covered their faces when Robert entered, then just as quickly dropped their veils when they learned he was the Western doctor. The Afghan physicians saw at least a hundred patients a day, and Robert found himself consulting on conditions he rarely saw in the United States—severe fistulas, abnormal communications between vagina and rectum or vagina and bladder due to tears during delivery and obstructed or prolonged labors; fungating cancers of the cervix and vulva; women with blood counts so low he couldn't understand how they managed to remain upright. For the first time he had a patient with an abdominal pregnancy, the result of a ruptured Fallopian tube that originally contained the pregnancy. The fetus had continued to grow and the placenta was now attached to other organs in the woman's abdomen. He and Doctor Mathir always referred these difficult cases to Peshawar's main hospital.

During his first week at the Afghan Women's Hospital Robert met Doctor Salim, the Pakistani anesthesiologist. He arrived on a morning when they had two hysterectomies scheduled. Doctor Mathir, by virtue of her seniority, always acted as Robert's first assistant, while the other physicians took turns as second assistant. It was only after Mathir felt totally at ease doing a procedure, as had happened with cesarean sections before Robert's coming to the hospital, that she permitted the other doctors to operate under her guidance. Robert felt reasonably comfortable allowing Mathir to do most of a procedure if they had an abdominal case, but she was much less confident with vaginal surgery. He patiently guided her through those cases. Zaida, the scrub nurse, did not need any guidance. She was as good as Sean had told him she'd be. Robert thought she was the best OR instrument nurse he'd ever worked with.

"What new catastrophes, Robert?" Sean invariably asked at dinner. The question was asked jokingly, but Robert knew Sean paid close attention to whatever he related. If there were problems at the hospital, Sean would do everything in his power to rectify them.

Samantha had her own horror stories. "Do you know what I learned today?" she almost shouted at one of their dinners. "Qasi, that creep we hired to oversee food deliveries to the orphanage, has been selling children to the Afridis. He tells the orphanage he's located relatives and delivers the child to the purchaser. Most of them are girls being sold into prostitution. Sean, I'm going to shoot that fucking bastard, excuse my French, Robert. Just when I think things can't get any worse, they do."

The more Robert learned about Samantha, the more he admired her. Like Sean and himself, she had grown up in a city, in her case Birmingham, England. The oldest of five siblings, she became responsible for their care after her mother died from pleurisy at the age of thirty-two. Her father worked in a factory. "That's why I never wanted kids of my own," she told Robert. "I've already raised a family."

Her father took to drinking heavily after her mother's death, often hitting the children when he was at home.

"It was only when James, the youngest, was finally out of the house that I was able to leave Birmingham for London. It was inevitable, I suppose, that I'd work for an organization like Save the Children."

One night a foot messenger from the hospital interrupted them during dinner. Robert recognized the man as one of the hospital's chowkidars.

"Please, sir," he said to Robert, "they need you at the hospital immediately."

"Do you know what's wrong?" Robert asked as he walked quickly alongside the man.

"A patient operated on this morning is very sick. Doctor Mathir is with her."

Two Afghan men stood in the shadows outside the hospital entrance, one of them smoking a cigarette. They stared at Robert as he approached.

"Husband and son of patient," whispered the chowkidar.

Robert was surprised to find Zaida anxiously waiting for him just within the door, out of sight of the two men.

"The vaginal hysterectomy patient from this morning is in shock," she told him. "Doctor Mathir is with her and has already called for Doctor Salim."

Robert entered the patient's room and found a worried-looking Doctor Mathir taking the blood pressure of an ashen-faced sixty-year-old they'd operated on ten hours earlier. Doctor Mathir, under Robert's direction, had performed the vaginal hysterectomy. Robert knew how badly she must feel because of this unexpected complication. He pulled back the blanket covering the woman and found the sheet saturated with blood. Her abdomen was markedly distended and she was gasping for breath. Robert lifted the woman's wrist. Her pulse was thready. "Can you get a pressure?" he asked Mathir.

"Nothing," Mathir said.

"She's bleeding from somewhere. We've got to open her up. Let's get her to the operating room. Do we have any blood?"

"Doctor Salim just arrived," said Zaida, sticking her head into the room.

"The woman's husband and son are waiting outside the hospital," Doctor Mathir said. "We can ask them to give blood."

She accompanied him to where the two men were standing. They gawked at the Afghan doctor's bare face as if they'd never seen a woman's face before.

"Tell them their mother is hemorrhaging and needs blood," said Robert.

Mathir listened impatiently as the two men spoke to one another, then turned to her. The younger man gesticulated wildly. She snapped angrily at him and turned to Robert.

"They won't give blood," she said. "They are afraid. They say you can point a gun at them and kill them, but they won't give blood."

"His wife, his mother?" Robert pointed at each of them. "Not even for her?"

She shook her head. "They will run to the bazaar and buy some. I told them the type."

"How do we know the blood is good?"

She shrugged her shoulders.

"We don't have much choice. Tell them to hurry."

He dashed back inside and began scrubbing while Doctor Salim covered the patient's face with a mask and gave her oxygen. Zaida was already in position at the table, her instrument tray ready.

Robert drew his scalpel vertically down the woman's wrinkled abdomen while Mathir was still at the sink. Zaida assisted him, blotting the blood that followed the path of the blade. She stretched the thin abdominal wall to provide exposure and in seconds, Robert had entered the woman's abdomen, which was filled with dark blood and clots.

"Jesus," he muttered, scooping out clots with his hands, then suctioning. "She's bleeding from everywhere."

Rather than the one bleeding vessel he'd expected to find, blood oozed from every pedicle they'd tied off that morning. The ligatures were all intact. She was also bleeding from every place they'd sutured in the peritoneal lining and fascia. He looked up at Doctor Mathir as she entered the room. "Either she's got a clotting problem or her tissues are very poor from malnutrition," he told her. "There's no loose vessel I can see. We'll just re-suture every place that's oozing and apply pressure." While they were working, another nurse entered. She held out two plastic bags of blood. Doctor Salim jumped up from his stool at the head of the table and took them from her. He hooked the first bag to the patient's IV and squeezed it. The intravenous tubing turned a solid crimson as the blood flowed through it.

I hope to hell that it's the right type, Robert thought.

"How's she doing?" he asked as he sutured.

"Her blood pressure is coming up and her pulse is better," said Salim.

"Hook up the second unit as soon as this one's in," said Robert.

After re-suturing every oozing pedicle and closure line, Robert applied pressure with wet laparotomy pads. He watched the clock for five minutes, then slowly lifted each pad. The bleeding was controlled.

"She's dry now but we'll have to watch her carefully tonight," he told Mathir. "Check her vitals and hematocrits frequently. You'd better tell those two—" He restrained himself. "Those two gentlemen outside to get another two units of blood. I'm sure she'll need them. If anything comes up tonight, send someone to my room."

Robert thanked them all for their assistance. He looked at his watch. It was too late to go back to Sean's. Except for a brief glance, he ignored the two men waiting outside the hospital. They sat with their backs against the fence, their partouks wrapped around them. He walked wearily through the quiet streets back to his room. The usual light show was in progress in the skies over Torkham, the Afghan border town, flares bursting like a Fourth of July celebration in progress. But the night was quiet, not even a sporadic gunshot. He thought of how enigmatic the Afghans were. Fearless as warriors, yet too terrified to donate blood; eager for large families, yet unwilling to provide semen for sperm counts; and terrified of betrayal by women.

"Hard to understand," he said aloud as he entered his room. He peeled off his clothes and moments later was fast asleep.

The following morning, Friday, the hospital waiting room was empty. Zaida was sitting with the patient he'd operated on during the night.

"Don't you ever go home?" he smiled.

"I slept in the room with her. She's much better."

The patient, who looked twenty years older than sixty, smiled toothlessly, her gums showing. Robert checked her vital signs and palpated her abdomen. It was soft, all the distention of the night before gone. He nodded approvingly.

"Tell her she's doing fine," he said to Zaida. "Do we have a blood count from this morning?"

Robert looked at the chart she handed him. Doctor Mathir had checked her hematocrit at four. It was better than he anticipated but she still needed more blood.

"Do we have any more blood for her?"

"We have two units in the refrigerator."

"Let's transfuse them today and check her hematocrit after the second one. You should go home and let one of the other nurses take care of her."

"The hospital is my home. The room where I live is too quiet, too dark."

"I understand your husband is in the United States."

"Yes, he is in New York City. He works in an Afghan restaurant."

"He'll bring you to America?"

"Yes, *inshallah*. He is working on it. Maybe before the end of this year."

How will this hospital ever replace her? Robert wondered.

19

The Refugee Assistance Land Cruiser bounced over rough roads through a bleak, wind-blasted region of rock and desert, the irrigated fields and orchards of the Vale of Peshawar now miles behind. Three young girls grazing their flocks of sheep and goats on the sparse vegetation watched the vehicle approaching and turned their backs to it, pulling their chadors over their heads. Ahead, to the southwest, the hills they would traverse baked in the late morning sun. Robert sat in back. Sean sat next to Zaheer, the driver. He twisted around in his seat every time he spoke to Robert, raising his voice to overcome the engine noise and the juddering of the vehicle on the dirt road.

They were twenty-five miles out of Peshawar heading to the camps in the Kohat valley when Sean pointed directly ahead. "The town that we're coming to in that gorge is Darra. It's off limits to foreigners but we have a pass so we can drive through. Every shop, all seventy or eighty of them, sells one product—guns."

They crept slowly along the dusty highway, which was also Darra's main street. Japanese pickup trucks, dented and sun-bleached, were parked in front of every shop. Stacks of rifles, machine guns, rocket and grenade launchers, all visible through open doors and raised gratings, lined every wall and counter. Turbaned Afghan mujahideen carrying AK-47s filed in and out of the stores. Their chests were draped with full bandoliers of cartridges, enough to decimate a regiment. Those warriors standing outside on the street followed the Refugee Assistance vehicle with suspicious eyes. God help the Russians, Robert thought. Interspersed among the weapons shops were chaikhanas, the tea shops of Pakistan. The men seated at the small round tables kept their weapons within arm's reach.

"There are factories behind these gun stores," said Sean. "These people are skilled craftsmen. Most of the shops and factories are family businesses with skills passed from father to son. They're capable of making any weapon you want, from a twenty-two caliber pistol to an antiaircraft gun."

Robert flinched at the unmistakable sound of gunfire, erupting one moment from one direction, then abruptly from another.

"They're testing the merchandise," Sean said.

"Can we look inside the shops?" Robert asked.

Sean shook his head. "Foreigners aren't allowed to get out of their vehicles here."

They drove on and the town receded into the distance. A one-eyed man sitting at the side of the road caught Sean's attention. The small wooden stand behind him was lined with boots and other items.

"Stop for a minute," Sean said to Zaheer. "Check out what this guy is selling," he said to Robert.

Robert hopped out of the car and inspected the leather boots, belts with stars and CCCP lettering on the buckles, Russian military caps, and insignia patches.

"They strip all this stuff off Russian bodies," said Sean, who'd come up behind Robert.

"*Shoravee*," said the Afghan, a big smile creasing his bearded face as he pointed first at the display, then at his vacant eye socket.

"He's telling us everything is Russian. Including the bullet that took his eye."

Robert bought a belt for less than a dollar and got back into the car. He ran the stiff leather through his fingers, trying not to think about the fate of its Russian owner.

They bounced for another hour over rutted, rock-covered roads before emerging from the Kohat pass. Ahead of them sprawled the first of the refugee camps. Sun-baked hovels and mud-walled lanes made up a small part of the camp, but the majority of the refugees lived in canvas tents provided by UNHCR.

"The Afghans try to give the camps the feel of their villages back home," Sean said, gesturing toward the mud houses, "but they can't build the houses quickly enough. Some of these people have been in tents for years. Those newer cinderblock buildings under construction are clinics to replace the tents and primitive buildings we're using now."

"That's the clinic?" Robert asked, pointing at a dilapidated structure of mud and stone with a dry thatch roof. Two lines of Afghan women in burqas, most of them sitting on the ground and holding children, waited outside.

"Afraid so," laughed Sean. "Much of our work consists of setting up medical facilities and income-generating projects. We also help them dig wells and latrines. But everything takes time and depends on availability of funds. You know the old saying about Rome not being built in a day."

A smiling young man in a shalwar kameez approached them as they stepped out of the Land Cruiser.

"Here's Doctor Ali, one of the Afghan physicians," Sean said.

"Welcome to our camp," Ali said to Robert.

"Doctor Morgen is working at the Women's Hospital in Peshawar," Sean said. "Would you mind giving him a tour of the camp while I check how things are going?"

"We have a maternal and child health clinic, a general medical clinic, an immunization section, a laboratory, and a dispensary," Ali said proudly, his English slow and deliberate. He pointed out each building and tent to Robert as if their existence, no matter how primitive, was a minor miracle.

"There are three doctors here," Ali said, "but we also use paramedical personnel. We do much training. We teach traditional birth attendants modern methods of managing childbirth. We train lady health visitors to be community health nurses in maternal and child care. We have a special feeding program that uses food supplements, and we try to teach the mothers how to give better nutrition. It is difficult because everyone is so poor. Malnutrition is very common. You will see two-year-olds who weigh less than seven kilos."

"Isn't food provided by the World Food Program and UNHCR?"

Ali looked at the ground for a while before raising his eyes to Robert's. "On paper every refugee gets enough food. But the reality is different. The Pakistani government controls much of the food distribution so . . ." He made a helpless gesture with his hands. "There is much corruption," he said softly.

They paused in front of the precariously built clinic Robert had asked Sean about earlier. At least fifty women and children squatted on the ground.

Young Afghan girls, no more than eight or ten years old and wearing brightly colored, loose-sleeved dresses, carried infants in their arms. Some of the garments, intricately embroidered in front, were strikingly beautiful. Every girl had her head covered with a chador, the long sheet of fabric trailing down her back. They reminded Robert of the gypsies he had once seen in a French market town.

"That is our maternal and child health clinic."

"Do many women die in childbirth?"

"Very many. Most are anemic and they have many babies, as you can see." He made a sweeping motion with his arm to encompass the crowd in front of the clinic. "It is a fact that more women die in childbirth in one month in this country than in an entire year in North America, Europe, Japan, and Australia, combined."

"Do you see many infections?"

"We have tuberculosis, dysentery, malaria, and respiratory infections. Very many sick people."

"Where is the nearest hospital?"

Ali looked surprised by the question. "In Peshawar."

"But that's almost three hours away."

"Yes, and they must travel by bus."

"All these people waiting outside the clinic—the women, the little children—they're all sick?" Robert asked.

A fleeting smile crossed Ali's face. "Not all," he said. "For some women, it is the only way to get out of the house. For them, it is a social event, a chance to speak to their neighbors."

A young woman came up to them, her brows furrowed. She clutched her chador tightly below her chin and spoke to Ali in rapid Pashto.

"This lady is a traditional birth attendant. She says she has a patient who is bleeding very heavily after having her baby. Could you please see her?"

"Of course."

The woman led them to a small tent, one of many set on an expanse of parched brown earth the size of three football fields. Its entrance, a loose flap of canvas, was blocked by a tall Afghan with a henna-dyed beard, his head swathed in a dirty white turban. The young woman spoke to him, gesturing toward

Robert. He forcefully shook his head. Doctor Ali interceded and the conversation between him and the bearded man grew heated. Finally, Ali turned away in disgust.

"He will not let you see her because you are a man," Ali said.

"Did you explain that I came here from America and want to help his wife?"

"He knows that. He doesn't care."

The young woman slipped past the man into the tent. She returned moments later and spoke to the red-bearded man in a pleading voice. He turned away from her. She looked at Ali, her voice quavering and her gestures frantic. She seemed on the verge of tears.

Ali again argued with the man, his voice rising as his anger mounted. The man stared at Ali impassively, then disappeared into the tent.

"He is very stubborn," Ali said to Robert. "His wife is bleeding heavily. The birth attendant says she is pale and will probably die soon. I told him her only chance is if we take her to the hospital in Peshawar. She may not survive the trip, but here she will die before night comes. He says he will let her die before he lets her go to Peshawar. He says he can always get another wife."

Robert had to hold himself back. He wanted to push his way into the tent and carry the woman out in his arms, beating the husband if he had to. Unconsciously, he clenched his fists. Ali gently touched his shoulder.

"There is nothing we can do. Many of these people think in an old way."

"You mean they hate women."

Ali grimaced. "In Afghanistan, in Pakistan, outside of big cities, that is the way people think. It is very complicated, and difficult for someone not from this culture to understand."

I understand all right, Robert thought. He knew the young Afghan doctor had tried his best. Not wanting to embarrass him, Robert restrained himself from venting his anger. He and Ali walked in silence for a few minutes. They came to an outdoor school. A class of about forty young boys sat on the ground in front of a black-bearded teacher in a faded blue turban. Each child wore a shalwar kameez and an embroidered cap. The teacher pointed at a blackboard set up on an easel next to his chair. His voice rose and fell monotonously, each of the children repeating his words.

"They are studying Koran," Ali said to Robert.

The teacher glanced at the visitors, then turned his attention to the blackboard.

"No girl students?"

"In this camp, we have a big fight. The mullahs do not want the girls to go to school."

"Isn't there anything you can do? If the camp is supported by International Refugee Assistance, can't Sean do something?"

"In other camps, girls go to school. Everything is okay. Here it is a problem."

Not a straight answer, Robert thought. He'd had enough. Doctor Ali was doing his best to put a good face on things, but if what Robert had seen so far in the camp was indicative of its people and its administration, he needed to talk to Sean. Scanning the row upon row of canvas tents, he spotted him in the midst of a group of men digging a latrine.

Robert walked up to the hole, already chest deep. Sean, sweat running down his face, was explaining something in his halting Pashto. He looked up and saw Robert.

"How's the tour going?" Sean asked.

"Interesting. My first time in the fourteenth century."

Sean smiled. "It takes some getting used to." He hoisted himself out of the hole.

"Isn't there something you can do about getting girls to attend school in this camp?"

"Ali told you the problem we're having, I see. It's taken us months to get them to allow us to teach the girls how to sew so they can sell what they make. We still haven't been able to persuade the mullahs about school."

"But your organization supports the camp. Shouldn't it have the final say?"

Sean tugged at his ear lobe. "I know it's hard to understand, but we have to respect their culture, no matter how misguided we think their beliefs are. Unfortunately, in this camp we're up against a very conservative group of mullahs. Their mindset is the most rigid of any we have to deal with in our nine camps. We try to use gentle persuasion."

"I just met some Neanderthal who wouldn't let his wife go the hospital in Peshawar. She's bleeding to death after her delivery and all he says is that he can get another wife."

"That's true. He can get four more if he wants."

"Shit."

"I know you're upset, but this is an Afghan enclave in Pakistan. You're not in the States, Robert."

Robert bristled at Sean's rebuke. "I may not be in the States but I find it impossible to stand by and watch someone die because she happens to be female. Respect for someone else's culture is fine, but not when they're killing women and preventing girls from getting an education.

"You'll feel better," Sean said gently, "when you see the progress we've made in the two camps we'll visit tomorrow. The girls in those camps do attend school and many of the people live in more permanent homes instead of tents."

"I don't mean to sound so critical. I know you're doing your damndest here. It's just . . ." Robert raised his hands in a gesture of helplessness.

Sean nodded. "You're not the first by any means to have this reaction. It takes a lot of getting used to. I know. I went through it myself."

"Another thing I wanted to ask you," Robert said. "I don't think I've seen more than a dozen young men in this camp. Where are they all?"

"The men come and go. None of them stay for long. They come back from fighting the Russians in Afghanistan to see their families, pick up supplies in Peshawar, then cross the mountains again."

"Where do they cross the border?"

"There are more than three hundred passes in the mountains of the Hindu Kush, many of them known only to the Pathans. Some Afghans cross as individuals but more commonly they cross in groups led by *maliks,* their tribal chiefs. Entire villages sometimes cross over into Pakistan. Many of the men stay just long enough to get their families settled, then go back to fight."

"Have you been to Afghanistan?" Robert asked.

Sean shook his head. "I'd be in serious trouble if the New York office found out I'd done that."

A young clean-shaven man wearing his brown partouk draped across his chest in spite of the heat ran up to them. His embroidered skullcap had slipped to one side of his head. In his arms, draped in a blood-stained blanket, a screaming child between one and two years of age writhed.

"Please," he said in heavily accented English, "American doctor come with me. Doctor Ali busy helping other doctor."

"What happened to the baby?"

The Afghan peeled the blanket back from the baby's head. A deep, jagged laceration had torn away a portion of the baby's scalp. The wound was actively bleeding.

"Russian guard see baby's mother and father trying to cross border. He shoot them. Both dead. Bullet hit baby, too. Another man carry it across."

Robert followed him into a tent used as a first-aid station. He cleaned the struggling infant's wound with antiseptic and applied pressure until the bleeding stopped. He saw no damage to the underlying bone.

"Stitches?" the Afghan asked.

Robert shook his head. The laceration was too wide, too jagged, and had too much missing tissue to approximate the edges. He applied antibiotic ointment, covered the wound with gauze pads, and wound yards of gauze around the child's head to hold the dressing in place.

"Keep it clean," he said, "and it will heal."

The Afghan thanked him and Robert left the tent. Sean was waiting where Robert had left him.

"It's tough to see children getting caught up in this war," Robert said.

"It's like Sam says, they suffer the most."

They spent the night at the organization's base in Hangu. Robert joined Sean and two representatives of UNHCR for dinner, the four of them sitting on folding chairs around a fire. They welcomed the night's cool air after the blistering heat of the day. The base cook served them naan and grilled lamb, and cups of sweet tea. Robert, preoccupied with the situation at the refugee camp, said little. Enervated by the heat of the day, they all retired early. Robert had a tent to himself but found it impossible to sleep. Stepping outside, he wandered in small circles, looking at the star-filled sky. Uncertain about his religious beliefs, Robert considered himself an agnostic for want of a better word. If there was a creator, a supreme being capable of creating such galactic perfection on high, why was this creator incapable of mitigating the suffering below? Why did he permit women to bleed to death and children to be shot? Even while asking himself this, as millions had asked it before him, he knew it was a question without an answer.

Robert visited two more camps the following day. As Sean had promised, both camps were a marked improvement over the first one. Permanent mud-brick houses outnumbered UNHCR tents. Hygiene was markedly improved with numerous latrines and privies. Malaria and intestinal diseases were not as prevalent as in the first camp. Each camp had more than one well, giving the refugees better access to fresh water. Volunteers taught women to support themselves, mainly by sewing and embroidery, and girls did attend school.

"These camps have been in existence longer than the one you saw yesterday," Sean said. "And the religious leaders have been more reasonable."

"Maybe you should bring the mullahs from the other camp here to see what can be accomplished."

Sean laughed. "It's not that easy with Afghans. Even the mullahs are at odds with one another. If I've learned anything in my time here, it's the need for patience. Quiet diplomacy still seems to work the best—if you're patient enough."

They spent a second night in Hangu to permit Sean to conclude his survey of the two camps on Friday morning. It was midafternoon when they began their ride back to Peshawar. As they emerged from the Kohat pass, the sky above the snow-covered peaks of the Hindu Kush in Afghanistan was suffused with the orange glow of the setting sun. The serene beauty of the mountains was deceptive, thought Robert, for all around rivers of blood flowed.

20

At the end of his second week in Peshawar, Robert picked up his notebook, determined to finish his letter to Lynn. The words *Dearest Lynn* were still the only ones he'd written. His impressions of Pakistan would be easy to write about, but he'd wanted to sort out his feelings about Lynn before putting his thoughts on paper. He knew now that it would take time, perhaps a lot of time.

He thought back to his first winter in Vermont, when Alyssa's mood had grown as dark as the long nights. On Groundhog Day, the newscast hadn't been a mood elevator for either of them. They didn't believe in the shadow nonsense, but hearing that six more weeks of winter were in store was still discouraging. Six weeks if we're lucky, Robert remembered thinking. The locals had told him of snow as late as May.

They'd received a birth announcement from the Finkels early in February. Robert had often thought of Lynn but avoided mentioning her to Alyssa. He'd worried about the course of her pregnancy and as January came to an end, he wondered if he should call her. Surely, he thought, they'd receive some news once she delivered. Not only had Lynn promised to let him know, but he couldn't imagine Mike not informing Alyssa. Alyssa opened the small envelope.

"Wonderful!" she exclaimed. "Mike and Lynn had a seven pound boy. They named him Joshua and Mike says everything's fine."

She passed the card to him. It announced the birth of Joshua R. Finkel. Mike's short note said *It's great to be a daddy. Lynn's fine. Hope you guys are well. Talk to you soon.*

"That is good news," Robert said, feeling a wave of relief washing over him. Then the realization hit him that he now had two sons.

"What is it?" Alyssa asked.

"Why?" he asked.

"You looked like you suddenly thought of something important."

"No, I was just thinking how thrilled they must be."

"Maybe we can get together in the summer," Alyssa said, obviously cheered by the thought. "They can stay with us or we can go down and see them. I'll try to get up to Montpelier when the roads are good and pick out a gift for the baby." As an afterthought, she said, "I wonder what R stands for. I don't know why they used the initial instead of printing out the middle name."

Robert said nothing. He knew Alyssa had invited them up during their first autumn in West Roylestown, but Mike had told her Lynn didn't feel up to the long drive. She'll probably find another excuse not to come this year, he thought.

In May, Alyssa told him that Mike Finkel had called earlier that morning.

"Oh?" said Robert, surprised. "How are they?"

"Fine. The baby is three months old. They're doing great."

"Did you invite them up?"

"Of course, but Mike said Lynn wasn't up to traveling yet."

Alyssa, wearing a bikini, was stretched out in a lounge chair in front of the house. It was the first really warm weather of the spring and it had improved her mood considerably. Davey was digging in a sand pile Robert had made for him.

"If a neighbor drives down the dirt road and sees you in that swimsuit, there'll be an accident," Robert said.

"What neighbor? The deer and raccoons?" She frowned momentarily, then smiled at him. "Do we have any gin and tonic water? I know it's early, but it's Saturday and this is perfect weather for it."

"I'll see what we have."

"Bourbon and water okay?" he asked as he came out. "I'll have to pick up some gin and tonic in town."

"Make mine weak and then come sit with me."

"You have the anemic one," he said, handing her the drink. He sat down next to her on the edge of the lounge.

"Do you know why Mike called?" she asked.

Robert's heart pounded. "I was wondering," he said, trying to keep his voice level. "Except for the birth announcement, we haven't heard from them."

"I called Mike yesterday at work and left a message for him."

"Oh?" Robert said, relieved.

"I asked if he had any psych contacts in Vermont. I told him I'm looking for work."

"Did he?"

She shook her head. "He used to know someone in Burlington, but he's moved on." She smiled sadly. "He sends you his best and he wants to know when we're moving back to the city."

"What did you tell him?"

"Nothing," she said, turning her head away.

Alyssa called the Finkels again during the summer but was unable to reach them. Her message on their answering machine went unanswered.

"They must have rented a place for the summer," she said peevishly.

In December, when Alyssa told him about the job she'd found in Westchester, Robert wondered if she'd called Mike Finkel to let him know. Several times he was on the verge of asking, but let it drop. Robert also wondered how Mike and Lynn would react if they learned she had an apartment in Scarsdale. Would they think the Morgens were splitting up? Lynn would probably be perplexed. Joshua, her baby, was now almost a year old. He had had no contact with her since her visit to his Manhattan office, but he knew instinctively she would be critical of Alyssa's move to New York. He could only guess at Lynn's relationship with Joshua, but he suspected she would never consider moving under any circumstances and leaving her son behind, not even if he was four years old.

One ritual that Robert and Davey followed the year Alyssa was away was telling bedtime stories. Robert sat on the edge of Davey's bed and made up a story for him. If Robert had permitted it, Davey would have been reading his books well past midnight. Storytelling allowed Robert to turn the light off and ease his son into sleep.

"You tell good stories, Daddy," Davey said to him one evening as Robert stood up to leave the room.

Robert sat back down on the edge of the bed and tousled his son's hair. "You think so, huh?"

Davey nodded forcefully and Robert laughed.

"Well, you're a good audience."

Robert thought about what his son had said as he sat in the kitchen later that evening. The newspaper was spread open on the table in front of him, but he paid no attention to it. He chuckled when he recalled the story he'd told Davey at bedtime, the tale of a giraffe and a mischievous spider monkey who become the best of friends.

"What happened next?" Davey had asked, laughing when Robert described the monkey using the giraffe's long neck as a slide.

"I'll tell you tomorrow," he said, leaning over to give Davey a kiss. "Now it's bedtime. See you in the morning, kiddo."

Maybe he said I tell good stories, Robert thought, because he wanted me to keep going. He decided that wasn't the case since Davey hadn't complained when he turned off the light.

Robert pushed the newspaper aside and went to his desk to look for paper. He poured himself a scotch on the rocks, sat down at the desk, and began writing the story he'd told Davey. The ice in his drink melted. It was eleven-thirty when he looked up. Three hours had flown by without his noticing.

From that evening on, Robert wrote every night after he put Davey to bed. His son was the perfect audience for his tales. If he didn't like a story, he was outspoken about its faults. Robert laughed to himself when he realized he was using Davey as a critic, but he found his son's responses helpful.

So what am I going to do with these stories? he asked himself. One thing he knew, he wasn't going to show them to Alyssa when she came on weekends. He hid them in his desk, then took them out as soon as she'd gone. Why am I afraid to show them to her? he asked himself. He already knew the answer. She'd laugh at him.

He'd written a dozen stories by the time summer was over. Whenever he entered Davey's room to tell him "I have a new story for tonight," Robert felt a sense of accomplishment. The look of eager anticipation on his son's face was Robert's reward.

It usually took three or four nights for Robert to finish the telling of the story. Davey often interrupted to ask questions. "What does that mean, Daddy? Why did the fox do that? I thought the little boy wanted a dog." No inconsistency escaped Davey's attention.

"Well, that's the end of the story," Robert said whenever he finished reading one. "What do you think? Is there anything you'd change?"

For a child not yet five, Davey's critiques amazed him. He picked up on the parts of the stories over which Robert had labored, always prefacing his remarks with "I'd like it better if . . ."

November in Vermont that year was brutally cold, too cold for snow. For three consecutive weeks, nighttime temperatures plummeted to twenty-five below zero. Alyssa opted not to come up on one of those weekends. "I can't stand it when it's that cold," she told him on the phone.

"It's cold in New York, too."

"Not twenty-five below. You're welcome to it."

That weekend, without Alyssa to criticize him, Robert sat with his children's stories, more than fifteen now, all typed, spread out on the kitchen table in front of him. I don't know anything about children's book publishing, he told himself. There's no one I can contact. Even as that thought occurred to him, he knew it wasn't entirely true. Lynn Finkel illustrated children's books. She would be the obvious person to call. But he hadn't spoken to Lynn in more than two years.

Robert drummed his fingers on the table and asked himself why he hadn't made any attempt to talk to her and why he hesitated even now, when he merely needed information. It wasn't because he didn't think of her. If anything, the opposite was true. Alone in his bed at night, he often remembered their one afternoon together. He wondered if she ever thought of him.

Be honest, he told himself, why won't you call? He picked up a pen lying on the table and quickly wrote on a piece of paper: Because you still care about her. Because you think she'd prefer not to be reminded that you fathered her child. Because you look upon it as being unfaithful to Alyssa. Because you don't want to do anything that might rock the boat with Lynn's marriage or with yours.

He looked at what he'd written and tore the page into pieces.

No matter how much you like her—or even love her—he thought, she and her husband were your friends. You can call. Thanksgiving was just a week off, and if the children's stories weren't a good enough excuse, the approaching holidays certainly were.

He stood up and walked to the phone on the kitchen counter. Nine o'clock on a Saturday night. It wasn't too late to call. They might not even be at home, in which case a babysitter would probably answer. Again, he hesitated, walking down the hall to his son's room to check on him, even though he was sure he was asleep. For almost two hours that afternoon the two of them had stacked firewood, trying to keep warm. By the time he tucked Davey into bed a half-hour earlier, his son's eyes had been closing.

Robert stood in Davey's doorway, listening to his breathing. Reassured that he was asleep, he returned to the kitchen and thumbed through his address book until he found the number. He held his index finger poised above the phone, then pressed the buttons. Lynn answered on the third ring and he felt his heart pounding when he heard her voice. It's not too late to hang up, he told himself.

"Hi, Lynn."

"Robert?"

"Yes. How are you?"

"I'm fine. It's so good to hear your voice. Is anything wrong?"

"No. I'm calling to wish you all happy holidays."

"Well, the same to you."

"And to ask you something about children's books."

"You've come to the right place for that," she laughed.

"Am I calling at a bad time?"

"Not all. Joshua is asleep. Are you and Alyssa and Davey well? I think about you—about all of you—often."

"Yeah. I think about you—all of you—often, too."

They both burst out laughing.

"We're a pair, aren't we?" Lynn said.

"When I saw the photo you sent of Joshua last Christmas I almost fell over. I have a photo that looks just like that—it's in the album of my baby pictures."

Lynn laughed again. "I'm not surprised. He looks just like you, you know."

"And Mike hasn't noticed?"

"I told you he wouldn't."

"I take it he's not home?"

"No, he's out. And Alyssa?"

"She has an apartment in New York."

"What?"

"It's not what you think."

Robert told her what had transpired during their time in Vermont, focusing on Alyssa's unhappiness at her inability to find work.

"So when this Westchester County job was offered to her, she took it. That was back in January. She comes up to Vermont almost every weekend. A couple of times last summer Davey and I went down to stay with her in Scarsdale."

Lynn's silence began to weigh on him.

"Anyway, it's only supposed to be a temporary arrangement. She's hoping this job will lead to something closer to home."

Again, the silence.

"You're very quiet, Lynn."

He heard her sigh. "Robert," she said softly, "take your blinders off."

"Really, Lynn, it's not permanent. She'll be coming back. She says it will be easier to get something up here if she's coming from a job. So I don't know what you mean when you tell me I'm wearing blinders."

"If you don't know, I'm not going to explain it. Now, what were you going to ask me about children's books?"

He told her about the stories he'd written and asked if she'd be willing to look at them. "If they're no good, just tell me. And if you think they have possibilities, well . . ."

"I try to be honest—brutally honest—always."

Her remark bothered Robert, as did the change in the tone of their conversation. What had he said to upset her?

"Just send them down," she said, "and I'll tell you what I think."

Robert couldn't think of what else to say. "Give Joshua a hug for me," he said at last.

"And give Davey one for me."

With that, she hung up. Robert was bewildered. He went over their conversation in his mind. It had started so well, the connection between them flowing easily, and suddenly she'd become silent and withdrawn. Why had that happened? It was when he'd told her about Alyssa's move to New York, but why should that have troubled her? She couldn't possibly think that Alyssa was involved with Mike again. He tried to make light of it, telling himself that just because he was a gynecologist it didn't give him special insight into the mind of a woman. But it troubled him enough so that he had difficulty falling asleep that night.

Five months passed before he heard from Lynn again. In April of 1986, three months after initiating divorce proceedings, Robert arrived home on a Sunday evening from his weekend with Davey. Preoccupied with Davey's reaction to his news about his forthcoming trip to Pakistan, Robert turned on his answering machine, paying no attention to messages until he heard Lynn's voice. He hadn't heard from her since their telephone conversation in November and assumed she thought his stories didn't merit a phone call. "I have good news," she said. "Call me."

It was a little before ten but Robert decided to take a chance on awakening her. Lynn answered on the first ring.

"I hope I didn't wake you."

"No, I was lying here reading. Congratulations, Robert."

"What do you mean?"

"I showed your stories to the editor of the book I'm working on and she passed them on to two of her colleagues. The upshot is the publisher has agreed to publish two of them. And they want me to do the illustrating."

"I can't believe it. That's great."

"It's unusual for them to accept stories from unpublished writers without an agent. But you'll get an agent now, I'm sure."

"I don't know how to thank you. I'm really grateful, Lynn. I needed some good news. Alyssa and I have split."

"What do you mean?"

"I filed for divorce in January."

She was silent for a moment. "I'm not surprised," she said finally. "What about Davey? Is he still with you?"

"He was until December. Then she said she wanted him down there to spend the first week of January with her parents. She told me they wanted to celebrate his fifth birthday with him. Like an idiot, I brought him down and she wouldn't let me bring him back to Vermont. I didn't know what to do. Obviously I didn't want to make a scene and have a battle in front of Davey. So I saw a lawyer up here. He said that even with joint custody, the court would never let Davey live with me now that she had him. Joe Ross referred me to a bigshot lawyer in Manhattan and he pretty much said the same thing. So that's the whole sad story. I've been screwed out of having my son."

"I'm so sorry, Robert. That's awful. I never knew she could be that devious. So, it looks like she's riding high. She has her son and her lover."

"What do you mean?"

"You're not the only one going through some major changes. I'm divorcing Mike."

"Are you serious?"

"Remember when you called and told me Alyssa had moved to Scarsdale?"

"When you got angry with me and told me I was wearing blinders?"

"Well, you weren't the only one wearing them. I may have suspected Mike still loved her, but I didn't expect him to start cheating on me. Not with a baby who wasn't even two years old. But he'd been coming in late a lot, giving me half-assed excuses. So when he told me he had a meeting one evening I followed him from his office."

"Don't tell me."

"Right to her building in Scarsdale."

"Did you confront him there?"

"No. I kicked him out that night and saw a lawyer the next day."

"You mean this was going on before January? Before she took Davey from me?"

"I think it's been going on since last fall."

"I feel like an idiot. What did Mike say when you told him you knew?"

"The usual bullshit. Maybe we could work it out. I told him to go work it out with Alyssa, that I was through with him."

"So where is he now?"

"Where do you think? In Scarsdale. He took an apartment in the same building as Alyssa." She gave a short, bitter laugh. "The same one-bedroom Alyssa used to live in. You know, I had no idea whether or not you knew what was going on. There was no way for me to know that you and Alyssa were getting a divorce. I thought of calling you, but I decided against it. If you wanted to live in la-la land, I told myself, that was your business."

"I wonder if it would have made a difference in Davey being able to live with me. I'll bet Alyssa's just waiting for our divorce to be final before she moves Mike into her place. Maybe I should tell my lawyer what's going on."

"How would you prove it?"

"You know what I can't understand, Lynn? How can you live with someone for six years and never really know the person? I hear all kinds of stories from my patients, but somehow, I never thought I'd be deceived and not know it was happening."

"Sometimes we don't want to know. It's painful."

"Yeah, you're right. This is so weird. I still can't believe it. You know, when you first told me about Mike and Alyssa having been lovers before we met them, I got angry. I knew it was true, but I didn't want it to be. Not because I'm a prude, but because she'd never told me about it. It was like she was deceiving me. You knew because Mike told you. But she wanted to keep me in the dark. Well, like you said, I was wearing blinders, and now we're both in the same situation."

"At least I get to keep Joshua. I wish it had been that way for you."

"Me, too. I'll always be kicking myself for taking Davey down to her."

"Don't blame yourself. You didn't know what she was planning. At least you have the satisfaction of knowing you were the one always thinking of Davey, trying to accommodate her. She was the devious one. Anyway, to lift your spirits a bit, my editor says you'll be receiving a formal proposal from the publisher this coming week."

"Great. I'm really looking forward to working on this with you. And now I have some more news." He told her about his departure for Pakistan at the end of the month.

"That's exciting, Robert. Can we get together before you go? Now we don't have to worry about being uncomfortable in front of our spouses. And I would like you to meet Joshua."

"I fly out on a Sunday so I'll be in New York on Friday to spend the next day with Davey. We can meet then. You can bring Joshua."

"That's Mike's weekend with Joshua." She hesitated for a moment. "I have an idea though. What are you doing this coming weekend?"

"Nothing, but I'm on call for my practice."

"I've never been to Vermont. How would you feel about my coming up with Joshua?"

"I'd love it. But it's a long trip for a weekend, especially with a baby."

"What if I came up during the week, on Wednesday or Thursday? I can bring my work with me and do it while you're in the office. I'm sure Joshua will sleep for most of the ride."

"I—"

"Look, if it makes you uncomfortable, Robert, then—"

He laughed. "I was going to say I'd love to see you and Joshua. Wednesday's my afternoon off. Why don't you leave Wednesday morning?"

"I will. I have a pen in my hand, so I'm ready for the driving directions."

Robert hadn't felt such a heady mix of excitement and nervousness in many years. He lectured himself about the need for caution. Don't be impulsive just because you're feeling sorry for yourself, he said. He hated clichés, but the old adage about going from the frying pan into the fire seemed apt in this case. He'd spent only a few intimate hours with Lynn. He really didn't know her at all. Just well enough to make a son with her, he thought, mocking himself. It wasn't enough to base a relationship on.

No matter what he told himself, no matter what had happened between them in the past, no matter what constraints he vowed to put on his feelings with respect to Lynn, he couldn't deny his anticipation.

He also thought about what Lynn had told him about his writing. He felt a sense of accomplishment in actually managing to sell two of his stories. But he'd believe it only when he held the publisher's proposal in his hands. He had no idea what they were offering him, but it would not make him rich. That didn't matter. Suddenly the future seemed full of possibilities. Alyssa had asked him what he'd do when he returned from Pakistan and he hadn't had an answer. He hadn't wanted to contemplate the obvious—a return to his practice in Vermont. Now perhaps, he wouldn't have to. Other roads were beckoning. He was going to Pakistan. He was going to be a published author. Life didn't have to be a straight path from which he couldn't deviate, like being on a down escalator from birth to death with no means of escape. There were side roads, branches, all kinds of possible routes to take. And what did it matter if he didn't know what awaited him at the end of those byroads? He'd find out eventually. All he knew was that something good was happening. For the first time in a long time he felt optimistic.

21

Shortly after one o'clock on Wednesday afternoon, Robert stood by the living room window nervously watching for Lynn's car. He'd arrived home from the office only a half-hour earlier. It was a beautiful day, one that hovered on the cusp between winter and spring. Sunlight bathed the patches of snow on the lawn and glinted on the ice-covered hilltops in the distance, but the first green buds were sprouting on the birches, and only that morning Robert had noticed the shoots of crocuses and daffodils emerging from the bulbs he'd planted around the house in the fall.

Just then a car slowed at the entrance to the driveway, hesitated for a second, then turned in. Robert grabbed his windbreaker and headed out the door. Lynn stepped out of the car just as he reached it.

"It's good to see you," he said.

"Almost three years, Robert. Can you believe it?"

She looked exactly as he remembered her, although her hair was longer. They approached one another tentatively. Moments later he held her in his arms. The fragrance of her skin that he had dreamed about so often now filled his nostrils and he kissed her neck. She spoke his name softly before he kissed her lips.

A short cry from the rear seat of the car interrupted them. Lynn opened the door.

"Hi, sleepyhead," she said, unfastening Joshua from his car seat. "He fell asleep in Springfield," she laughed, looking at Robert.

She lifted her son from the car seat and kissed his cheek. Robert studied the child with bemusement. Joshua, except for the shape and color of his eyes, looked like Davey. Had the two boys been in the same room, anyone who didn't know their parents would think they were brothers.

"This is Mommy's friend, Robert," Lynn said.

"Hi, Joshua," Robert said, smiling at the boy. "Can I hold you?"

The boy turned his face away and clutched his mother tightly.

"Shy and still sleepy," Lynn said. "Josh, look where we are." She turned slowly so the boy could look in all directions. "Robert, it's beautiful here." She breathed deeply. "And the air is so clean. I don't know if my dirt-filled New York City lungs can tolerate it," she laughed.

"You must both be starved," Robert said. "Come on in and we'll have some lunch."

"I have our bags in the trunk."

"I'll bring them in for you."

"You're getting heavy, Josh," she said, putting him down and taking his hand. "Let's go see Robert's house."

They followed him inside and Lynn paused on the threshold. She gazed at the wood-paneled living room, its walls lined with bookshelves. "Oh, Robert, it's lovely."

"That's exactly what I thought the first time I saw it."

"I can't believe Alyssa wanted to give this up—the house, the woods, the hills . . ."

"There's a job waiting for you with the Vermont Tourist Office," Robert laughed.

"Seriously, I think this is incredible. And it's so quiet. What a great place to write."

He gave Lynn a tour of the house. Joshua spotted Davey's Tinkertoys. He pointed at them and looked at his mother.

"Can he?" Lynn asked.

"Of course." Robert handed the box to the boy. "Come into the kitchen, Josh. You can play in there while your mother and I make some lunch."

"It must be so hard for you without Davey," Lynn said.

Robert nodded. "At first it was terrible. I hated to come home in the evening. The house was so empty, lifeless."

"I know what you mean. I don't know how I'd endure it now if I didn't have Josh."

"Do you miss Mike?"

She looked at him in surprise and laughed. "Not one bit. Isn't that strange?

"And you? Do you miss Alyssa?"

"Not one bit," he smiled. "That's the advantage of growing to dislike someone. You don't miss them when they're not around.

"Well, let's see what there is to eat."

"Oh, good, cream of tomato soup," Lynn said, taking the can from the cupboard. "Josh loves it. I'll bet Davey does, too."

"Let's see what else we have. There's wheat bread, cheese, lettuce, mayo . . ."

"Let me wash up and I'll help you make the sandwiches," Lynn said.

"I like Tinkertoys," Joshua said while his mother was out of the room. They were the first words he had spoken to Robert.

"That's great. What do you like to make with them?"

"Big houses," he said, throwing out his arms. He grew pensive for a moment. "My daddy lives in a big, big house now," he said.

"Bigger than the building where you and your mom live?"

"Uh huh, as high as the sky."

"My little boy, Davey, lives in a very big building, too. Someday you'll have to meet Davey." He turned to look at Lynn, who had just come back into the room. "Mike never took Josh over to Alyssa's?"

"I don't think so. You know, Josh, Robert is going away on a long trip but when he comes back, maybe you'll be able to meet his little boy, Davey." She looked at Robert for confirmation.

"That's right, Josh. When I get back I'll make sure you and Davey get to know one another."

"Where are you going?" the boy asked.

"To a country called Pakistan."

"Robert is a doctor, Josh. He's going to Pakistan to help poor people." Joshua looked at him warily.

"You don't like doctors?" Robert said.

The boy shook his head.

"Because they give you shots?"

Joshua nodded.

"But I don't. I never give children shots."

Joshua looked from Robert to his mother.

"It's true, Josh. Robert never gives children shots, so you can relax."

"You know," Robert said, while they were eating, "Alyssa tried to reach you last summer to invite you up here. When she couldn't, she figured you were probably away on vacation."

"We did go to the Jersey shore for a week. It's just as well she didn't reach us."

"You wouldn't have come?"

"I wouldn't have been comfortable." She smiled. "Besides, Alyssa may be self-involved, but I don't think she would have missed Joshua's resemblance to you."

Robert nodded. "That's why I'm surprised someone else hasn't noticed."

Lynn shrugged her shoulders and lifted her hands. "Some people see what they want to see."

"Who, mommy?" said Joshua.

"Little pitchers with big ears," Lynn laughed. "Probably puzzled by how cryptic we're being. Well, like you," she said. "You see the sandwich you're eating, right?"

He nodded.

"He's sure a cute kid," Robert said.

"Narcissist." Lynn mouthed the word at him.

"How about a walk after lunch? I'll show you the property and then we can hike in the woods. I still have Davey's old carrier, so I can put Josh on my back."

Robert led them to an old logging road and they trudged up, avoiding the muddier areas where snow was rapidly melting.

"Josh, listen," Lynn said. They stood quietly, listening to the rustling of squirrels in the underbrush and the rat-a-tat of a woodpecker above them. She pointed up into the tree. "There he is. See him. He has a red spot on his head."

"Alyssa and I ran into a black bear on this trail," Robert said. "It was during our first spring in the house."

"No kidding! Oh, I'd love to see him."

"He sure scared Alyssa. She ran all the way back to the trailhead."

Lynn smiled. "I know it's mean of me but I would have liked to have seen that."

They hiked for almost two hours, then headed back as the sun began to descend behind the hills to the west.

"Do you want me to take him, Robert? He's heavy."

"No, I'm fine. You know, I haven't had such a nice day in months. The snow was too deep and the weather too cold to do this with Davey the end of last year, and when I see him now we're always in the city. It's too long a drive to bring him here just for weekends. I'll have him for a month in the summer though, so he'll spend it here."

"Where do you stay in New York?"

"In Massapequa with my parents."

"I'm sure they're glad to have the chance to see you both."

He nodded.

"Down," said Joshua, pointing at the ground.

Lynn lifted him out of Robert's carrier and he ran ahead of them. Lynn took Robert's arm. "Don't fall in the mud, Josh," she called.

"It'll wash off," Robert said. "It's nice to see him enjoying the outdoors."

Robert flipped through his record collection when they arrived back at the house. As dusk descended, Joshua sat on the kitchen floor with his Tinkertoys while Robert and Alyssa prepared dinner. Classical music played in the background. It's incredible, Robert thought. Like we've been doing this together for years. Unconsciously, he smiled to himself.

"What are you smiling about?" Lynn asked, looking up from the chopping board at that moment.

"I was just thinking how comfortable all this seems. Do you realize we barely know one another? We spent some social evenings together and, well, one very special afternoon, and we haven't seen one another in three years, and yet . . ."

"I know. I feel the same way."

"Mommy," said Joshua, "where are we going to sleep?"

"Are you tired already? We haven't even had dinner."

He shook his head.

"You can have Davey's room," Robert said, "the room where you found the Tinkertoys."

"Where will you sleep, mommy?"

"Robert has enough rooms for everyone. He won't make me sleep outside."

"Do you have more toys?" Josh asked Robert.

"Let's go to Davey's room and see," Robert answered.

He opened his son's closet and removed Davey's toy box. "Here are blocks and some little cars and . . ." Josh had already picked up two of the miniature cars and sat down on the floor next to the box. "You can play with everything in here if you like," Robert said, heading back to the kitchen.

"He's a lovely child," he said to Lynn.

"You're not just saying that because he looks like you?"

"I'd say it even if he didn't," Robert laughed.

"And don't you like the little devil's question about where his mommy is going to sleep? I wonder what he's thinking."

"It is an interesting question," Robert said.

Lynn placed the knife alongside the cutting board and walked up to him. "I think you should know one thing, Robert. I invited myself up here because I really wanted to see you and I wanted you and Joshua to know one another. But I don't have any ulterior motives. We're both in situations that are new for us and I don't want us to do anything because we're on the rebound or because—because we were once together. What I'm trying to say is don't feel pressured into doing anything you don't want to do. I value your friendship and if that's what we ultimately have, that's fine."

Robert placed his hands on her shoulders and lowered his lips to hers. "This is exactly what I want to do," he said.

After dinner Robert kindled a fire in the living room. Josh sat on his mother's lap as she read from books Davey had left behind. Only one thing missing to make this scene perfect, Robert thought. Lynn looked up from her reading and smiled wistfully at him. She knows what I'm thinking, he told himself, shrugging in reply.

"Do you know what I think, young man?" Lynn said to Josh.

He smiled coyly at her and shook his head.

"Yes, you do know," she said, tickling him. "You've had a long day and it's time for bed. Let's show Robert what a big boy you are. Did you know, Robert, that Josh always goes to bed without a fuss?" She winked at Robert.

Robert put down his book and followed Lynn and Joshua to Davey's room. She sat on the edge of the bed and tucked him in.

"Are you comfortable? Cozy?" Robert asked.

Joshua looked at him with a serious expression and nodded. Robert leaned over and planted a kiss on his forehead. "I'll say goodnight then. And the nightlight is on in case you wake up during the night. Do you remember where the bathroom is?"

Josh turned to his mother, a questioning look on his face.

"Josh still wears Pampers," Lynn said. "Getting him bowel trained was easy, but peeing in the toilet is a different matter."

"It was the same with Davey. He was past three when he made up his mind to stop wearing Pampers at night."

"Oh, good, then there's hope," Lynn laughed.

She followed Robert back to the living room and sat down on the sofa.

"Can I join you?" Robert asked, picking up his book from the arm of his chair. Lynn patted the seat next to her.

"What are you working on?" he asked.

"Just doing some preliminary sketches for a book I received last week about a girl and her cat. It's quite good actually. I've worked on this author's books before."

"Davey still has every book you've given him. He took them with him to Alyssa's. I've always thought your artwork was excellent."

"Flatterer. I'm looking forward to doing the artwork for your books."

"I still can't believe the publisher wants them."

She leaned over to look at the jacket on Robert's book. "Thesiger. I haven't read anything by him."

"He's an explorer. I guess I'm an armchair adventurer."

"You'll be having some adventures of your own pretty soon. Are you looking forward to Pakistan?"

"Yes, but feeling a little guilty about it, too."

"What do you mean?"

"You know. The divorce, which might be final about the time I get back. I worry about how Davey is taking it. He doesn't say much, but I know how upset he is. And now I'm disappearing from his life for six weeks."

Lynn nodded. "Divorce is hard, but I'm sure Davey will work his way through it. You shouldn't feel any guilt, Robert. You still have your own life to live.

"Now, describe to me where you'll be."

"Here, I'll show you," he said, standing up and pulling a *National Geographic Atlas* off one of the bookshelves. He opened to a map of Pakistan and pointed. "Peshawar."

"It's right on the border with Afghanistan. Will it be dangerous?"

"I don't think so. I have a friend there, Sean Cooper. He's the one who told me about International Refugee Assistance."

"How did you meet him?"

"It's a funny story actually. He was a patient of Joe Ross. During our first year here in Vermont, Sean dropped in on us out of the blue. He was on his way to Burlington to visit his brother and Joe had told him to visit us. Joe promised to call us, of course, to tell us Sean would be coming. Well, you know Joe. It must have slipped his mind. So there's this big guy with red hair and a beard standing on our doorstep with a gigantic malamute, his mother's dog. He worked overseas for years with American Friends Service Committee before taking on the job in Peshawar working with Afghan refugees. International Refugee Assistance sponsors a women's hospital in Peshawar and that's where I'll be working, training Afghan physicians."

"I think it will be fascinating."

"It'll be nice to see Sean again. He's one of those people whose heart is really in the right place. I liked him right away."

"Alyssa knows you're going, I assume."

He nodded. "I told her."

"Did she have any comment?"

"She accused me of having always wanted to run off."

Lynn looked at him incredulously, then laughed. "You should have told her 'Yes, far away from you'."

Robert smiled. "She doesn't have much of a sense of humor these days."

"I sound terribly catty, I know," said Lynn. "It's just that Alyssa has always rubbed me the wrong way. More so now."

Lynn went back to her sketching while Robert read. An hour had passed when Lynn stifled a yawn. She put her pad and pencils aside. "That's enough sketching for tonight."

"Can I get you anything to drink?" Robert asked.

She rested her head on his shoulder. "No, I'm fine, just a little sleepy. Must be the air. I'm so relaxed, Robert. Thank you again for letting Josh and me come to visit, and for such a nice day."

"I'm the one who should be thanking you."

She shifted on the sofa to face him and Robert took her in his arms, kissing her deeply.

"Can we look at the stars for a minute before we go to bed?"

They stepped outside and Lynn squeezed his arm. "I can't believe it," she said. "I'd forgotten a sky could look like this." She turned in a slow circle, looking up. "Do you know your constellations?"

"A few of the more obvious ones like Orion. Can't miss the three stars in his belt."

"It's so beautiful here." She shivered suddenly. "And chilly."

"The nights are still very cool," he said, putting his arm around her shoulders.

"Come," Lynn said, "show me where I'm to sleep. It'll feel good to crawl under the covers."

"You have two choices," Robert said, walking down the hallway with his arm around her. "This is the guest bedroom." He showed her a room with a double bed and small dresser, opposite the one where Joshua slept. "And this is my bedroom." Robert led her to the master bedroom at the end of the hall.

Lynn silently surveyed the room with its queen-sized bed. "Which one would you like me in?"

"I think you know the answer to that."

"I want to hear it from you."

"You're in the right room."

She smiled at him and kissed his cheek.

"And since I'm a perfect gentleman, you can use the bathroom first."

Lynn removed her toiletries bag from her suitcase and headed for the bathroom.

"Clean towels are on the shelf," Robert said.

Am I doing the right thing? he asked himself as he undressed. But he had offered her a choice. If there was one thing he'd noticed about Lynn, it was that she seemed sure of what she wanted. She didn't say no, he told himself. He slipped into a bathrobe while waiting for her to come out.

"No hair wash tonight or I'll look like Medusa in the morning," Lynn said, emerging from the bathroom with a towel wrapped around her body.

"I'm sorry I don't have another robe," Robert said. "You can have mine."

"I don't need it. I'll slip under the covers." She unwrapped the towel and tossed it to Robert. He felt his heart thudding as he looked at her. "You're lovely," he managed to say.

"I told you," she said, climbing into bed, "you're a flatterer."

"A truthful one."

"I seem to recall our doing this before," Lynn said when he joined her after his shower. "A long time ago."

"You don't know how many times since then I've fallen asleep with that afternoon in my mind."

She looked at him. "Even when you were still with Alyssa?"

"Even then."

"And I thought it was just me dwelling on it like a lovesick schoolgirl."

"What will Josh think if he finds us here?"

"What's wrong with my being in bed with his father?" she giggled.

"Seriously."

"We'll probably be up before him. You're working tomorrow, aren't you?"

"Yes, and I have a seven-thirty meeting."

"See. No problem. Now stop worrying." She embraced him and pulled him down on top of her.

"I never thought I'd hold you like this again."

"I've always heard good things happen to those who wait," she whispered in his ear.

22

Lynn and Joshua stayed with him for the entire week, but for Robert time ceased to have any meaning. He'd never been happier and refused to think about Lynn leaving. How can this be? he wondered. If a voice were to whisper in his ear that it had always been this way, that he and Lynn had been together for years, it would have been entirely plausible, more believable, in fact, than the few days they'd been together.

Robert juggled his patient schedule into half-days so that he could take Lynn to some of Vermont's quaint towns: Middlebury, Newfane, and South Royalton; they walked through covered bridges and hiked trails in the Green Mountain National Forest, Joshua on Robert's back in the child carrier; and twice, when they knew they'd arrive home later than Joshua's dinner time, they stopped at an inn to eat.

Robert soon received his contract from the publisher, along with a modest advance. The contract was better than he'd anticipated. They also took an option on two more stories.

"It's funny how things work out," Robert said. "Two weeks ago I was at loose ends, anxious to get to Pakistan. And now so much is happening, I almost wish I could delay my departure."

"Don't be silly. It'll give you something to look forward to on your return. I can't wait to hear your impressions and know everything you're doing there. Do you realize the only places I've been in my thirty-eight years are some Caribbean islands and Hawaii? That was enough adventure for Mike. Give him a swimming pool and a lounge for sunbathing and he thinks he's found heaven."

"If that's the case, he and Alyssa will be in a state of mutual bliss."

They laughed as they thought of their ex-spouses lying next to one another in lounge chairs.

"Today New York, tomorrow Miami Beach," Robert intoned in a shrill voice. "Anyway," he said, "when I get back I'll have some serious thinking to do, like what I want to do when I grow up, where I want to be, what to do about Davey—and about us."

Lynn placed her hand on his arm. "Do you know what I've always found? When I take things one step at a time, the rest seems to fall into place."

"If I had Davey, I'd feel I had the world at my fingertips. We could live anywhere. You and I could do our writing and illustrating here, or in Europe, or—"

"I'm flattered that you're including me in your fantasies, but I fantasize, too. I can't imagine any fantasy that would make me happier than I am at this moment. All I know is that it will be important for you to remain close to Davey and include him in your life as much as possible. Work, place—all that will follow. You're young and healthy, and if you want to know what I think, you already have the world at your fingertips."

Robert held her close. "I'll keep that in mind."

On Wednesday evening, one week after Lynn had arrived, they sat on the sofa, Robert reviewing the editing suggestions from the publisher and Lynn completing the sketches of 'the girl and her cat' book.

"Josh and I will be going in the morning, Robert."

He sighed deeply. "I couldn't bear to bring it up," he said. "I just assumed I'd follow you down on Friday."

"It's better if I leave tomorrow. You've got to pack and take care of your practice. I feel that we've monopolized your time."

"I wish I could see you in the city on Saturday."

Mike will be coming to pick Josh up for the weekend and you'll have Davey Saturday. What time is your flight Sunday?"

"I have to be at Kennedy by four."

"Where will you stay Saturday night?"

"I was thinking of driving out to my parents after I drop Davey off in the evening, but . . . ."

"You can stay with me, Robert, and I'll drive you to the airport. I'd like that."

"So would I. What if Mike shows up?"

"He won't." She smiled. "Do I tell him he can't stay with your ex?"

Robert laughed. "I guess not. That's what I'll do then."

On Thursday morning, Robert loaded Lynn's bags into the trunk while she strapped Joshua into his seat.

They stood facing one another behind the car. She placed both her hands in his. "Thank you for a wonderful time. I'll see you Saturday night—I'll make dinner."

"Thanks for coming," he said, kissing her.

Lynn leaned into the car. "Thank Robert for letting us stay in his home and for showing us such a nice time."

"Thank you," Josh called. "Nice time."

Robert laughed, then leaned in and kissed the boy's cheek.

"Drive carefully," he called, as the car rolled down the driveway, Lynn waving goodbye.

He watched her drive down the dirt road until she was lost to sight, then continued to stare after her, as if he could visualize exactly which curve she was on as she headed toward the intersection to pick up the paved highway. Robert placed his hands on his face and breathed deeply, trying to detect the aroma of Lynn's hands where they'd rested in his. He tried to imagine every detail about her—her gray eyes, the freckles on the bridge of her nose, the curve of her lips as she smiled, the fragrance of her smooth skin, the contours of her breasts beneath his hands.

The sun crept above the eastern hills and Robert shielded his eyes as he watched the deserted dirt road. Life's got a lot more twists and turns than that old road, he thought. He laughed to himself when he thought of Joshua's abbreviated 'nice time' remark. He realized, too, that he was falling in love with Lynn.

Robert felt strange as he stepped off the elevator in Lynn's building on Saturday evening. The last time he'd been here was more than three years ago, when he and Alyssa had come for dinner. At that time Lynn and Mike were a unit, just like he and Alyssa. Joshua didn't exist. Maybe Mike and Alyssa were fantasizing about each other even then, but he certainly never thought of Lynn as anything more than a friend. If anyone had told him what the future held, he would have accused them of having either a vivid imagination or a mental disability. Everything had changed, for him at least, when Lynn asked him to father her child. Had he been honest with himself, he would have admitted back then that anything was possible.

He stood before Lynn's door, a suitcase in one hand and a large cardboard carton bound with heavy twine in the other. He listened for a moment before ringing the bell. Silence. He placed the carton on the ground and pressed the buzzer.

Lynn threw her arms around him as soon as she opened the door. Robert stepped inside, set his suitcase down, and carried the carton in from the hallway.

"My goodness," Lynn said, "what's in there?"

"Drug samples, medical supplies, spare instruments. The New York office of International Refugee Assistance sent me a list of things the hospital desperately needs."

Lynn attempted to lift the box and managed to get it a few inches off the floor.

"Robert, how can you possibly carry this? It must weigh at least seventy pounds."

"I'll manage," he laughed. "Looking on the bright side, I won't have to bring it back with me."

"Let's go in the kitchen. Dinner is just about ready and I've opened a bottle of wine."

Lynn poured the wine and raised her glass to him. "Here's to a wonderful, safe trip."

"And here's to the homecoming," Robert added. "I'll miss you.

"Mmm, this wine is delicious." Robert lifted the bottle and read the label.

"I thought the rioja would go well with dinner. We're having paella."

"My God, Lynn, you've gone all out."

"Better reserve judgment till you taste it. It's the first time I've made it. At least we know we have good wine."

"This is delicious," Robert said later, taking his first bite.

"Thank you. So what did you and Davey do today?"

"I drove him out to my parents in the morning so I could say goodbye to them. Then it was back to Manhattan and the Museum of Natural History. He can't get enough of that place since he discovered dinosaurs."

"And he knows them all, right?"

"Every single one. He even corrects me if I misidentify one. And get a load of this. He's reading the Edgar Rice Burroughs *Tarzan* books."

"Wow! They're not too hard for him?"

"I guess not. He told me he just finished *The Yearling* and it made him cry. Would you believe it? And he takes out at least a half-dozen books every time he goes to the library."

"I wonder if his brother will be that smart."

Robert laughed. "It's so funny to hear you say that."

"It's the truth."

"Our truth."

"Right," she said, raising her glass.

Robert gazed around the dining room. "Do you know how long ago it was that I was last here?"

"I was thinking of that before you arrived."

"Life's full of surprises, isn't it?"

"Yes, and some of them are delightful."

He nodded. "You don't feel at all funny about the two of us sitting here?"

"Did you feel funny when I was in Vermont with you?"

"No."

"There's your answer."

"Did Mike pick up Josh this morning?"

"Yes. He said he called Wednesday evening and wondered where we were."

"What did you tell him?"

"The truth. Visiting a friend, and Josh was with me.

"By the time you get back, Robert, I'll have finished the artwork on the cat book." She gestured toward a manuscript and drawings on the sofa in the living room. "And I'll have the preliminary drawings done on at least one of yours, maybe both. You'll have to tell me if they meet with your approval before I do the final work."

"As if there could be doubt."

"Writers have their concepts and artists have their own, you know."

He reached across the table and squeezed her hand. "We'll have a meeting of the minds."

"I've missed you so much that right now I'm ready for a meeting of the bodies."

"I love a woman who speaks her mind," Robert laughed.

"But I'll let you have dessert first and you can finish your wine."

They lay in Lynn's bed that night, her head nestled on his shoulder, while outside, six floors below, the muted sounds of car horns and sirens drifted up.

"I'm not used to the sounds of the city any more," Robert said.

Lynn lifted her head to listen. "To me, that's white noise. I'm sure you don't miss it. I remember how quiet it was in Vermont and how wonderful the skies were at night. I have to laugh when I look up at the sky here. If I'm lucky, I'll see one or two stars."

Lynn rolled on top of him and plastered his face with kisses. Slowly she slid down his body until she had him in her mouth. Robert moaned with pleasure, then whispered, "Enough. I don't want to come." He climbed up behind her and entered her from the rear while he reached around her to fondle her breasts. They reached orgasm at the same time. Lynn collapsed beneath him and they both laughed.

"It's a good thing Josh isn't sleeping in the next room," Robert said.

"He wouldn't be asleep after that," Lynn said. "God, that was great."

They made love again during the night, then again when they awoke in the morning with the sun streaming into the bedroom window.

"That should help you remember me," Lynn said.

Robert clasped her to him, trying to imprint the feel of her body.

After breakfast, they walked the streets of the city until lunchtime. They had a leisurely lunch at Rocco's in the Village, then caught a cab for the ride back to midtown. Lynn insisted they leave early for the drive to JFK. "You country yokels forget about things like traffic jams," she said admonishingly when he argued it was too early. She was right, of course, and it was four-fifteen when they pulled up to the curb near the Lufthansa terminal.

"Remind me always to listen to you," Robert said.

"Sometimes, anyway," she laughed. "Shall I park and help you carry things in?"

"I can manage."

He unloaded his suitcase and carton from the car and embraced her. "Thank you, thank you."

"You'll write?"

"What do you think? God knows how long a letter will take to get here, so don't worry if you don't hear for a while."

"And you'll take care of yourself? And bring yourself home to me in one piece?"

"Stop worrying."

"You know I'm in love with you, don't you?"

A policeman approached to tell Lynn to move the car. Robert kissed her. "I love you," he said, then he picked up the suitcase and carton and disappeared into the terminal. He looked around once but Lynn's car was gone.

23

Robert had been in Peshawar for four weeks when he received his first letters from the States, two from Lynn and one from his mother. He had finally completed his letter to Lynn and mailed it almost two weeks earlier, which meant it might just be arriving. He had told her of his work at the hospital, his hosts, and his impressions of the refugee camps and Peshawar. When it came to writing about more personal matters, Robert found himself stymied. *It's not supposed to be a love letter, for Christ's sake,* he said to himself, exasperated. He limited that portion of the letter to mentioning the wonderful days they'd spent in Vermont and asked her to remember him to Josh. He said he looked forward to seeing her soon. Even in closing, Robert found himself sweating over what words to use. If he signed it *Love, Robert,* he wondered if that implied too big a commitment. Finally, he opted for *Affectionately, Robert.*

Lynn, in her letters, expressed her concern for him and wondered when she'd be receiving his first letter. She told him that she was hard at work, finishing the book she'd been working on and doing the preliminary sketches for his books, that Joshua was fine, and that she couldn't help stealing glances at the calendar and counting the days until his return. She had signed both letters, *Love, Lynn.*

He had hoped Alyssa would drop him a note about Davey in reply to the three letters he'd sent to his son, but that was not to be.

That same week, Sean and Samantha introduced Robert to a new guest, a personable young American built like a fullback on Notre Dame's football team, which was where, in fact, Jack Malloy had attended school. Malloy worked with USAID in Peshawar, where he'd been stationed for the past three years.

"Do you have surgery scheduled for tomorrow?" Sean asked Robert.

"No, Doctor Mathir's mother is having surgery and she's taking the day off. Why?"

"You're making a little trip."

Robert looked from Sean to Malloy. "The Khyber Pass?"

"Jack arranged it," Sean said.

"Wonderful."

"And on Friday, if you like," Malloy said, "you can come along with me and two friends to Swat. A little overnight R and R. Pretty country—river, mountains, cool, fresh air. There's a hotel there and we're planning on spending the night."

"Sounds great if Sean has no objection."

"No problem on this end."

"Good. We'll be leaving about eight. You'll only need an overnight bag, but bring a warm jacket. Where should we pick you up? Here or at your room?"

"Whichever. I'll be ready."

The landscape grew starker as the USAID Jeep approached Jamrud, where the fertile Vale of Peshawar met the Khyber Pass. Jamrud, about ten miles west of Peshawar, was the site of a fort built more than one hundred fifty years earlier. They drove under an arch, the gateway to the Khyber, where the driver stopped at a checkpoint. An armed Pakistani wearing a bulky green sweater over his shalwar kameez approached the vehicle. He had an impressive gray moustache and an olive green beret with red insignia that matched the insignia on his sweater.

"He'll be our guard as we drive through the pass," said Robert's Pakistani driver.

"Why do we need a guard?"

"The Afridi people sometimes make trouble. It is safer."

Looking at the old weapon the guard carried, Robert did not feel reassured. "What kind of rifle is that?" he asked. "I've never seen one like it."

The driver laughed. "Enfield three-o-three, an old rifle from the British wars."

The guard opened the rear passenger door, greeted them with a *salaam aleikum*, and slid in behind them. He planted the stock of the rifle on the floor of the car and cradled the weapon so that its muzzle was plainly in sight through the passenger window.

The road began to climb through barren, brown hills. Overloaded trucks groaned their way up the incline, clouds of choking dust rising behind. The driver rolled up his window each time they passed one of the struggling vehicles, then rolled it down again until they came to the next truck. Robert spotted the tracks and tunnels of the old Khyber Railway cut from the rockface above the road. Another truck, its enormous cargo covered with a tarp fastened with ropes, came down the road toward them. Its driver pulled as close to the edge as possible and they passed within inches of each other.

"Fruits and vegetables from Afghanistan," the guard said.

"There's still traffic across the border?" Robert said.

"Yes, but it is dangerous. Many trucks are destroyed in the fighting and drivers are killed." He said something in Urdu to the driver, who shrugged and nodded. "Ahead, around that next curve," the guard said, "we will be at the high point of the pass, Landi Kotal. That is as far as we go."

Robert spotted a red marker whose white letters announced: KHYBER RIFLES WELCOMES YOU TO KHYBER PASS. The insignia beneath the letters was the same as that worn by the guard.

"You're with the Khyber Rifles?" Robert asked, turning to the guard.

"Yes. We are going to stop at a fort that we garrison."

A dirt road veered off to the left and they swung onto it, winding their way up to a fortress-like structure.

"Khyber Rifles fort," the guard said.

No one back home would believe this, Robert thought. Driving through the Khyber Pass with a Khyber Rifles guard riding shotgun and stopping at the Khyber Rifles fort.

They drove past an antiaircraft gun emplacement surrounded by sandbags. Three soldiers dressed like the guard in the car sat within the sandbagged perimeter.

The guard indicated where the driver should park and they all got out. Robert noticed a group of about ten Afghans sitting on the ground. Half of them had their partouks, the brown blankets that served as cloaks or prayer mats, wrapped around them to ward off the morning chill. Their heads were covered with turbans or skullcaps. They sat quietly, staring at the panorama that unfolded to the west. Brown hills covered with rocks and rough scree rose above them off to the left, while to the right of the pass a railroad tunnel gouged out of the brown hillside was visible. In the far distance, Robert made out the pale blue Hindu Kush range. Snow still covered the higher peaks. From this vantage point, Robert looked down at the road and border crossing, where a few trucks were halted on each side of a barricade. A broad valley with irrigated green fields and scattered mud-brick houses was visible on the Afghan side of the border.

"That is Torkham in Afghanistan," the Khyber Rifles guard said.

The Afghans looking intently off to the west were not watching the border or the village, however. Their gaze was directed skyward. Robert caught sight of two planes, the sun glinting off their wings as they swooped into steep dives. Small clouds of smoke rose from the valley floor.

"Those are MIGs bombing mujahideen positions," a voice said behind Robert.

He turned to confront a handsome soldier wearing dark reflective glasses. A thick black moustache hid his upper lip. He had the same olive green cap and bulky sweater as the guard who had accompanied them in the vehicle. His waist was encircled by a wide leather belt adorned with an ornate silver buckle bearing the Khyber Rifles insignia.

"I am Major Tuma," he said, extending his hand to Robert. "Welcome to the Khyber Rifles fort."

He motioned to one of the soldiers and moments later, two men approached them, one carrying folding chairs and the other a tray with tea and cups.

"Please," Major Tuma said to Robert, indicating that he should sit.

The morning chill began to dissipate as the sun rose behind them. Robert cradled his teacup in his palm, relaxed in his chair, and sipped at the sweetened tea. In my wildest dreams, he thought, I could never conceive of a scene like this. I'm a spectator at a war drinking my tea in total comfort. The soldier standing next to them refilled their cups as Robert and the major talked. Again and again, the MIGs dived on their targets. Clouds of dust were visible when the bombs hit, yet they heard nothing. The men at the antiaircraft emplacement alertly watched the skies.

"You see where the MIGs are dropping their bombs beyond the village," Major Tuma said. "Look to the left of there. Distance is hard to judge from here but perhaps one or two miles from where the bombs are falling you will see something moving."

"I see them. What are they, trucks?"

"Those are Russian tanks and APCs, armored personnel carriers. Usually the mujahideen don't let themselves get caught in the open. This group must have gotten careless."

"Do the Russians ever fly across the border here?" Robert asked.

"They cross the border but usually avoid the fort. They know we're ready for them. Have you ever been in Afghanistan?"

"No."

"Some Americans and Europeans go, especially reporters and medical personnel. The mujahideen take them across."

"What happens if they're caught by the Russians?"

The major laughed heartily, revealing gold crowns on his lower molars. "Then it is not so good." He made a slashing motion with his hand across his neck.

Robert was back in Peshawar in time for dinner with Sean and Samantha. Both of them had been to the Pass but they were eager to hear Robert's impressions.

"I still find it hard to believe that we're sitting here having a nice dinner in a reasonably safe place while such a short distance away people are fighting and dying."

"It does have something surreal about it, doesn't it?" Sean said. "It might surprise you to know that the mujahideen now control eighty percent of Afghanistan."

"How can that be? The Russians have all the air power and armor."

"And at least a hundred thousand men," Sean said, "but still, all they really control are the large cities and the supply route from the northern border down to Kabul. They've got isolated outposts throughout the country, but the soldiers rarely venture out. From what I hear, the Russian army is totally demoralized. They've taken a lot of casualties. Many of the soldiers are trading their weapons for hashish."

"It sounds like they're mired in a Vietnam of their own making."

"Exactly. And with the Americans providing Stinger missiles to the mujahideen, Russian air supremacy doesn't mean much. Sure, they destroy thousands of villages, but that just makes for more support for the mujahideen. The Soviet government doesn't tell the people at home what's really going on, but enough news comes in from western sources like VOA and the BBC so that they're aware things aren't going well for them."

"Do you think the Russians will pull out?"

"Not any time soon. Too much face to lose."

"Even if they do," Samantha interjected, "it will take many, many years to rebuild that country. And who knows what will happen when the Russians go? The Afghans have a long history of fighting one another. I have a feeling these refugee camps will be around for a long time."

"And that means we will, too," said Sean, smiling tenderly at her. He turned to Robert. "Incidentally, do you realize a month has gone by since you arrived?"

"I've been so busy I haven't really been keeping track of time."

"The hospital staff says you're the best thing that's happened to them. They're busy, they're learning a lot, and they appreciate the lectures you've been giving them. They don't want you to leave."

"Well, that's very flattering," Robert said. "Did you tell them I'm not going yet? That I still have two more weeks until another volunteer arrives?"

"They know that. They just wanted me to tell you how they felt. Who knows, maybe you'll come back. Sam and I sure hope so."

"Thanks. You've both been great."

"By the way, Jack Malloy called. The trip to Swat is confirmed. He'll pick you up after breakfast. And Doctor Mojarri is planning to take you to one of the Red Crescent hospitals on Sunday morning."

"Everything I'm seeing is fascinating, but I hate taking time away from the hospital. I feel like I'm letting them down if I'm not available."

"They have to swim on their own, too. I think Doctor Mathir is beginning to feel more secure. Wouldn't you agree?"

"Yes, I would."

"Anyway, you'll be back in time for the afternoon clinic on Sunday. The visit to the Red Crescent hospital will be an eye opener for you."

"Everything I've seen has been."

24

Robert was surprised the next morning when Jack Malloy drove up to Sean's house with two young women in the car. "Elizabeth Holmes and Karen Barker," he said, introducing them. "They work at USAID and will be going with us to Swat."

Jack, Robert guessed, was about thirty-five and the two women, Karen and Elizabeth, even younger, twenty-seven, twenty eight at the most. Robert wondered if he'd been invited along to make up a foursome or, in view of how much older he was, as a chaperone for Karen and Elizabeth.

Malloy was like a kid on vacation during the drive. He passed cans of beer to them from a cooler on the floor of the passenger seat. Robert endured the discomfort of having his legs wedged between the cooler and the door. While drinking his beer, talking and laughing, Jack negotiated his way through the insanity of Pakistani traffic with total aplomb. It made Robert feel as if he were on a college outing, the difference being that Jack proved himself surprisingly knowledgeable about the area they drove through. Even while bantering with Karen and Elizabeth, he called everyone's attention to any place of interest they passed.

Driving through the Peshawar Valley, he pointed out the plantations of tobacco and sugar, as well as miles of orchards, along the road. "The Vale of Peshawar," he said. "Rich agricultural land. This whole area, including Swat and Peshawar, was a principality called Gandhara about two thousand years ago.

"And this place, Charsadda," he said, when they were about fifteen miles out of Peshawar, "was the capital of Gandhara and a major Buddhist pilgrimage site. There's not much here now. Whenever the locals find something old they try to sell it."

"Can we do some treasure hunting?" Karen asked.

"I'd love to find a Buddha figure," Elizabeth said.

Jack pulled the Land Cruiser to a stop alongside a table of artifacts, behind which stood a somber-faced Pakistani.

"Probably all junk," Jack said, "but let's look."

They got out of the car and examined the shards of pottery and fractured Buddha figures.

"Oh, look at this," Elizabeth said, picking up a Buddha figure missing its head. "It would have been perfect."

The Pakistani stared at the two women at first, then averted his eyes. Both women had their heads uncovered. Karen, a blond, wore her long hair loose. The hot wind sweeping across the baking fields blew strands of hair across her face, causing her to flick them away constantly with her fingers. Elizabeth had the nervous habit of playing with the end of her ponytail. The Pakistani, while trying to interest Jack and Robert in the pieces he displayed, threw sidelong glances at the women.

"Let's walk through the ruins and into the fields for a few minutes," Jack said, "and see if we spot anything on the ground."

"What do you both do at USAID?" Robert asked Elizabeth, who walked next to him as they followed an irrigation ditch.

"Both of us edit and type up the reports that come in from the field," Elizabeth said. "Then they're compiled for different offices."

Suddenly, they heard Karen, who had fallen behind, yell.

"What happened?" Jack said, turning to her.

"That kid threw a rock at me and it hit me in the back."

They noticed a boy of eight or nine standing about fifty feet behind them. A tall, white-gowned figure stood behind the boy, one hand resting on the youngster's shoulder. He had a long, stringy gray beard and his head was covered with a white cap.

"Let's go back to the car," Jack said. He glared at the old man, who was bent over whispering something to the boy.

"What was that all about?" Robert asked.

"A lot of these rural places are very conservative. That guy was a mullah and told the kid to stone the women because their heads were uncovered."

"Stupid bastard," Karen said.

"Hey, you know where you are, fourteenth century Pakistan. If you play by their rules, you avoid trouble. All it takes is a kerchief."

"Well, I'm not playing by their rules," Karen argued. "Let them get a grip. They look at us like we're prostitutes because we don't walk around veiled. They're sick people."

"I agree," Elizabeth said. "Whenever I'm close to a Pakistani man, it gives me the creeps. Even in the office."

"It's upsetting," Robert said diplomatically, "but still, we're in their country."

"And they can keep it. I was looking forward to my assignment here, but after six months, I'm sick of it. I wish I was back in Milwaukee."

"If you wore a burqa or chador, you'd feel liberated," Jack teased. "You wouldn't have to worry about sex-starved Paki men."

Karen pouted as they continued driving. Robert was beginning to wonder why Malloy had asked the two women along. He suddenly thought of Lynn and tried to imagine what she must have been like at the age of Karen and Elizabeth. A hell of a lot more mature than these two, he decided. He imagined her sitting in the rear seat, alertly watching the country they drove through, listening raptly to Jack's comments. He missed her.

"There are two roads to Swat," Jack said when they reached Mardan, the first major town they came to. "We'll take the main one over the Malakand Pass. That way we'll reach Mingora, the biggest town in Swat, by early afternoon."

"Is that where we'll be spending the night?" Robert asked.

"No, Mingora is too big, too crowded. The place I'm shooting for is a village called Miandam. The sunsets there are the best in Pakistan. If we're lucky we'll make it before the sun goes down."

They had already crossed the Malakand Pass when Jack pointed to a line of hills on the left. "See that big hill up there. That's where Churchill Picket is. When Churchill was a young officer during one of the British wars, he almost died in a skirmish there. The view from the top is great but we'd use up too much time getting to it. Actually, where we are now is a major crossroads. If you follow the road to the northwest it'll take you to Chitral. If you head northeast you'll get to Gilgit and Hunza, and eventually cross into China through the Khunjerab Pass."

"That's part of the silk route, isn't it?" Robert asked. "Have you ever done that trip?"

"I tried last year and it ended up a nightmare. The road was blocked by a massive landslide and we never got through. I wasted almost a week of vacation time."

They were on their second sixpack as they wound their way north to Mingora, passing terraced fields and orchards. Robert kept his eyes on the road and on Jack, trying to ascertain if his driving was impaired in any way. Jack Malloy seemed to have a hollow leg when it came to beer.

Mingora was as Jack had described, bustling streets crowded with shoppers and buses. Robert was glad they weren't going to be spending the night there. It would have been like being back in Peshawar.

"You're all probably hungry," Malloy said, "but we'll lose too much time if we stop for lunch. Let's grab something and eat in the car." He swerved off to his right and stopped in front of a small open air café. The aroma of frying food wafted through the rolled down windows of the Land Cruiser. Jack ordered *samosas*, puff pastries filled with meat and vegetables, and *pakoras*, deep-fried flour balls flavored with spices.

"Jesus," Robert said when Jack handed him a bundle of carefully wrapped newspaper, its outside hot and already stained with grease. "You must have ordered enough for ten people."

"Good, huh?" Jack said, pieces of his samosa spilling down his chin as he drove.

The bundle was still half-full when they finished eating.

"Anybody gets hungry later, there's plenty left. Now let's wash it down with another beer."

The highway as it left Mingora ran above the raging waters of the Swat River on their right. I wouldn't want to be rafting that river, Robert thought.

"The river's high," Jack said. "From the snow melt." He leaned forward to see the river better, taking his eyes off the road.

"This road's a little hairy," Robert said, nervously peering down into the waters below.

"The ledge this road's on was blasted out of the rock face," Jack said. "Before it was built, maybe sixty years ago, people had to cross the river back and forth on bridges of wooden slats and ropes. They called them suicide bridges."

"I won't complain about the road then," Robert said.

It was late in the afternoon when they reached the fertile farmland of Fatehpur. Both women were asleep in the back seat. Jack laughed as he looked in the rearview mirror. "They're okay, just a little young," he said to Robert, as if reading his thoughts. "I promised them a trip to Swat weeks ago, so here we are."

"Well," Robert said, maybe some of what they've seen will rub off on them."

The valley narrowed and the scenery began to look like postcards of Switzerland. Jack turned off on a dirt road about a mile outside of Fatehpur and they wound their way up through pine-covered hills, patches of snow still visible on the north-facing slopes. The windows were rolled down and Robert could feel the cool air rushing down the valley.

"That's it just ahead, Miandam. The women will be surprised when they open their eyes. We're up at six thousand feet."

"This is spectacular," Robert said, scanning the evergreen-covered mountains. "I can't believe how cool it is. And you made it in time. The sun is just going down."

"There's a small hotel about a kilometer ahead of us on the left. I've stayed there before. We can get our rooms and go watch the sunset."

"Wow!" came a cry from the back seat. "Where are we?"

"We took a shortcut to Switzerland," Malloy said.

"I believe it," Elizabeth replied.

"Snow!" Karen said. "In May."

Their hotel was a rambling wooden structure built in the style of a mountain resort from the time of the Raj. Its exterior walls, rotted and peeling in places, showed signs of age. The lobby, too, had seen better days, its stuffed chairs sagging and stained. The guestrooms were basic but clean. The women shared one room, Robert and Jack another. They slipped into warm jackets after checking in and pulled worn wicker armchairs up to the verandah railing. The western sky was layered in flaming red and orange as the sun sank rapidly behind the mountains. A pink glow lingered as the blue of twilight descended on them. Robert was certain the temperature dropped another twenty degrees when the sun disappeared.

"Where do we get dinner?" Elizabeth asked, her interest in the sunset waning rapidly.

"Tired of finger-food, huh?" Jack said. "They serve dinner here. Not great, but okay. Anybody notice how much beer was still in the cooler?"

"One six-pack left," Robert said, "last I looked."

"That's what you think. I have six more in the trunk. Nothing like beer in the mountains. Frat parties in college gave me my taste for beer, but my love for the mountains came a lot earlier. I grew up in Washington state. Ever been in the Cascades?"

"No, I haven't," Robert replied.

"Beautiful. Did a lot of hiking there when I was a kid."

The hotel's restaurant was cavernous and gloomy, its ceiling lined with dark wooden beams. Every table, covered with a bleached and faded tablecloth, was empty. The waiters, clad in none-too-clean shalwar kameezes, padded around silently in their sandals.

"I think we're the only guests," Robert said.

"Yeah, not many tourists these days," Malloy said. "Makes it kind of nice to have the place to ourselves, doesn't it?"

"Tonight we have lamb," their waiter said.

They waited to hear what else was available but the waiter was silent.

"That's it?" Jack said. "Lamb?"

"Lamb, mint jelly, and peas, sir."

Robert chuckled in spite of Jack's consternation. "Right out of the Raj, isn't it?"

Jack cast a disparaging look at his food when it came. "I think this was cooked in the days of the Raj. The meat's overdone and the peas are right out of a can."

Night arrived early in the mountains and they stood outside on the verandah after dinner, shivering in the cold air.

"I can see my breath," Karen said.

Stars twinkled above them, a novelty after Peshawar, where dust obscured the night skies.

"It's peaceful here," Elizabeth said, yawning. "You wouldn't know there's a war on."

"Yeah, that's why I love this place," Jack said. "It sure as hell ain't for the food. Let's go to my room and have some beer before we crash. I even have a deck of cards."

25

Two days with Jack Malloy and his friends was more than enough. The alcohol abuse of the one and the immaturity of the others made Robert feel like a college dormitory resident. On the bright side, the weekend jaunt was a reminder that there was more to Pakistan than its grim, overcrowded cities and sere interior. He quickly forgot Swat's sparkling river and cool mountains, however. After Robert made rounds at the hospital on Sunday morning, Doctor Mojarri drove him to Peshawar's Red Crescent Hospital. The hospital was a stark reminder, if Robert needed one after his visit to the refugee camps and Khyber Pass, that a brutal war was taking place a short distance away.

Peshawar seemed to be a city of hospitals. Robert noticed more hospitals on his walks through Peshawar than he recalled seeing in Manhattan. In addition to the hospitals for Pakistanis, some public, others private, there were hospitals geared specifically to the care of the war's wounded. Some were run by the International Committee for the Red Cross, others by Red Crescent and various political organizations. Sean had warned Robert what to expect at the Red Crescent Hospital.

"You'll have to remember that these hospitals are there not only to treat the war wounded of Afghanistan, but to impress visitors, especially Americans, with how awful the Russian enemy is. It's another way to make sure the aid and dollars keep flowing in. Anyway, you'll find it a valuable experience."

Robert and Mojarri were greeted by Doctor Anwar, the Pakistani director of the hospital. He immediately led them out onto a veranda that encircled a courtyard planted with red, yellow, and pink roses. "Our patients are enjoying the morning air before the heat comes," he said. Robert gazed across the veranda.

Dozens of wheelchairs with young, bearded Afghan men, all amputees, were crowded along the walkway.

They stopped in front of each man and Robert, with Mojarri and Anwar translating, heard how the wounds were incurred. The stumps of legs were usually caused by land-mine explosions. "The Russians drop the mines from planes along mountain roads," said Anwar. "They're small, the same color as rocks and dirt, and difficult to spot. The ones they drop for children are very colorful. That's why many children in Afghanistan have missing hands. These men you are seeing—" He raised his arm in an encompassing gesture. "They are the lucky ones, the ones who were able to survive the trip across the mountains after their injuries. Most of the wounded mujahideen die before they can get help." The three men stopped in front of a black-haired Afghan, twenty-five years old at most. His right leg was missing. He looked at them, his dark eyes intense.

"This is Hassan," Anwar said. "He speaks English."

"You are from the States?" Hassan said to Robert.

"Yes. Where did you learn your English?"

"I learned in university. Then I taught English in Kabul before the Communists came. They arrested me and brought in teachers of Russian."

"Why did they arrest you?"

"My speaking English made me—" His hand fluttered in the air before he found the word he wanted. "Suspect. They wanted Afghans to learn Russian."

"How long did they hold you?"

"One year, three months, and two days. The worst year, months, and days of my life. All prisoners were tortured. When they released me, I joined the mujahideen."

"It was the Russians who tortured you?"

He grimaced. "It was my own people. But their Russian masters told them what to do."

"Did you lose your leg to a mine?"

"Most of the men you see here did. Me, no. We attacked a Russian tank and I was hit." He smiled. "But we destroyed the tank. My companions placed me on a donkey. I rode all the way to the border."

"How long did it take you to get to the hospital?"

"Four days. They tied my leg with a—" Again, he fumbled for the word.

"Tourniquet?" Robert said.

"Yes, tourniquet. When I arrived here—" He made a chopping motion with his hand.

"Are you going to get an artificial leg?" Robert asked.

"*Inshallah.* I am waiting. America very good. They help us in our *jihad.*"

"Maybe in one month he will get his leg," Anwar said. "Others have been waiting longer."

"The Red Cross has a prosthesis center here in Peshawar," Mojarri said. "They try to make the prostheses as simple as possible so they can be repaired if need be when the men go back to their villages."

"They must be very busy," Robert said.

"You cannot imagine," Mojarri said. "The Red Cross hospital is doing maybe two thousand amputations every year. And that is just one hospital."

"What will you do after you get your prosthesis?" Robert asked Hassan.

"Go back to Afghanistan to kill Russians."

Anwar patted his shoulder and the three men moved on. "Don't think he is not serious," Anwar said to Robert. "For these men it is a jihad, a holy war. Let us go now to meet some of the patients inside."

Robert and Mojarri followed Anwar into a large ward, where again they stopped before each patient. The first four were quadriplegics, paralyzed from the neck down. "The people you see with them are all relatives," Anwar said. Two men were being tended to by young boys who were holding bottles of soda with a straw for the patients to drink. The other relatives were old, bearded men, who sat talking earnestly to the wounded men. Many of the patients were burn victims, who were in different stages of the grafting procedure. The most grotesque of the wounded were those who had facial wounds, one missing part of his jaw, another with an ugly charred crater where an eye should have been.

They were suddenly interrupted on their rounds by a young man in a gray shalwar kameez who spoke to Anwar and pointed to the veranda entrance. Three tall, bearded men in spotless flowing white robes and *kefiyas* stood in the doorway. Anwar excused himself and headed toward them.

Robert looked questioningly at Mojarri.

"They are Saudis," Mojarri said, an unmistakable tone of derision in his voice. "They contribute a lot of money to mujahideen groups and also to the hospital. But the Arabs are not popular here." He did not elaborate.

"I am sorry," Doctor Anwar said, returning, "but I must leave now. My visitors are very important people and their schedule does not permit them to wait while we complete our tour."

Robert and Mojarri thanked him for showing them around. Robert looked around the verandah at the faces of the young Afghans once more. Most were staring into space, fingering amber prayer beads and reciting passages from the Koran. His gaze fell from their serious, bearded faces to the stumps of their missing limbs. What must they be thinking? he wondered. How soon they'll be able to return to their jihad? What life will be like with one or both legs missing in a world of steep mountain passes?

Robert had a great deal on his mind while he worked at the hospital clinic that afternoon. Mathir scheduled four surgeries for the next two days, so he knew he would be busy and he was grateful for that. He returned to his room after leaving the hospital, made himself a cup of tea, and sat outside. There hadn't been much time for introspection during the month he'd spent in Pakistan, but now he was extremely troubled. He'd had no reply to any of the letters he'd sent to Davey. For that, he blamed Alyssa. Not long ago Robert couldn't have imagined going a full month without seeing his son. He could only hope that Davey was well and coping with his absence.

The image of the damaged young mujahideen fighters in the Red Crescent hospital flashed through his mind at that moment. What must their parents think, having raised their sons only to see them become amputees? And I, he thought, assailed by pangs of guilt, I have a son and I'm partly responsible for putting him in a situation where he's torn between two parents. Would he become as crippled emotionally as the mujahideen were physically?

It was unusual for Robert to become mired in maudlin thoughts. He asked himself, why now? Perhaps it was because his time at the hospital in Pakistan was approaching an end. There was so much he'd have to confront when he returned home.

It wasn't only his relationship with his son that was troubling him.

When he realized he missed Lynn during the ride to Swat, it was the first time in almost a week that he'd thought of her. Consciously or not, for some reason he had tried to distance himself from Lynn, to put aside his relationship with her. Not even the books she was working on, his books, that he'd been so excited about when he learned they would be published, interested him since his arrival in Peshawar. He had to admit to himself, too, that signing his letter to her with the word 'affectionately,' instead of 'love,' troubled him. Why had he done that? Why had there been no hesitation on Lynn's part in signing her letters, *Love, Lynn*. He knew the word 'love,' when used to end a letter, had many meanings, ranging from friendship to passion. He could just as easily have signed his letter that way, using it as a synonym for 'affectionately,' so why hadn't he? After all, he had told her the last time he saw her that he loved her. What made him shy away from that word now?

He tried to make his mind go blank, closing his eyes and cutting off all thought. He focused on the chorus of birdsong that rose every night as dusk approached. With the stealth of a spy, the word he had been unconsciously trying to suppress crawled through his defenses. Commitment. He was afraid of it, especially now, so soon after the debacle of his marriage to Alyssa. His fear of commitment was the reason for avoiding the word 'love.' It was why he wouldn't permit himself to think of Lynn, why he had difficulty in writing to her. But Lynn had asked nothing of him, he reminded himself. She had told him that even if their relationship evolved into nothing more than friendship, that was fine. Didn't he believe her? Or was the real reason for his fear the knowledge that he had fallen in love with her and was fighting against it? God, it's all so complicated, he thought. And at my age. I thought I was past all this—this emotional tumult.

His tea had grown cold long ago. He carried the cup into the room and frowned when he glanced at his watch. Sean had told him to arrive earlier than usual this evening since they were having guests for cocktails at five, to be followed by a buffet dinner. It was almost five now and he hadn't even showered. But it wasn't a shower he wanted at that moment. He felt the need to sit down and write a long letter to Lynn, a letter in which he would try to explain the struggle taking place within him. Perhaps that was the only way to understand his feelings.

"It'll have to wait," he said with irritation.

26

Voices drifted out from the living room and patio as Robert knocked at the door. Sean greeted him. "How was your visit to the Red Crescent hospital?" he asked.

"Depressing."

"That it is. Like me, you probably wonder what kind of future these men will have. It's tough enough for men with two legs to survive in Pakistan and Afghanistan.

"Come meet our guests. We've got two people from Medicins sans Frontieres, the French medical outfit."

"Doctors Without Borders?"

"Yes, you'll like them. And there are two from Victory Medicine, an American organization based in Alabama. They're new arrivals."

"I suspect they're spooks," Samantha whispered to him in passing.

Sean introduced Robert to Jean Viliers and Simone Roussel, a French physician and nurse. Sean had been right. Robert knew he liked both of them after chatting with them for only five minutes.

Je parle francaise, Robert informed them. *Le preferiez?*

Their faces lit up but they assured him English was fine.

"Have you been into Afghanistan?" Jean asked Robert.

Robert shook his head. "Have you?"

"Yes, two times, but it is not enough. The Afghans are desperate. Thousands of villages and most of the hospitals are destroyed. People receive no medical care. We bring in what medicines and supplies we're able to and run clinics for them. It's, what do you say in English, a drop in the bucket? But we must do something. Almost a million Afghans have died in this war."

"You're not afraid of being captured by the Russians or the Afghan Army?"

"Of course we are, but the mujahideen are careful. They take us over the mountains and we do most of our traveling in the country at night to avoid the helicopter gunships. Still, we worry. We know the Russians and their puppet government have many spies in Peshawar and something can always go wrong."

"How long do you stay when you cross into Afghanistan?"

"Usually two weeks. There's too much chance of an informer telling the Russians if we stay longer." Jean looked at Robert quizzically. "Would you like to come across with us next time?"

"Very much, but when will that be? I'll be at the Afghan Women's Hospital for another two weeks, then I'm scheduled to leave Pakistan."

"We never know exactly when we're leaving. The mujahideen tell us only hours ahead of time. We think it will be in about two weeks."

It would be a crazy, dangerous thing for me to do, Robert thought, but also a chance to see firsthand what's happening there.

"If you decide to join us, please don't tell anyone at the hospital. The fewer people who know, the safer it is for us." He handed Robert a card with the Medicins sans Frontieres address and phone number. "You can always leave a message for me and I will meet you."

"If I decide to go, I have to tell Sean. He'd have to change my return flight."

"That is no problem. Sean can be trusted."

Robert, stepping out onto the patio with his drink, couldn't believe he was seriously considering going into Afghanistan. He was joined at that moment by the two Americans from Victory Medicine, Roland Smith and Frank Poole. Smith, with his porcine face and cruel mouth, bore an unsettling resemblance to Sheriff Bull Connor, the segregationist sheriff of the sixties.

"I'm a health adviser," he told Robert in answer to Robert's question about what he was doing in Pakistan.

"What does a health adviser do?"

"We try to find out what we can do to keep the resistance groups fighting the Russians healthy. We learn what they need and try to get it for them."

Poole, who at six-four towered over his companion, was even more guarded. He was a bland-faced beanpole of a man with heavily lidded eyes. "I'm an economist," he told Robert. "Like Roland, I find out what the Afghans need and relay the information so we can get it to them."

Robert was about to ask if that included weapons, but decided they'd never give him a straight answer. Their elusive replies to Robert's questions confirmed for him that Samantha had been right: they had to be CIA.

Later that evening, Sean drew him aside. "I couldn't help noticing the intense discussion you were having with Jean and Simone."

"They're great people. Totally dedicated."

"Did they offer to take you across?" Sean's voice was barely above a whisper. "I'd think twice before doing it," he said in response to Robert's nod. "It's dangerous as hell."

"But a once in a lifetime opportunity."

"If you're captured you can count on it being once in a lifetime. When will this happen?"

"They don't know yet. About the time I finish at the hospital. I'll have to give it more thought. If I tell them yes, can you change my flight reservation?"

"That's not a problem."

"Have you tried Abdul's *nargisi koftas*?" Samantha asked, joining them. "They're delicious." She pointed with her fork at the fried meatballs in onion sauce on her plate.

"I'll get some now," Robert said. "They look good. Incidentally, those two . . ." He gestured with his chin toward Smith and Poole. "You're right."

Samantha laughed. "Pretty obvious, isn't it?"

Robert was cleaning his plate when Samantha sidled up to him. "You're right about the koftas, too," he told her. "They're wonderful."

"Sean told me what you're thinking about," she said softly. "It's frightfully risky, Robert. Jean and Simone, they're very young and have no family responsibilities. You have a son."

"I appreciate your concern, Sam. I have to think about it some more."

Back in his room at the end of the evening, Robert struggled with his new dilemma. To go or not to go. One moment he told himself he was crazy for considering it, the next he couldn't contain his excitement. Personal safety was a major consideration, of course, but there were others. As Samantha had said, he had a son. If anything was going to hold him back, it was Davey. How could he place himself at risk when Davey, only five years old, needed him so much? But if he didn't do it, would he always have regrets? Not as important a consideration but one he still had to take into account was his practice. How would Todd Jones feel about caring for Robert's patients for weeks longer than he'd planned? And then there was Lynn. What would she think if he delayed his return by weeks? He knew she'd be accepting if he explained it, but it was difficult when he was so far away. Like his practice, the matter of the two children's books was secondary, but if Lynn completed the art work, she'd want his input. The publisher, too, might not like the idea of his being out of the country and out of reach for a prolonged period. In spite of all these considerations, Robert already knew the answer he would give Jean.

He sat down on the bed and picked up his notebook. For the next hour, he filled page after page, his thoughts coming faster than he could put them on paper. He hoped Lynn wouldn't think he'd gone off the deep end when she received the letter, but he suspected she would be understanding. In his brief time with her he sensed she could intuit what he was thinking anyway. *I guess this is what's called spilling your guts,* he wrote, as he reached the end of his letter. *If I had to sum it up, I'd say I believe I'm in love with you and it terrifies me. Does any of this make sense? The new project will take me into remote country, so I won't be able to get any letters out. I'll do my best to get home by the end of June or early July and I'll tell you all about it then.* He signed it, *Much love, Robert.*

27

Robert left a message at the Medicins sans Frontieres office for Jean to call him at the hospital. On a Wednesday evening, he met Jean and Simone outside an Afghan restaurant near Shoiba Bazaar. The Pakistanis and Afghans passing turned to look at them, even though Simone had her head covered. The restaurant's patrons, all men, stared at them as they entered. Those with their backs to the door swung around on their chairs. An Afghan waiter materialized as soon as they crossed the threshold, looked nervously from Simone to the men inside, then led them to a dark stairwell, where they climbed to a room on the upper floor. Its sole occupant was a sheep. A young man in a soiled shalwar kameez stained with old blood poked his head in the door. The waiter snapped at him brusquely in Pashto and he tied a rope around the sheep's neck. He dragged it from the room, returning moments later with a piece of cardboard to sweep the sheep droppings from the floor into a small pile just outside the doorway. The waiter in the meantime carried in a low table and cushions. When they were all seated on the cushions around the table, their knees crossed uncomfortably under them, he asked them if they wanted tea or soda, then disappeared from the room.

"In English, you would say quaint, no?" Jean said, smiling.

"Very."

Jean stepped onto the open wooden balcony outside the window and called to Simone and Robert to join him. It was already dark, the last vestiges of light no more than pale blue and purple streaks just above the western horizon. They peered down into the crowded street and saw the young man who'd cleaned their room placing cuts of lamb on a grill almost four feet long. The hot charcoal flared into orange and red flames as fat dripped onto it.

The waiter reappeared with their drinks and they sat down again. He handed each of them a slab of *naan*, a flat bread that would serve as their plate, and a cloth napkin, more gray than white. The smell of grilled lamb drifted through the window, making them all hungry.

"We've eaten here once before," Simone said. "The customers downstairs had the same reaction. They are not accustomed to having a woman in the restaurant. The food is delicious in spite of how—" She grasped for the word. "Primitive. Yes, that is the word."

The waiter brought in an enormous tray of lamb and set it down on the table in front of them. He placed a metal dish on the table for bones and scraps. The lamb was succulent, the best Robert had ever tasted. For the first ten minutes, they ate without speaking and the lamb quickly disappeared.

"That was delicious," Robert said.

"We are not finished," Simone said.

Robert didn't know what she meant until the waiter reappeared with more naan and another tray, as large as the first, of roasted lamb. He removed the empty tray and set the full one down in its stead.

The three of them now ate slower, too full to continue but unable to stop.

Robert wiped his mouth and hands with his napkin. "I've decided to join you," he said.

A smile creased Jean's face. He wiped his hands and extended his right hand to Robert. "*Merci,* Robert. That's wonderful."

"I am very happy," said Simone. "It will be very good to have another physician with us."

"Have you told Sean?"

"I will tomorrow."

"Please," Jean said, "tell no one else."

"What will I need when I go across?"

"A warm jacket and sweater for the mountains. The nights are cold. Good boots. You will be doing a lot of walking. The Pathans, they never tire. They carry a piece of naan next to their body—" He pointed down his shirt.

"—and they walk for hours, living only on naan and tea. You must keep up. They will not wait for you if you fall behind."

"I'll keep up."

"It is exhausting," Jean said, smiling.

"But exhilarating, *n'est pas?*" Simone added, looking from one to the other.

"Yes," confirmed Jean, "exhilarating. And you will develop a great love for the Afghan people. They endure everything without complaint."

"And they are very generous even though they have so little," Simone said.

There were a few pieces of meat left on the tray but everyone declined.

"I've never had such delicious lamb," Robert said.

"It must be because they recite verses from the Koran before they slaughter the sheep. I have been told the animal does not struggle."

Jean's expression was serious and Robert couldn't tell if he was being facetious.

"We should come here again before—" Simone looked quickly around to make certain the waiter was not nearby. "—before our crossing."

"I'd like that," Robert said.

They agreed to contact Robert at his room or at the hospital as soon as they heard from their mujahideen guide. Their conversation ceased while the muezzin's call to prayer came clearly through the open window. They listened intently, as if hearing it for the first time.

"This will be a big caravan," Jean said almost as an afterthought, in a voice barely above a whisper. "We will carry many supplies."

Jean and Simone accompanied Robert back to his room. They shook hands and agreed to meet again at the same restaurant in ten days if Jean had received no word.

On his bed Robert found a note from Sean and two letters. *These arrived at the office today. Hope you enjoyed your dinner with Jean and Simone. Let me know about changing your flight.*

The man is prescient, thought Robert. He picked up the two envelopes, one from his parents and one from Lynn. Still no word from Alyssa about Davey.

I still haven't received a letter, Lynn wrote. *I try to reassure myself that it's because the mails are slow and I wonder now if you received my earlier letters. I wish I knew you were alright. I've completed the artwork for one of your books and I hope to have the other one done by the time you return. Joshua wants to know when we'll see the nice man with the Tinkertoys again. Otherwise, everything is the same. Take care of yourself. Love, Lynn.*

Robert didn't know if he was imagining it, but he detected a self-protective, guarded quality in the brief letter, almost as if she wondered whether he had written to her, and if he truly was going to return. Lynn, too, must be realizing how new and fragile their relationship was, he thought. He wondered if she'd find his recent letter reassuring or if it would only confirm her doubts.

His mother's letter surprised him by the deterioration in her handwriting. It was the writing of an old person, as was the subject matter. She enumerated all of their aches and pains, related who among their acquaintances had died, and complained about his father, who refused to take her to a movie or a restaurant. That's new, he thought. He'd never heard her carping at his father. She made no mention of her teaching and he wondered if she still gave piano lessons. She also said nothing about Davey, which meant Alyssa had made no attempt to contact them or to arrange for them to see their grandson.

Troubled by his mother's letter, he sat down and wrote to his parents first. He realized there was little he could do to buoy his mother's mood, so he kept his tone light. He told them, too, that he'd be busy with another project and would be returning several weeks later than he'd thought, but not to worry. *I'll bring Davey to see you,* he wrote, *as soon as I get back.*

He wrote next to Todd Jones, thanking him again for covering his practice and explaining that he'd be returning later than he'd anticipated. Finally, he wrote another letter to Davey. He had no idea whether Alyssa gave their son his letters or tossed them in the trash. He imagined his ex-wife sarcastically telling him when he returned that no letters had arrived.

Jean didn't call that week. Sean had cancelled Robert's scheduled flight and rescheduled it for a month later. "If you're back here before that," he said, "we'll just reschedule it again."

On Saturday Robert set out to meet Jean and Simone at the Afghan lamb restaurant. He drifted through the shadowed streets of the bazaar at dusk. As he approached Shoiba Bazaar the air was heavy with a smoky residue. Jean and Simone stood in front of charred and smoldering beams, all that remained of the restaurant. Part of its façade had fallen on the huge grill, now resting on its back with its twisted legs protruding skyward, giving it the appearance of a mortally wounded insect. An eerie quiet had settled on the street.

"What happened?" Robert asked.

"A bomb. Early this afternoon. Fifteen people dead."

"Jesus! Who would do such a thing?"

"*Khad,* the Afghan secret police. They're controlled by the Russians."

"But why bomb a restaurant?"

"Because it was run by Afghan refugees and they knew foreigners often ate here. They try to frighten us. *Tant pis.*"

Dejected, they walked several blocks in silence to a Pakistani restaurant. The overcooked tandoori chicken did nothing to improve their moods.

"This is the place they should have bombed," Jean said petulantly.

"No word yet?" Robert asked, giving him a few minutes to get over his pique.

Jean shook his head. "How many days do you still have at the hospital?"

"Monday is my last day. The new doctor will be arriving."

"They will let you stay in your room?"

"Yes, Sean said it was fine."

Jean nodded. "Sean, he is a good man."

The day before the new physician's arrival, Robert sat down to lunch next to Sahar, Doctor Mojarri's Pakistani assistant. He had had very little opportunity to speak to her during his six weeks working at the hospital.

"Do you have children?" he asked, assuming that like most Pakistani women in their thirties she had several.

Sahar was an attractive woman with arching black eyebrows and soft brown eyes that often appeared to conceal pain. Robert seldom saw her smile.

"I have two. My daughter is with me, but my son is with my husband."

"You're separated from your husband?"

"Yes."

Robert wondered if he should persist with his questioning, but he almost felt she was pleased that someone cared enough to ask.

"Did your son choose to live with his father?"

"Choose? No, but this is Pakistan and a woman has no say. His father wanted him, so he took him."

"I'm sorry. There's still a lot I don't understand about Islam and its traditions."

"This has nothing to do with Islam," she said, trying to keep her voice down. She chose her words carefully, but she was angry. "For most men here, Islam is an excuse for suppression of women. What the Koran says and what Pakistani men do are as different as day and night. If I went to court and told the judge my son cries for me, begs me to let him live with me, do you know what the judge would say? He would say I couldn't satisfy my husband, even though I was the one who threw him out. Everything would be my fault. And since my son is male, the judge would say he belongs with his father." She brushed away a tear. "So," she said, trying to regain control of herself, "what do you think of your experience working at the hospital?"

"I hope the doctors got as much out of my being here as I got out of working with them. It's been a wonderful experience for me."

She looked at him, her eyes flashing, and he knew she was not thinking about the hospital or about his experiences there, but about her son. "Be glad you live in America," she said.

Our experiences aren't that different, he wanted to tell her, but instead he sipped his tea. No sense trying to disabuse people of the notions they hold, he said to himself.

28

Everything had happened so quickly that Robert found it hard to believe he was actually on his way to Afghanistan. On Monday, his last day at work, the hospital staff had presented him with a black Afghan vest lavishly embroidered with gold thread and small mirrors to show their appreciation for his help. It might have been the height of Afghan fashion, but Robert had to smile when he pictured himself wearing it in the States. They also gave him a brown woolen Chitrali cap, which was to prove much more useful. Robert wore it pulled down over his ears as he marched through the frigid mountain passes of Afghanistan.

At dinner Monday evening, Sean had introduced him to Elroy Chambers, an OB-GYN from Tallahassee, Florida, who would be taking Robert's place at the hospital. He sat opposite Chambers at the table and realized that six weeks earlier he himself had been the new arrival. The time had passed so quickly.

"You look a bit perplexed, Robert," said Samantha, passing him the salad.

"I was just remembering my first day here. The weeks have flown."

"Sean tells me it's been a good experience for both you and the hospital," Chambers said in a slow drawl.

Robert nodded. "Better than good. You'll enjoy working with the Afghans."

"When will you be flying home?" Chambers asked.

Sean caught his eye, raising his brow in warning.

"I'm not sure. I'll be staying on for a while to do some sightseeing."

"No word?" Sean said later as Robert was leaving to go back to his room.

"No. I'm getting concerned."

Robert fretted as he walked back to his room. He knew he couldn't remain in Peshawar indefinitely, waiting for something that might or might not happen.

As he fumbled with his key in front of his door, a figure stepped out of the shadows.

"Robert?"

"Jean, is that you? You scared the hell out of me."

"Yes. We go tonight."

"Tonight! When?"

"Be ready in two hours. I will come to get you. Put these on and take only what you absolutely need." He handed Robert a folded shalwar kameez, a partouk, and a small knapsack. "Boots and warm clothes are most important."

"What do we do about water?"

"I have iodine tablets. Do you take any medicines?"

"No."

"Good."

Before Robert could say another word, Jean had disappeared back into the shadows.

In his room, Robert rummaged through his suitcase for underwear and socks. He tucked his passport into the neck pouch he'd wear under his Afghan shirt. He retrieved his toothbrush from the bathroom and picked up his razor. Holding the razor in the palm of his hand as if he were weighing it, he debated for a moment, then tossed it into his suitcase with everything else he was leaving behind. If he was going to dress like an Afghan, he might as well let his beard grow and look like one.

He picked up the phone on the night table and dialed Sean's number.

"Hey, what's up?" Sean asked when he heard Robert's voice.

"It's tonight."

Sean was silent.

"Can I leave my suitcase here?" Robert asked.

"Sure. It'll be safe. There's still time to change your mind, you know. Have you really thought this through?"

"If I don't go, I'll always wonder. I think you understand." He heard Sean talking to Samantha in the background.

"Look, you take care," Sean said, "and come see us as soon as you're back. Hold on. Sam wants to say something."

"Robert, you're really leaving?"

"In two hours. Jean's picking me up."

"I'll say a prayer for you."

"Thank you. Don't worry, I'm coming back."

Two hours later a soft knock sounded on his door and Jean, dressed in a shalwar kameez like Robert's, led him out to an old truck, the driver concealed in the darkness of the cab. Jean and Robert stopped and looked up and down the street. It was empty and, except for the idling of the truck's engine, there wasn't a sound. The two of them climbed into the cab and the driver shifted into gear. He drove slowly down the deserted street, past the shuttered shops and market.

"If for any reason we're stopped, pretend to be asleep and let the driver do the talking," said Jean.

"Where's Simone?"

"She'll be meeting us at the rendezvous point."

It was a moonless night and they drove for hours. Robert could see nothing but the poorly paved road ahead of them. When lights appeared in the distance, the driver slowed and turned off the main road, following dirt tracks through the foothills until the lights were behind them.

"They may be Pakistani checkpoints," Jean said. "Safer to go around them."

Robert dozed on and off through the night. He was jolted awake when they left the main road and wound their way down a rock-strewn dirt track to a dry streambed. A flashlight beam flickered once or twice ahead of them and the driver slowed to a stop.

"Where are we?" Robert asked.

"Just south of Dir. What is the expression in English, as a crow flies? As a crow flies we are less than twenty kilometers from the border."

They stepped out of the truck into a night colder than any Robert had experienced in Peshawar.

"We're already quite high," said Jean, seeing him shiver. "But we'll be heading up another thousand meters, maybe more, before we reach the border."

Shadowy figures moved all around them and Robert heard the stamping of hooves and the snorting of animals. A horse whinnied softly. Suddenly two figures appeared directly in front of them, one of them resembling a tent in the darkness.

"Here's Simone," Jean said.

Simone, a burqa draped around her but pulled back from her face, greeted them. The tall Afghan at her side wore a woolen Chitrali cap. He disappeared into the darkness immediately after Simone introduced him to Robert.

"Mohammed is our guide," Jean explained to Robert. "Were you stopped?" he asked Simone.

"Yes, but no problem. They saw the burqa and assumed I was Mohammed's wife."

Robert's eyes gradually adjusted to the darkness. Men were packing boxes onto mules and horses. Robert counted at least twenty animals, but knew by the snorting and pawing that there were more.

"This is our biggest supply train of the year," Mohammed said when he reappeared. "It also means it's our most dangerous. We must keep moving until the first light appears, then we look for cover. When dusk falls, we resume our march. We should reach the first village after two nights' march. It will be light in about two hours but by then we will be in the mountains, away from the road. After we camp and hide the animals, we will eat." He glanced at each of them in turn. "You must keep up. Do not fall behind."

They started off a few minutes later, several of the mujahideen dropping behind to walk at the rear of the procession. They drove the train of pack animals with soft clicks of their tongues. Every mujahideen Robert had seen carried a rifle or AK-47 and a full bandolier of cartridges slung across his chest. He had no idea how many warriors were accompanying the supply train, but given where they were headed, he hoped there were many.

29

Robert shivered in his lightweight down parka as he followed the shadowy forms of Jean and Simone. He envied the French physician and nurse the dexterity they had gained from their previous trips across the rugged mountains. Tripping frequently on rocks, Robert cursed beneath his breath. He'd lost track of how long they'd been on the move.

Icy winds whistling off the mountains lashed them like whips. Robert panted during the steep uphill climb. He pulled his woolen cap down as far as it would go and hunched his shoulders into his parka. He followed Jean and Simone mostly by sound, lifting his head every now and then to make certain their shadowy forms were still ahead of him. Keep up. Keep up. He repeated the mantra to himself. If he'd halted in his tracks, he had no doubt the mujahideen behind him would have walked their pack animals over him.

He glanced up at the stars, and for a fleeting second thought of Vermont. He was thousands of feet higher than any place in Vermont, and there were more stars than he'd ever seen. The new moon had not yet made its appearance, which was why, he guessed, the mujahideen had chosen this night to begin their march. Robert had no idea where they were. Mohammed had said they'd be marching for only a few hours this night, which meant they'd be camping on the Pakistani side of the border. They wouldn't cross into Afghanistan until the following evening.

The first faint light of dawn appeared on their right. Moments later, as if they'd sprung out of nowhere, the dark shapes of the mountains towered above them. The trail they were on disappeared behind cliffs directly ahead of them. Robert's breathing was labored at this altitude. He couldn't begin to imagine breathing thinner, colder air if they had to cross peaks as high as those in the distance.

A sharp whistle sounded ahead of them and the caravan came to a halt. The men behind him pulled the lead animals down a track Robert hadn't noticed. Mohammed, accompanied by four men, came up to them.

"We camp here for the day," he said.

Robert looked around to see where the mujahideen were leading the supply train, but all the animals had disappeared.

"Where'd they all go?" he asked.

Mohammed laughed. "There is a narrow valley down there, almost hidden by the peaks."

While the animals grazed on the sparse vegetation, most of the mujahideen knelt and prayed. Their backs arched in unison as their foreheads touched the ground. When they'd finished, one of the men, a boy really, built a small fire under an overhang of rock. A slab of naan and some dried fruit were thrust into Robert's hand by one of the men. He hadn't eaten in almost twelve hours, but was more thirsty than hungry. What he most appreciated was the cup of black tea Mohammed handed him.

Just seeing the sun rising was enough to make him feel warmer, although the chill of night lingered at this altitude. Robert removed his knapsack and, following the example of the mujahideen, wrapped himself in his partouk and reclined on the ground, his head resting on his knapsack. Moments after lying down, Robert was asleep.

For the remainder of that long day, Robert dozed on and off, lulled to sleep by the droning of flies and bees. Hidden in the shadows of the rock face, he was protected from the sun's heat. The mujahideen passed around more naan and tea in the afternoon. Robert counted twenty men in the camp, but others were posted in front and behind them as sentries. The youngest of the mujahideen were no more than fourteen or fifteen. Mohammed, who Robert guessed to be in his forties, appeared to be the oldest.

"Time to go," Mohammed said, as dusk approached. Robert's watch indicated it was almost six and the animals were already loaded. As the sun sank below the ridge line to the west, the caravan was strung out on its original track through the mountains. Streaks of red crossed the darkening sky and then the last vestiges of light faded entirely.

Robert lost all track of time as they climbed. At some point, they crossed the snowline. Plodding along half-asleep, he was startled by the crunch of snow beneath his boots. Step followed step on the snow-covered track, the dark figures of Jean and Simone barely discernible ahead of him. Their only light came from the star-studded sky above and the eerie contrast between snow and rock face.

Sometime during the night, they began to descend and Robert heard the sound of running water. The caravan stopped and he could hear Mohammed's voice close by. "After the animals drink, we'll cross the river. It's low here, but the water moves quickly and the bottom is slippery. Place yourself next to an animal and hold on to his pack while we cross."

Robert, his fingers gripping the rope around a horse's pack, felt the pull of the current around his boots. He placed his feet as flat as possible on the slick rocks beneath the surface, slipping in spite of his caution. One moment he'd been tripping over rocks on the trail, the next he was slipping on them in the river. The horse threw his head when Robert lost his footing and tugged sharply on the rope to prevent himself from falling. "Easy, easy," Robert said.

They came out of the river onto flat ground, but within a half-hour they were climbing again. Without their seeing him, Mohammed had dropped back until he was between Robert and Jean. "One month ago," he said, "it was impossible to cross the river. The melting snow made the river too high."

"Where are we?" Robert asked.

"Welcome to Afghanistan, my home," he said.

30

Mohammed's words made Robert's heart skip a beat. They'd made it. Somewhere in the darkness they'd crossed a line visible only on a map and they were now in occupied territory.

As their climb became steeper than any they'd done in Pakistan, Robert's feeling of exhilaration subsided. He heard the scraping of hoofs behind him and the curses of an Afghan trying to control a horse struggling to get its footing on a patch of ice. Although Robert could see nothing on either side of him, he knew their track was no more than a dozen feet wide. Mohammed had warned them that there were sheer drop-offs in some places. Any animal, or human for that matter, who slipped over the edge might plummet hundreds of feet to the rocky gorges below.

Robert, tripping over rocks, tried to adjust his way of walking. The more he tensed up, the clumsier he became. Several times the sound of rockfalls rumbled behind him, provoked by one of the animals stepping too close to the edge of the trail. His only clue that they were nearing the summit was cloud cover that wouldn't lift. He could no longer see stars or the shadowy forms of Sean and Simone in front of him. The only sounds Robert heard were those of his own breathing and the panting of horses behind him. His chest ached with the effort of the climb and he felt lightheaded. Whatever altitude they were at had to be more than twelve thousand feet. The cold was intense. It penetrated his parka and hat. The fur-lined gloves he wore were next to useless. His fingers ached and he wondered if they were frostbitten.

Suddenly their uphill climb ended. They walked for a short time on a level, shrubless plateau, then descended. The cloud was once again above them and he was able to see Jean's dark form in front of him. Behind him, the curses of the mujahideen became more frequent as loads shifted on the animals, threatening to hurl them off the track. Walking was now even more difficult. Robert and his two French companions slipped frequently on the loose scree, their thin pantaloons offering little protection as they slid against sharp rocks on the trail.

Robert had never been so happy to see the first light of day, until he heard the commotion behind him. He turned and watched in horror as four mujahideen struggled to prevent a horse from toppling over the edge of the track. The animal's hind legs were hanging off the trail and he pawed frantically, his belly touching the ground. The horse snorted in terror as one of the men removed boxes of cartridges from its back while the others held on. Robert realized that if the horse went over, it would take the men with it. Freed of the weight, the horse dug in with his front hooves, pulling himself up. It trembled and shook itself when they managed to get him back on the track. One of the mujahideen held the horse's lead rope and calmly lit a cigarette. The others replaced the load.

As the sky brightened, the caravan halted for the men to pray, then resumed its march. They walked in single file down steep switchbacks. For the first time Robert was able to see the individual mujahideen stretched out ahead of him. The lead man was at least thirty meters ahead of the others, zigzagging his way across the trail.

"What's he doing, Jean?" Robert asked, pointing at the man.

"He looks for mines. The Russians drop them on the trail."

Something else to worry about, Robert thought. Automatically, his gaze dropped to the rock-covered trail. The ground was littered with spent cartridges. The burned hulk of an upended armored personnel carrier appeared suddenly among the boulders along one side of their path.

The trail descended into a broad green valley that opened out below them. The early morning mist was just burning off as the sun rose. Wildflowers covered the fields, their sweet smell enveloping the tired men. The droning of bees filled the air with a steady hum. Robert lifted his face toward the sun as it crept over a ridge to the east, then quickly lowered it as mosquitoes swarmed around him. At the opposite end of the valley a stream cut its way through rock walls. Fed by snowmelt, its water moved quickly, rolling loose boulders in its course.

A smaller valley angled off abruptly from the larger one and they headed toward it. From a distance, Robert saw the remnants of a bombed village spreading over the valley floor. Only two mud-brick houses remained intact. They made their way through the debris of mud walls and shattered houses and were met by a small group of children who ran from one of the houses toward them.

Mohammed walked quickly toward the three foreigners. "We will stop here for breakfast, then take cover in caves above the valley until nightfall."

Behind a wooden fence alongside one of the huts, an old woman was cooking over a stone oven. Chickens pecked their way across the ground. Two old men looking like illustrations from a children's Bible with their long gray beards and turbans, chased the children away. They carried slabs of naan out to the mujahideen. On top of each piece was a bit of scrambled egg. When they'd all been served, the two men carried out trays with clay cups of black tea. The Afghans squatted on the ground as they ate. Mohammed frequently looked up from his naan and tea to watch the sky.

In front of the other house, a man with one leg sat on the ground leaning against the wall. One side of his face was obliterated by burn scars, the eye socket replaced by taut white tissue. He smoked a cigarette, staring into the distance with his remaining eye, paying no attention to the new arrivals. The pungent aroma of hashish wafted toward them.

"Did the Russians destroy this village?" Robert asked Mohammed.

He nodded, still looking up at the sky, now intensely blue.

They'd been resting no more than a quarter-hour when Mohammed stood up and gave the order to resume walking. They wound their way up a narrow path almost invisible from the valley, passing a complex of caves in the rock face on one side of the trail. The mujahideen herded the animals into one of the caves, which opened at the back into what appeared to be a small extension of the valley. Towering rock walls surrounded the patch of green making it difficult to spot from the air.

A few of the younger warriors kept watch over the animals while the others crawled into caves. Robert, Jean, and Simone entered a cave together. Light filtered in for about twenty feet; the rear of the cave was in darkness. Jean removed a plastic bottle from his knapsack and filled it with water from an urn in the cave.

"The villagers leave water here for the mujahideen," Jean said as he poured iodine into the bottle.

They passed the bottle around, Jean adding more iodine each time they emptied and refilled it.

"It's easy to get dehydrated in the mountains," Jean said.

"I'm so tired," Simone said, reclining on the ground and closing her eyes.

Prior to joining the mujahideen supply train, Robert had thought his boots were broken in. He'd worn them numerous times hiking in the woods in Vermont. Now, after a twelve-hour overnight slog through the mountains, his feet felt like raw hamburger. He was almost afraid to remove the boots, fearful that he wouldn't be able to get them back on again. Grimacing, he tugged them off, then gingerly removed his foul-smelling socks. His feet were blistered where the boots had rubbed. Where he'd worn holes in the socks, the flesh was raw and bloody.

Jean kneeled to inspect Robert's feet. He shook his head in commiseration and opened his knapsack.

"This is almost the total of my first aid kit," he said, passing a tube of ointment to Robert. "Better put some of this antibiotic on the raw areas."

Robert smeared the ointment on the sores, then lay back and rested his head on his knapsack. He tossed his partouk on haphazardly as a blanket and within minutes was asleep.

A throbbing sound, like the rapid beating of a heart, jolted him out of a sound sleep. He thought he'd been dreaming until he spotted Jean at the mouth of the cave peering out.

"What's wrong?" said Robert.

"Helicopter gunship," Jean said. "It's above us now."

Robert caught a glimpse of the helicopter between the sheer walls of the cliffs lining the narrow valley. It hovered five hundred feet above them.

"Maybe he sees the animals," Robert said.

"The valley is in shadow," Jean said, trying to sound optimistic. "I think he is moving away."

The drone of the rotors grew fainter as the gunship moved off in a southwesterly direction.

"They'll be back," Jean said.

Robert looked at his watch. It was almost four. He had slept eight hours, yet felt like he'd only had a short nap. Simone hadn't stirred, even with the gunship above them.

"Did you sleep?" Robert asked Jean.

"*Oui,* until our Russian friends showed up." He pointed toward the sky.

One of the elderly Afghans they'd seen earlier down at the hut poked his head into the cave. Seeing the two men awake, he entered carrying a tray with tea. From inside his partouk, tied firmly around his chest, he removed a frayed cloth wrapped around three flatbreads. He placed the tray and cloth on the ground, then disappeared again, returning with half a watermelon resting on the palm of one hand and pieces of dried fruit clutched in the other. He mumbled in Pashto.

"I think he is apologizing for offering us so little," Jean said.

"Thank you, thank you," Robert said, hoping the man knew how appreciative they were.

Simone sat up and rubbed her eyes. The old man stared at her as if she were an apparition, then fled from the cave. She brushed her hand through her short brown hair and smiled sheepishly. "No covering."

"Do you think it's okay to go out to—"

"Yes, it is okay," Jean said. "I have to go, too."

"And so do I," Simone said.

They followed Jean out of the cave, he and Robert heading toward some large boulders below the trail. Simone scuttled toward a rocky outcropping in the opposite direction.

While they were eating, Mohammed stepped into the cave. He smiled broadly. "Did the Russians wake you up?"

He laughed when they nodded.

"We leave in forty minutes. Be ready, please."

"It'll take me that long to get my boots on," Robert said, washing his naan down with tea.

31

The mujahideen were already leading the fully-loaded horses and mules down the trail when Robert, Jean and Simone left the cave. They retraced their steps through the broad valley, the mountains in the distance drenched in a mauve patina. Mosquitoes whined around their ears.

Far off to the west, the setting sun glinted off two objects hurtling down from the sky. The MIGs pulled out of their dives. The muffled sound of bombs hitting their targets reached them moments later. It was reminiscent of Robert's visit to the Khyber Rifles fort near the border, only this time he was on the other side of that line and the MIGs were much closer. As far as the occupying Russian soldiers were concerned, he and his companions were fair game.

By the time the mountains turned purple and the last streaks of pink light were about to be swallowed by nightfall, they were back on their original trail and climbing once again. Robert thought about the destruction in the village they'd left behind. Afghan civilians suffered terribly for the successes of the mujahideen. The Russians, frustrated by the hit and run tactics of the resistance, struck back at their only stationary targets, the villages of Afghanistan. And yet, in spite of their homes being pounded into rubble, the villagers continued to assist the mujahideen. It was as if they knew the day would come, as it always had in the past, when the invader would be expelled, their homes rebuilt, the mosques again calling them to prayer.

Trudging higher into the mountains, tripping over shards of rock and slipping on ice patches, shivering in the winds whipping down at them from the peaks, wincing from the pain of his blistered feet, Robert tried not to think of how miserable he was. He reminded himself that millions of Afghans had struggled across these same mountain passes as they fled toward Pakistan. He imagined women, old men, children, all ill-clad and carrying their meager belongings, driving their animals ahead of them as they walked mile after mile. They carried with them the memory of their villages and crops, pounded into dust by Russian planes and artillery, and as if that were not enough to endure, Russian gunships crisscrossed the sky, hovering like predatory insects above the ragged lines of refugees.

Just watching the mujahideen living their warrior existence, Robert was awed by the physical endurance of the Afghans. Pitting themselves against the rigors of their environment only made them stronger and an even more formidable foe for the Russians.

In the middle of the night, the caravan halted on a high plateau. A crescent of new moon was visible through wisps of mist that floated past. It was bright enough for Robert to see his breath. The cold was more intense than he'd experienced so far. In front of the caravan, one of the mujahideen had started a fire to boil water. Mohammed distributed naan to each of them. Robert's mouth was so dry he didn't know if he'd be able to swallow the bread. He thought about his canteen, which he'd forgotten to put in his knapsack, lying on the dresser in his room in Peshawar. As if reading his thoughts, Jean passed him his plastic bottle of iodine-treated water. "Just a few swallows," he said. "It has to last."

"Come over here," Mohammed called from near the fire. As each of them approached, he thrust a clay cup of tea into their hands. Robert removed his gloves to let the heat of the cup warm his fingers, but the pain was so intense he put them back on.

"We start down now," Mohammed said as he collected the cups. "By first light we will be in the village."

Buoyed by the knowledge that they'd be in a village in a matter of hours, Robert nibbled at his slab of bread as they headed down the trail. No matter how primitive the settlement they were coming to, there'd be a place to lie down. His body craved sleep and warmth.

He glanced at the luminous hands of his watch. A little past three. Soon, soon, he told himself. At that moment he was blinded by an intense light directly in front of him. He caught a glimpse of the line of mujahideen, frozen into momentary immobility. Exploding mortar rounds and machine gun fire shattered the silence. Rounds of rifle fire cut the air and he felt a searing pain on the right side of his face. Horses screamed in fright. The mujahideen behind him shouted as they struggled to control the animals.

"Russians!" Mohammed yelled, racing up the path toward them. Jean and Simone were already running back in the direction from which they'd come. Robert followed behind them, stumbling over downed animals. He stopped to help an Afghan lying face down on the track, but saw the back of the man's head was gone. The shooting became more intense, non-stop salvos obliterating the screams of men and animals. The ground thirty feet ahead of him heaved as it was hit by a rocket or grenade.

"Run, run!" Mohammed shouted, coming up alongside him. "Find cover."

Robert ran through the cloud of smoke from the explosion, tripping over Mohammed as the Afghan went down in front of him. Robert could see Mohammed lying prone on the rocky trail. His blanket lay at his side and blood was seeping through the back of his shirt. The yellow beams of the Russians' powerful lights swept across the path, illuminating the bloody bodies of mules and horses, their cargo spilled everywhere. Those animals still alive screamed in pain and fright. Two mujahideen knelt and fired their AK-47s in the direction of the lights, then ran as bullets whined all around them. One collapsed in a heap and rolled onto his back.

"Robert, here!" Simone screamed, frantically waving at him as she disappeared over the edge of the track on the right. Robert ran toward her and leaped over. He stumbled down a rock-covered slope and spotted Simone ahead of him, struggling to lift Jean from the ground. "Help me, Robert, he's hurt!"

Robert squatted next to them. The bright light was now above them but provided sufficient illumination for him to see Jean's face. Bloody saliva trickled down Jean's chin. His breathing was rapid, gurgling, as if he were blowing bubbles under water. Robert unzipped his jacket. The front of Jean's shirt was soaked with blood. Lifting the shirt, Robert saw the exit hole of a large caliber bullet on the right side of Jean's chest. Blood and bubbling air flowed steadily from the wound. Robert balled up a handful of Jean's shirt and pressed it against the wound, knowing that any first aid in this remote area was futile. Jean stopped breathing. Robert felt for a carotid pulse with his free hand. "He's dead," he murmured, as if he himself couldn't believe it.

Simone sobbed and started to crumple. Robert seized her arm. "Stop it!" he said "We've got to get out of here!" The firing had subsided and they could hear shouts in a language that sounded like Russian, not Pashto. He felt Jean's neck again. Still no pulse. This time his fingers touched Jean's neck pouch. Robert lifted it over Jean's head and stuffed it into his jacket pocket. Roughly, he pulled off Jean's knapsack and threw one strap over his shoulder. Gripping Simone's arm firmly, he tugged her down the narrow path, no longer able to see clearly as they ran further away from the Russian lights. For all he knew, the path might end in a precipice and their bodies would never be found. As much as he wanted to see daylight, he knew that darkness was their only protection. The rocks they stumbled over were getting larger.

"I have a flashlight," Simone whispered.

"No lights," Robert hissed. "Too dangerous."

Their path, covered now with boulders rather than stones, began to ascend.

"Try to stay close to me," Robert said, scrambling on all fours, feeling his way around the rock face blocking his passage. Keeping his palms on the rock, Robert scuttled crab-like to one side until he came to a narrow passage between two massive boulders.

"Simone," he called, his voice a harsh whisper.

"I'm here," she said. Robert felt her hand touch his boot.

"I think we can squeeze in here and get some cover until it's light." He wriggled into the space, his hands extended in front of him, and found that the cleft widened. "Give me your hand," he said, groping for her fingers.

Simone crawled behind him until they reached the rear of the rocks. They huddled next to one another, shivering in the intense pre-dawn cold. The voices they'd heard earlier were more distant and the gunfire had ceased. Now that they were no longer moving, Robert became aware once again of the burning pain on the side of his face. He touched the area gingerly. There was a pronounced gouge just below the right cheekbone, sticky with coagulated blood. If the bullet had entered a few centimeters more to the left, his body would be lying on the path with Mohammed's.

All we can do now, Robert thought, is stay here and hope the Russians didn't see us when we went over the edge. Even if they had, he doubted they'd hunt for them in the darkness. To the Russians, they were mujahideen, and the Russians avoided close combat with the mujahideen if at all possible, especially at night.

Simone reached for his hand and clutched it. "*J'ai peur,*" she said, trembling.

Robert, too, was afraid, but for both their sakes he had to control his fear. He placed his arm around her shoulders and held her close. "We'll be all right," he whispered.

How could this have happened? Robert wondered. The whole train of supplies lost. Mohammed and Jean and who knows how many other mujahideen, dead. Someone must have tipped off the Russians. Why else would they have set up an ambush on that particular trail? The only thing he knew with certainty was that it would be catastrophic for him to fall into Russian hands. He doubted they'd be lenient with an American traveling with mujahideen, even if he was a physician. Certainly they knew Medicins sans Frontieres was providing assistance to villagers in the country, but that was different. It wasn't the French who were assisting the Afghan resistance with money and arms, it was the Americans. If he and Simone were captured, his only chance for survival would be to pass himself off as a French doctor. That meant disposing of his passport and keeping Jean's, which he assumed was in the pouch.

He knew now that Sean had been right when he told him to think carefully about crossing the border, warning him, in fact, that he shouldn't do it. It wasn't as if Robert hadn't known about the risks involved. Like anyone else who puts himself in harm's way, he simply thought himself immune to danger. Perhaps, because of his arrogance, he deserved to find himself in this predicament. Self-pity won't get you anywhere, he thought. I've got to concentrate on getting us out of here.

Simone was shivering so badly he could hear her teeth chattering. Her entire body was trembling. She'd also lost her gloves. Robert slipped off one glove and put it on her right hand. She began to protest but he hushed her and held her bare hand with his gloved one, plunging his own ungloved hand into his parka pocket. They sat like that, partners in misery, waiting for the new day.

Gradually, gray light dispelled the darkness. Simone's eyes opened wide when she looked at him.

"Robert, you've been wounded."

"It's superficial," he said, hoping that was true.

He stood up to get a better idea of their surroundings. A rock face towered above them. The rough path they'd plunged down during the night ended abruptly, the rocks transformed into boulders. The boulder Robert and Simone hid behind was among the largest. There was no more than a square meter's space between the boulder and the cliff face. They were trapped, but making their way back to the trail where they'd been ambushed was unthinkable in the light of day. Either they'd be spotted from the air or by Russian troops still in the area. Now that dawn was breaking, Russian soldiers might begin searching for any survivors.

Robert had to hope, too, that if the Russians came upon Jean's body they wouldn't recognize him as a foreigner. Since Medicins sans Frontieres usually sent small teams in, not individuals, the Russians would know there were others.

"Let's try to find better cover," Robert said. "Maybe we can get higher up. If we're lucky we might find a cave."

Their legs were cold and stiff after spending hours crouching on the ground. Slowly and painfully, they eased their way around the rock face, searching above them for any way to ascend.

"Look," Robert said. "There's an opening in the wall."

About eight feet above them, almost hidden by a spire of rock was a cleft in the rock face. The pinnacle in front of it prevented it from being seen from the path. Robert clung to a narrow ledge while seeking toeholds for his boots. He was finally able to clamber up the scarp and extend his hand to Simone. The cleft was six feet high and wide enough for both of them to enter, but it quickly narrowed, ending about eight feet from its opening.

"We'll have to stay here until it's dark. We'll be able to see anyone coming down the path."

"I don't know what's worse," Simone said. "The cold or the hunger."

"You don't have any naan?"

"I lost it while we were running."

Robert reached into his shirt and pulled out a half-moon shaped piece of bread remaining from the night before. "Let's see if Jean had any," he said, opening the knapsack. Jean had saved almost his entire slab. In addition, the plastic water bottle was half full. The other items in Jean's knapsack were a small bottle of iodine and a tube of antibiotic ointment. Robert tucked them into his own knapsack.

They divided the bread and each took a few swallows of water. They made sure to eat only a small portion of the naan and save the rest. It might be the last food they'd see for a long time.

As the sun rose above the eastern ridge line, they positioned themselves in the mouth of the cleft to take advantage of its warmth. "Watch for any sign of movement on the path," Robert cautioned.

For a while, they listened in silence to the drone of bees. Flies, attracted to the raw wound on Robert's face, pestered them. The irony didn't escape him. They'd left thousands of dollars worth of supplies on the trail and didn't have a Band-Aid between them.

"Do you think we can find our way out of here?" Simone asked.

"We'll get back on the main trail and follow it east. It took us a little more than two nights to get here, so it shouldn't take much longer to get back if we keep moving. Maybe some mujahideen will find us and help us get across the border."

She lapsed into thoughtful silence.

"Jean and I are from the same town in France—Carpentras," she said suddenly, almost to herself.

Robert looked at her. "Are you Jewish?"

She gave him a surprised look. "No. Why do you ask?"

"My wife—my ex-wife—is Jewish and we visited Carpentras because she wanted to see the synagogue."

"So you know my town."

"Yes. I've traveled all through the Vaucluse."

"Jean's mother and my mother are very close—like sisters. They always thought Jean and I would marry, but we never felt about one another like that. We were friends. Dear friends."

She began to cry softly, folding her arms across her knees and burying her face.

Robert reached out to her and patted her back.

"I'm so sorry about Jean."

"If I survive, how will I tell his parents?"

Before Robert could answer, a droning sound, one he was now familiar with, distracted him. It was coming closer. He flattened himself against the cave wall and peered out of the entrance. A Russian helicopter coming from the north dropped out of the sky above the ambush site. Robert knew the Mi-24 Hind gunships were capable of carrying a dozen troops. He didn't have to say anything to Simone. She, too, moved backward into the shadows of the cleft. The noise of the rotors diminished as the gunship disappeared for a minute from view. Suddenly, it loomed up just ahead of them, rising vertically. It hovered for a few seconds, then disappeared above the cliff. Robert waited until he could no longer hear it, then crouched low as he left the cave and hid in the shadow of the spire of rock. He dropped to a prone position, turned his head to Simone, and put a finger in front of his lips. He motioned for her to move further back into the cleft.

Two Russian soldiers were climbing down the same path he and Simone had followed during the night. They carried AK-47s and were looking from side to side. About fifty meters from the cliff face, they stopped and spoke to one another. Robert saw their faces clearly. They were no more than boys, eighteen or nineteen at most. He heard the murmur of their voices. The taller of the two made a sweeping gesture with his arm and shrugged. Robert thought he heard the word *dukhi*. *Dukhi*, or phantoms, he knew, was the word used by the Russians to describe the mujahideen because of their ability to attack and disappear.

They turned and headed back in the direction from which they'd come. Robert waited until they were out of sight, then clambered back into the cleft.

"Are they gone?" Simone asked.

He nodded. "I don't think they'll be back, but there may be more of them around. We should stay out of sight."

For the rest of the day, they stared longingly at the sunshine and blue sky visible from within the depths of the cave. They took turns sleeping during the afternoon, but Robert only managed to doze. While Simone slept, he looked at the contents of Jean's neck pouch. He found his French passport, traveler's checks, and a photograph of Jean with two older people, whom he assumed were his parents. Jean had no beard in the photo and Robert saw from his passport information that he was thirty-two. Robert knew it would be futile to attempt to use that passport should the situation arise. Even if Jean had the beginnings of a beard in the photo, as Robert now had, there would be no resemblance between them. He transferred Jean's belongings to his own neck pouch and tossed the empty pouch into the depths of the cave. As the sun began to descend and the light outside faded, he stood up.

"We should go," he said, touching Simone's shoulder.

She awoke with a start. He handed her the plastic water bottle and she took a large swallow, closing her eyes as she did so.

"What time is it?"

"It's after five. Let's move out."

They cautiously made their way down the rock face, then followed the narrow path up toward the convoy route. They paused when they came to Jean's body, in the same place where they'd left it. Flies buzzed noisily around his face. The Russians must have assumed he was an Afghan, Robert thought. There was no sign that the body had been disturbed. Simone, her eyes welling with tears, looked at Robert imploringly. He knew she didn't want to leave him like that, but he shook his head. They had no shovels and they were close enough to the main track so that anyone up there would hear them moving rocks. Robert crouched low and listened intently as they approached the ambush site. The stench of death was in the air. He inched his way forward and lifted his head until his eyes were at road level. The full extent of the ambush's carnage was before him. Dead mules and horses, at least thirty of them, lay in pools of blood. Open boxes and packing cases were strewn everywhere, their contents looted by the Russians. Six mujahideen, including Mohammed, lay where they'd fallen. Their weapons were gone. The only sound was the buzzing of flies.

Simone joined him. She covered her nose and mouth with her hand. Tears ran down her face as she surveyed the scene. Robert pointed east and they clambered to their feet, ready to begin their trek back toward the Pakistan border. Taking advantage of the fading light to cover as much ground as possible, they jogged along the path. Robert hadn't removed his boots at all since the previous day, but somehow the soreness in his feet was gone.

Before the ambush, they had negotiated this ground in the dark and

Robert recognized nothing. The sheer drop-offs on both sides of the track were intimidating and they realized how lucky they'd been the night before to find the path that had led them to shelter among the rocks. Cliffs towered above them, gradually merging into taller snow-covered peaks. As soon as the sun disappeared behind them, the temperature fell. The mujahideen had known this trail, making it possible for the three foreigners to travel in relative safety merely by listening to the sounds of their companions and the footfalls of the animals in the darkness. Now, however, it was just the two of them, and they'd have to remain alert, careful not to get too close to the edge. They nibbled at the remnants of their naan as they walked, licking the crumbs from their hands.

The first stars were now visible in the sky. Even more important, the new moon was brighter than it had been the night before and provided a faint light. Their breathing grew more labored as they ascended to the ridge line. They paused to catch their breath when they were on the plateau. Robert tipped his head back to look at the panoply of stars above them. How could there be such beauty in the midst of so much death? he wondered.

"It's like seeing the face of God," Simone whispered, standing next to him.

They plodded along, hour after hour, gradually beginning their descent. Their hunger became more acute as the night dragged on, and the small swallows of water they allowed themselves did nothing to assuage their thirst. If they were lucky, when dawn came they'd find themselves in the vicinity of the village and cave complex where they'd spent the previous day. Not only would it be a familiar place where the remaining villagers would be sure to help them, but it would give them some idea of how many hours march they had ahead of them before they approached the border.

It was with a sense of both relief and apprehension that they saw the sky brighten ahead of them, a faint pink strip tracing the black outline of hills that might very well be Pakistan. Now that they were heading east, the light came upon them quickly. The caves that Robert hoped to find were nowhere in sight, the land dropping off on both sides of the path, merging with fields of rock and dry stream beds. As the sun rose, Robert was able to make out a smudge of green in the distance. He pointed it out to Simone. "I think that's our valley."

They continued to descend. Early morning mist lay over the valley, but soon they were able to see the bombed-out remains of the Afghan village. A cloud of brown dust hovered above it. On the outskirts of the village they could make out a smoldering pile of twisted metal.

"The two houses are gone," Robert said.

"Is it the same village?"

"It has to be. Look, there's the stream cutting through the corner of the valley. The Russians must have bombed the village again." He looked to the north, where the snow-covered mountains of the Hindu Kush were visible. Dropping his gaze back to the valley, he tried to discern the path they'd taken to get them up to the caves. With or without the caves, they'd have to take cover soon. The new day was upon them and there was no telling when the Russians would begin their air sorties.

They passed fields of sugar beets and tobacco, then the shattered trunks and branches of fruit orchards. The familiar smell of death assaulted their nostrils when they entered the village. Robert headed toward the rubble where the houses had stood. Charred bodies lay on the ground, some of them children. "Bastards," Robert growled, looking up at the sky.

Except for the corpses, it looked like there had never been life here, just remnants of walls the same color as the earth from which they'd been constructed. Only an occasional scrap of brightly colored material or a shattered piece of crockery held the clues to the existence of a village.

He poked through the rubble with his boot, searching for any food that might have survived the bombardment. He found only a dented, blackened tea kettle and a torn sandal.

"Listen!" he called to Simone. "Do you hear something?"

Dull thuds sounded in the distance, almost in the same direction toward which they'd been heading, but they saw nothing. No sign of MIGs or gunships in the clear skies. Robert headed toward the northern perimeter of the village where he'd seen the smoke. The stench of burning rubber mixed with the putrid smell of charred flesh. The wreckage he'd spotted from the track above the village was a Russian armored personnel carrier, or what was left of it. The ground was littered with body parts and fragments of Russian military uniforms. The charred remains of one corpse were still smoldering.

Robert wondered if the Russians had destroyed the last standing houses in the village in retaliation for a mujahideen strike against the APC. Another instance of civilians suffering for the successes of Afghan warriors.

"We'd better find those caves," Robert said, aware now of the heat from the rising sun.

They were both sweating as they made their way toward the hills northwest of the village.

"There!" Simone said. "Isn't that the trail?"

"That's it," Robert said, seeing the top of a cave opening behind scattered boulders.

They climbed the rocky path, bypassing the cave that opened into the pasture where they'd left the animals. Robert led Simone toward the cave they'd shared with Jean. She stopped outside the opening, her feet rooted to the ground. For a moment she swayed, as if she were about to faint.

Robert took her arm. "Are you all right?"

"I—" She raised her hand and covered her eyes.

"I know what you're feeling," Robert said. "But it's not safe standing out here."

"I'm sorry," she said. "I'm all right now."

As they were about to enter, two bearded Pathans stepped from the dark interior. They wore Chitrali caps and had partouks draped over one shoulder. Full ammunition belts were slung in bandolier fashion across their chests. They looked so unconcerned that Robert thought the two must have been watching them for some time. Slowly, they raised their automatic rifles and leveled them at the two strangers.

32

The older Pathan, whose beard was streaked with gray, spoke to them in English.

"Who are you?"

"We're with Medicins sans Frontieres, Doctors without Borders," Robert replied. "Our convoy was ambushed."

The older man translated for his companion, who nodded his head while observing them.

"My name is Abdur," their interrogator said. "My friend is Nazir. We heard the Russians had ambushed your supply train. Was Mohammed with you?"

"Yes," Robert said. "He's dead. I don't think any of the mujahideen survived. One of our doctors was killed, too."

Again, the man translated. *Shoravee*, said his companion, spitting in disgust.

"You're trying to make it back to where you crossed the border?"

"Yes."

Abdur shook his head. "It's not possible. Our men have attacked a Russian armored force east of here. Soon they'll be bringing in gunships and soldiers by the hundreds."

Nazir said something and Abdur laughed bitterly. "He says more Russians for us to kill. Our men were camped here yesterday evening when this Russian armored car approached the village. We took care of it."

"Boom!" Nazir said, spreading his hands in the air.

"The Russians' main force must have heard the explosion. They sent a gunship over. The helicopter dropped a flare and fired rockets at the only two houses standing. There was nothing we could do."

Nazir spoke quickly, his anger evident. The only word Robert made out was *Stinger.*

"My friend says if we had Stinger missiles, we would have shot the gunship out of the sky. But our group has none."

"Can you tell us a way we can get to the border?"

"For now, stay with us. The rest of the men will join us soon and we'll find out how the battle is going. We remained behind in case the Russians try to land troops here." He translated for his companion and laughed at Nazir's reply. "Nazir says we're missing all the fun. He's right."

"Won't the Russians try to follow your men here?"

A fleeting smile crossed Abdur's face. "They know better than to come looking for us. The Russians don't like leaving major roads and valleys. When night comes we'll take you to a village about thirty kilometers from here. The people will hide you until the Russians leave the area. Then someone will lead you across."

The two Pathans sat down in the mouth of the cave and motioned to Robert and Simone to join them.

"Are you hungry?" Abdur asked.

"Very."

Nazir stood up and disappeared within the cave, returning with naan and hard-boiled eggs.

"We got this from the villagers yesterday," Abdur said. "*Melmestia,* you know that word?"

Robert shook his head.

"It is the way of the Pathans. We have *melmestia,* being a good host, *nanawati,* giving asylum, and *badal,* vengeance. We live by these things."

Nazir handed Robert and Simone cups of hot tea and then brought two more cups for himself and Abdur. He said something to Abdur which made the man smile.

"Nazir heard me telling you about *pushtunwali,* the way of the Pathans. He said the Russians are learning about *badal.*"

"Do you think we can trust these two?" Simone asked Robert in French.

"We have no choice," Robert replied in French.

"I am an honest man," Abdur said, looking at Simone, "so I must tell you I speak French. I studied engineering in Paris."

She blushed. "Forgive me."

"When I spoke about *melmestia*, it does not only mean being a good host. It means taking care of guests. We are responsible for you and we will defend you with our lives."

"Thank you," Simone said.

"You are a nurse or a doctor?"

"Nurse."

"And you are a doctor?" he said to Robert

"Yes."

"Both my father and brother are physicians," said Abdur. "This young lady is French, I know. But you speak English without an accent. You are an American?"

"Yes, I am."

"My parents and my brother live in the States. In California. They left Kabul eight years ago."

"You didn't want to join them?"

"I can't blame them for going. Things were very difficult in Kabul when the Communists came to power. My father and brother lost their positions at the hospital. And my mother, who taught English at the university, was also fired. The Taraki government did not approve of their politics. At first I thought of going with them to America, but when the Russians invaded everything changed. My wife was killed in an air raid and I joined the mujahideen. I love my country and some day they will need engineers to rebuild Afghanistan. Many of our villages and towns look like this one. Big piles of rubble."

"Do you think your family will return?"

"I don't know. America is a wonderful country and they have good lives now. Safe lives."

"Abdur," Nazir called. He pointed to the sky.

They looked up to the north and saw the helicopters approaching before they heard them, four dark spots in the morning sky.

"Maybe better if we sit inside the cave entrance," Abdur said.

It was smoky in the cave from the small fire Nazir had built to boil the tea. He poured more water in a kettle and placed it over the orange embers. Robert took the opportunity to refill Jean's plastic bottle and added iodine.

A scuffing sound on the rocks outside startled them. Abdur and Nazir picked up their weapons from the ground next to them. They stood alert, one on either side of the cave entrance. They heard a soft whistle and relaxed, leaning their guns against the cave wall. Two Afghans appeared in the entrance. They looked in surprise at the two foreigners and spoke to Abdur. Frowning, he replied with almost a growl. One of the Afghans poked his head out of the cave and signaled with his arm. Robert and Simone gasped as two Russian soldiers, their hands tied behind their backs, were pushed inside. The two mujahideen who brought the prisoners were obviously surprised when they saw Robert and Simone. Robert made out the words Medicins sans Frontieres as Abdur spoke to the four mujahideen gathered around the prisoners. One of the Afghans brusquely shoved the prisoners to the ground next to Abdur.

"Do you speak English? Francais?" Abdur asked the two Russians, both of whom appeared to be in their early twenties and looked terrified.

They shook their heads.

"We'll learn nothing from them," Abdur said disgustedly.

The droning of a helicopter seemed to be just above them and the two Russians glanced at one another, then looked up hopefully. Extracting a knife with an eight-inch blade from the belt around his shalwar kameez, Nazir hissed at the Russians and placed a finger on his lips. Showing them the knife, he made a slashing motion across his neck with the edge of his hand. One of the Russians began to cry.

After a few minutes the noise from the chopper's rotors grew more distant. Abdur spoke softly to his companions, then turned to Robert and Simone. "My men destroyed a tank and two APCs. Many dead Russians. We lost two men. When the gunships arrived, my men broke off the battle."

"You attacked the Russians with so few men?" Robert said, looking at the four recent arrivals.

"The others are hiding until the helicopters leave."

"What will you do with these two?" Robert asked, looking at the Russians.

Abdur shrugged, but said nothing.

The hours passed slowly, all of them dozing or drinking tea. Nazir fed the Russians pieces of bread and gave them water to drink, but he didn't free their hands. The mujahideen took turns napping. As the sun went down, the cave entrance was enveloped in shadow. Nazir stepped outside, returning a few minutes later. He said a few words to Abdur, who got to his feet and picked up his weapon.

"The rest of my men are outside," Abdur told Robert and Simone. We'll leave here in a few minutes and head north. Don't get separated from us." He distributed naan to everyone, tearing the slabs in half to make sure there was enough to go around. All of them, except for Nazir and the two Russians, followed Abdur from the cave. Robert turned and took one final look at the two Russians, who stared at him with pleading eyes.

They walked single file up the trail, assailed by the ever-present mosquitoes, then began a steep uphill climb, clambering over boulders. The sun dropped below the western hills and Nazir still had not joined them. Robert turned to look behind them and saw Nazir on the trail, slipping his knife back into his belt as he walked quickly to catch up with them. Simone, following Robert's gaze, shuddered. Nazir caught up, passing them as nonchalantly as if he'd been busy cleaning up after a picnic.

Dusk descended quietly with no sound of distant gunfire or gunship rotors. Robert had the impression they were being led through a serpentine maze of rock. The mountains turned a deep purple and soon they were walking in darkness, the rising moon giving them barely enough light to see by. Robert and Simone, tripping or losing their footing on jagged pieces of shale, were certain that the mujahideen were annoyed by their clumsiness.

As always, Robert wondered how the mujahideen were able to endure these nights of forced marches. They seemed immune to the cold and unfazed by hunger and thirst. Some wore captured Russian boots, but others had plastic or canvas shoes offering little protection for their feet. Even in their down jackets, Robert and Simone were cold, yet the mujahideen with only their partouks to wrap around them never complained.

On all of these night walks, Robert could never tell how long they'd been marching. He'd glance at the luminescent hands of his watch, thinking they'd been on the trail for hours and find only a quarter-hour had gone by. At other times, he'd be surprised to discover they'd been walking for half the night. One moment they were ascending, then suddenly the trail would wind steeply down. It was not yet dawn when they heard dogs barking in the distance. Their path now led steadily downhill toward a light that flickered for a moment, then went out.

All Robert could surmise about their location in relation to the Pakistani side of the border was that they were north of Peshawar, how far north he didn't know. He realized now that his return to Pakistan might be delayed indefinitely. If he were to judge by the battles between Abdur's group of mujahideen and the enemy, the Russians maintained a large presence along the border in this area. He doubted the mujahideen would risk getting them across. They knew other routes, of course, trails that led through the upper reaches of the mountains. That would mean arduous hiking through intense cold and deep snow. He wondered if he and Simone were up to it. Just in the time they'd been in Afghanistan, they had lost weight, in his case at least six or eight pounds, and neither he nor Simone had any excess fat to begin with.

Another thought nagged at him. What if word of the ambush got back to Peshawar? How could it not? he asked himself. The Pathans were on both sides of the border and news spread quickly. As with the Kurds in Turkey and the Middle East, artificial boundaries meant nothing. When word did reach Pakistan, would everyone assume he was dead? If that were the case, the International Refugee Assistance office in Peshawar would notify the New York office, and they in turn would notify his parents, whom he'd listed as his emergency contact. Robert feared the effect on the two old people if they were hit with news of his death. And what about Davey? And Lynn? What would news like that do to them? The possibility of exposing people he cared about to the trauma of such tidings made him angry with himself. Samantha had reminded him of his responsibilities. You have a son, she had told him, whereas Jean and Simone were young and single. He had chosen to ignore her admonition, and now he was facing the consequences.

The mujahideen, Abdur had told him, would be responsible for their safety and do all in their power to get them back across the border. But Robert had seen enough carnage now to know that the mujahideen themselves were vulnerable. No one could truly guarantee their safety.

Simone's shadowy form moved down the trail in front of him. Her family in France would also receive news that she was missing and presumed dead. Jean's, too, he reminded himself. If he and Simone did live to make it back to their countries, Jean's family would learn the painful truth. What a mess, Robert thought.

The light he'd seen earlier flickered again. The silence was suddenly broken by a muezzin's cry of *Allah O akbar*, the call to morning prayers. What had appeared to be walls of rock ahead of them now took the shape of man-made walls. They were entering an Afghan village, the mud-brick houses hidden by thick ramparts. Off to the east, Robert glimpsed the black outline of mountains silhouetted against the first light of the new day.

The mujahideen moved silently through the narrow streets, the forbidding walls pressing in on them from each side. Someone had managed to quiet the dogs that had barked earlier. There were no lights and nothing in the village moved, yet Robert was certain everyone knew of their presence. The men ahead of him came to a sudden halt as they heard the squeak of a wooden door opening. A hand appeared holding a kerosene lantern aloft and the warriors mumbled their greetings as they passed inside. The short, white-bearded man holding the light evinced no surprise when he saw Simone and Robert. He shook hands with both of them. They entered a courtyard, the shadows of the mujahideen dancing on the walls as the old man raised his lamp higher. A large tree grew in the center of the open space, its branches spreading out to cover most of the courtyard.

Their host closed the door to the courtyard and opened another carved wooden door leading into a house the color of the clay upon which they stood. They filed into a reception area and took seats on the cushions lining the walls. Robert caught a glimpse of an elderly woman in the kitchen, her chador pulled away from her face as she bent over a Primus stove illuminated by a kerosene lamp. Two young men, strapping black-bearded Pathans, came out of the kitchen carrying trays of naan wrapped in cloth, and sweet green tea. They greeted Abdur warmly and mumbled their greetings to the others. They distributed the flatbread and tea and returned to the kitchen, emerging with trays of food—mounds of rice, bowls of mutton, and salad.

It was unlike any breakfast Robert had ever eaten but he was grateful for it. A young boy with a pitcher of water circled the room, pouring a small amount into the hands of each of them. Like the Afghans, Robert and Simone picked up rice and mutton with their right hands. They ate ravenously. It was their first meal since leaving Peshawar. Robert looked longingly at the bowl filled with chopped salad greens, and tomatoes. Since arriving in Peshawar, he had had no problem with intestinal upsets. Picking up a bug while traveling with the mujahideen would be more than an inconvenience—it might jeopardize his ability to keep up on the long slogs through the mountains. Simone, he noticed, was already eating salad. Against his better judgment, he ate a few mouthfuls of lettuce and some chunks of tomato. Not smart, he thought, but they are delicious. When the bowls were empty, the two men, who Robert learned afterward were Abdur's brothers-in-law, brought in slices of melon and a dish of dried fruit. The old man entered the room and sat down next to Abdur. They spoke softly to one another, both of them glancing at Robert and Simone.

"My father-in-law, Jamakhar, tells me there are many Russians in the area," Abdur said. "They were in this village two days ago, but did not destroy it like they have so many others. Jamakhar is the local *malik*, or chief. He and the other villagers pretend to cooperate with the Russians, and give them false information about the mujahideen. They see that my father-in-law has two grown sons living with him so they believe he is opposed to the mujahideen. But my brothers-in-law act as couriers between mujahideen groups and report on the movements of Russian troops. So far there has been no problem. But Jamakhar is afraid the Russians don't really trust the villagers and will return, especially after the recent heavy fighting near here. You have two choices. Either we must leave here and head further north into the mountains to another village, or you can remain and Jamakhar will hide you in the storage cellar under the house if the Russians come. If they find you, you know what will happen."

"We don't want to place your in-laws in danger," Robert said.

"My in-laws are accustomed to danger. Two of their sons and their daughter, who was my wife, have died in this war. They are not afraid for themselves, but for you. You must decide."

"If we stay here, where will you and your men go?"

"Wherever we can hurt the Russians. It depends on what intelligence we receive."

Simone touched Robert's arm. "It will be dangerous no matter where we go. If Abdur's in-laws are willing to hide us until it's safe to cross, I'd prefer to remain here."

"Then that's what we'll do. Thank you," he said to Jamakhar, looking directly at the old man.

Abdur translated and his father-in-law nodded, making reassuring motions with his hand.

"When will you and your men leave?" Robert asked Abdur.

"It's already dawn. It's too risky to leave now. When night comes, we'll go."

"There's no way to know how long we'll have to be here?"

Abdur shook his head. "Jamakhar's sons will let him know when it's safe. You'll have to trust them. As soon as the Russians move on, they'll arrange for you to get across. Perhaps we can make that happen sooner with an attack north or west of here."

As the sun came up, some of the mujahideen slept, others sat in the courtyard smoking in the shade of the tree. The warriors appeared more relaxed in the village, which surprised Robert. The villagers, he figured, all knew they were here in Jamakhar's house and would alert them to any impending danger. At intervals they heard the muezzin calling the faithful to prayer. Robert and Simone sat on their cushions and leaned back against the wall, dozing rather than sleeping in spite of their exhaustion.

Jamakhar and his wife, Shahla, brought tea later in the morning. For lunch, Robert and Simone ate *kofta*, Afghan meat balls, and rice, followed by watermelon.

"I hope we're not depriving them of food," Robert said to Simone.

Abdur, who walked into the room at that moment to join them, told them not to worry. "My in-laws do well. They have goats and sheep and tend their own orchards."

"Is the mosque nearby?" Robert asked when they again heard the muezzin's call.

"Do you wish to pray?"

Robert knew by Abdur's barely concealed smile that he meant the question only in jest.

"Do you pray?" Robert asked.

"Not in the way you mean. My relationship with Allah is a very personal one. We talk. And you two?"

Robert smiled. "My relationship with God is also a personal one."

Simone nodded in agreement.

Abdur sprang to his feet when they heard a shout from outside the house. He snatched his weapon from behind his cushion.

They stood in the doorway watching as Jamakhar spoke to an excited villager in the courtyard. He turned and called to Abdur, who in turn shouted orders to his men. The mujahideen picked up their weapons and filed past Robert and Simone into the house.

"We must hide," Abdur told Robert and Simone. "There is a Russian armored column approaching the village."

Jamakhar had already pulled up the carpet in the center of the room and opened a trapdoor. The mujahideen, carrying their weapons, descended into the dark interior of the cellar under the floor.

"There are eight steps," Abdur said. "Walk carefully and do not speak until Jamakhar says the Russian soldiers are gone."

Robert and Simone picked their way down the steps, hands reaching out from below to guide them. Abdur was the last one to come down. They all squatted or sat on the cold clay floor, their backs against the wall. The unwashed odor of the mujahideen filled the room, but it was too dark to see them. Robert could only hear their breathing. He pictured the old man replacing the carpet in the reception room and waiting at the door to greet the Russian troops. Perhaps Jamakhar and his sons would offer them sweet tea. Nerves of steel, Robert thought.

They felt a vibration through the walls of the cellar. Tanks, Robert thought. They must be right outside. As he had so many times in the past few days, Robert wondered what he was doing here. Was it his fate to die in this poor, wounded country? He refused to believe that, but what man believed that the next bullet to be fired was meant for him?

He heard nothing from the room above them. Either the Russians hadn't entered the house or the floor was too thick for sound to penetrate. Robert couldn't recall a time when he'd been in such utter blackness. He had thought it dark on the moonless nights with the mujahideen in the mountains, but there at least he'd had the comfort of the stars and the whiteness of the snow. Now time ceased to exist, as it had so many times since he'd crossed the border. He wondered what thoughts were going through the heads of the mujahideen. On the surface they were always calm, betraying no fear. Were they so accustomed to imminent death that they simply accepted it? He knew that Islam meant submission, and in moments like this he envied these warriors of Islam their blind faith.

33

A creaking noise above them roused Robert from the doze he'd fallen into. He heard the trapdoor being lifted and Jamakhar's voice.

"We can go up," Abdur said. "The Russians are gone."

One behind the other, they filed up the steps into the reception room. Abdur's father-in-law closed the trapdoor and replaced the rug.

They sat on the cushions and drank the tea brought to them by Jamakhar's sons.

Robert, sitting next to Simone, glanced at his watch and leaned toward her. "We were down there for two hours."

"It felt like an eternity," Simone said.

Abdur spoke to his men, then switched to English for Robert and Simone. "Jamakhar says the Russians searched every house in the village. They suspect we are close by. You can walk in the courtyard if you wish, but only go outside the wall if you have to use the facilities. The Russians sometimes return soon after they leave, hoping to catch some careless mujahideen."

Robert smiled to himself at Abdur's use of the word facilities. The communal outhouses, one for men and one for women, were so primitive and stinking he'd gagged each time he had to use it. Whenever Simone emerged from the women's facility, her face was ashen.

Several times during the day, Robert had watched Jamakhar's sons carry buckets of water from the communal well. Water from one bucket was poured into a plastic jug and used for hand washing. A bar of soap rested next to it on a metal ashtray. Anyone coming from the facility always headed immediately to the jug, for which Robert was thankful. The thought of coming down with an intestinal bug in this environment was too nightmarish to contemplate.

As the sun went down, Jamakhar and Shahla brought in trays with scrambled eggs and naan fried in oil. The mujahideen drank cup after cup of green tea, fortifying themselves for their night march. As the sun dipped below the hills in the distance, the men rose to their feet and picked up their weapons. Each of them shook hands with Jamakhar.

"We leave now," Abdur said. "Jamakhar will care for you as if you were his own family." Jamakhar interrupted and said something in Pashto. Abdur laughed. "He says you shouldn't forget he wouldn't have lived this long if he wasn't careful. He says to trust him and he will get you across when it's safe. God willing you will be back in Pakistan before too long."

"Thank you for everything," Robert said, shaking Abdur's hand.

Abdur, after saying his farewells to his in-laws, followed his men out the door. Robert and Simone were alone in the room. While Shahla cleared the trays, Robert suggested they go outside. The first stars were visible and the air was cool, not frigid as it had been in the mountains. It was a welcome relief from the daytime heat.

They strolled slowly around the courtyard.

"When were we expected back in Peshawar?" Robert asked.

"Usually we're gone no more than two weeks on these trips. I'm sure they've received word by now about the ambush. They must think we're all dead."

"We probably would be if it weren't for Abdur and Jamakhar."

She nodded, a worried expression on her face.

"What's wrong?"

"I hope they don't send word to my parents."

"I'm concerned about the same thing. I wish there were some way to let them know in Peshawar that we're all right."

"Perhaps it's better that they hear it from us if—when we are across the border. If the Russians were to learn that we were here . . ."

Simone didn't have to finish her thought. Robert nodded in agreement.

As much as they would have liked to remain outdoors, the mosquitoes soon drove them inside.

It was still dark when Robert awoke with a cramping pain in his abdomen. He was covered in sweat and threw off his partouk. The cramping became more urgent and he cursed silently. Reaching into his knapsack, he removed his penlight and stumbled toward the door. It was open. He turned to shine his light into the room. Simone was gone.

Robert crossed the courtyard and pushed open the door. He raced to the outhouse, hoping he'd make it in time. His diarrhea was explosive, the cramps doubling him over. He clutched at his abdomen. At least a quarter hour passed before he trusted himself enough to return to the house. He felt feverish and weak.

He heard his name whispered from within the house as he washed his hands in the courtyard.

"Simone?" he answered.

"Robert, I'm sick."

"Me, too. I'm sure it was the salad."

For the remainder of the night, each of them dashed repeatedly outside.

"I feel so weak," Simone said as dawn came.

"Do you have a fever? I feel like I do."

"Yes, I think so. And we have no medicine."

Shahla entered the room with tea, looked at each of them, then called to her husband.

In response to Jamakhar's questioning look, Robert pointed at his stomach. Simone held hers, too. Jamakhar spoke to his wife and left the room. He returned with a small bottle of white tablets and handed two pills to each of them. Robert passed his bottle of iodinated water to Simone, then he swallowed his pills.

"I think he's giving us aspirin," Robert said.

Shahla, in the meantime, carried in bowls of yogurt and poured sweet green tea for them.

In spite of having no appetite, they forced themselves to swallow the yogurt and tea.

They slept on and off throughout the day, too exhausted to sit up or go outside except when they had to use the facility. Fortunately, their diarrhea had subsided and Robert was sure they'd be better by the next morning. They declined lunch and dinner, only drinking the tea that Shahla brought.

Day followed day with no message from Jamakhar. They occasionally heard the distant thuds of artillery rounds or bombs. MIGs streaked across the sky almost daily, high enough to avoid any missiles fired by the mujahideen. Their days were measured by the punctual chanting of the village muezzin. With nothing to occupy them, Robert and Simone sat and talked about their families and their lives at home. Sheltered under the branches of the walnut tree in the courtyard, they escaped the direct rays of the sun.

"I keep thinking about Jean," Simone said. "It is difficult to imagine life without him. He was like my brother."

"Do Jean's parents have other children?"

"There is another son, younger than Jean. He attends university in Lyon.

"How old is your son, Robert?"

"Davey is five. He lives with his mother in New York. I have a picture of him if you'd like to see it."

"I would like very much to see it."

Robert pulled out the photo of Davey sitting on the woodpile in Vermont from his pouch. "He was four in this picture."

"He is a beautiful child. You are divorced?"

"In the process."

"It must be difficult for all of you."

Robert nodded. "I worry about Davey. He wants to live with me, but . . ."

"His mother wants to keep him with her, yes? One of Jean's friends in France is in a similar situation. Children become a—a—pawn—is that the word?—when their parents fight. The mother and father are so angry they ignore what the child wants. It is very unfortunate."

"Very. And you, Simone? Are you involved with anyone?"

"Now, no. In the past, yes. For three years. But he left for America to study for an advanced degree in physics."

"What happened?"

Simone shrugged. "He didn't come back."

"Did he ask you to join him in America?"

"I do not think his wife would have liked that." She smiled.

"He married an American?"

"*Oui.* I was very hurt, but now, four years later, *tant pis.* It is life, no? I tell myself there is a reason for everything. Not being involved with anyone permitted me to work with Medicins sans Frontieres and come to Pakistan."

"You don't regret it? Not even now?"

"No. Not even now."

By the beginning of July, the daytime heat was so oppressive it was too hot for them to sit in the courtyard until after the sun set. And then they had to contend with the mosquitoes. They passed the days dozing or sitting in the reception room, eating melon and drinking tea, telling each other about books they'd read or movies they'd seen. Simone was as anxious as he was to be on the move, but they were totally at the mercy of Jamakhar's judgment. They looked meaningfully at him each time he entered the room, but with the sounds of battle still audible during the day, they knew the Russians were only a few miles away.

Their departure took them by surprise. They had just stepped into the courtyard as the sun sank behind the mountains when they heard the unmistakable sound of a helicopter gunship. They looked up but saw nothing. They looked at one another as if to confirm they weren't imagining things. Turning in a circle, Robert scanned the horizon. There was nothing but sky, streaked with orange and pink.

Suddenly, the gunship appeared to rise straight out of the ground on the outskirts of the village. It headed in their direction, only fifty meters above them, close enough for them to see the crew in the cockpit and the muzzles of the machine guns. Paralyzed where they stood, Robert and Simone watched helplessly, expecting each moment to be their last. They were blinded by a massive explosion, the shock wave knocking them off their feet. It was as if they'd been caught in an earthquake. Fragments of seared metal and parts of bodies rained down on them as they scrambled to their feet, racing for the door. Shards of blackened metal, some of them large enough to kill a person on impact, fell into the courtyard and onto the roof of the house.

Robert and Simone almost collided with Jamakhar and his sons, who held the door open for them. Shahla stood behind them. Jamakhar mimicked the firing of a weapon at the gunship. His sons looked out at the jumble of debris in the courtyard. Exultant grins transformed their faces. The lower half of a body, its uniform smoking, lay next to a large piece of one rotor. The old man spoke sternly to his sons and their smiles vanished. One of them ran to the door in the perimeter wall and opened it. He peered out in both directions, then turned to nod at his father.

Abdur, cradling a Kalashnikov, pushed his way past his brother-in-law, a small group of mujahideen following him into the courtyard. Ignoring Robert and Simone, he spoke urgently to his father-in-law. The old man called to his two sons and they joined the conversation. Abdur broke away from the group and approached the two foreigners.

"It's no longer safe here. You will have to leave immediately."

"Did your men shoot down that helicopter?"

Abdur pointed to a tall Pathan, so thin he was almost skeletal. "RPG, a rocket-propelled grenade. Ali has good aim. But now there are many Russians coming this way. They may bomb this village."

"What about your in-laws? What will they do?"

"Like all villagers, they have their valuables buried in a cave in the mountains. As soon as we leave, they will drive their flocks up to the high country."

One of Abdur's brothers-in-law left his father and came up to them.

"This is Samaludin," Abdur said, introducing him by name for the first time. "He will lead you to the border."

Robert and Simone looked warily at the young man. After putting their lives in the hands of Abdur and Jamakhar, it was difficult for them to fully trust someone who until then had only served them tea.

"You must trust him. He knows this country better than anyone. If anyone can get you across, it is Samaludin. But now you must hurry. Get your packs and jackets."

For several minutes there was a commotion in the house as Samaludin's brother, whose name Robert never learned, distributed flatbreads. Robert and Simone slipped on their jackets and backpacks. By the time they looked up

Abdur and his fellow mujahideen were gone. They were never able to thank him.

Fragments of debris from the destroyed helicopter still smoldered in the courtyard. The sickening smell of burning flesh hung in the air.

Jamakhar and Shalah, each carrying a gnarled sheepherder's stick and a cloth bag with food, hastened ahead of them through the courtyard toward the door leading to the street. Robert and Simone followed. Samaludin brought up the rear. He took a final look around the courtyard, as if he might be seeing it for the last time, then pulled the door shut.

For the first time since their arrival, Robert and Simone saw other villagers. Old men, women, and children, some driving goats and sheep before them, headed up the lane to the trail leading from the village. Abdur and the mujahideen had vanished. Even as they fled, they heard the chanting of the muezzin in the mosque that neither Robert nor Simone had ever seen. Shalah suddenly turned and ran back toward them. In spite of her age, which could have been anywhere from sixty to eighty, she moved quickly, surprisingly agile on the uneven, stone-covered earth. She stopped before Simone and silently placed a necklace of lapis lazuli beads over her head and around her neck. Simone lifted the blue stones in her hand and looked down at them in astonishment. Before she could thank the old woman, she had raced back to her husband. They watched her follow Jamakhar and Samaludin's brother into a stubble field thick with grazing sheep. Soon the three of them were waving their sticks, pressing the sheep uphill.

Thinking they were supposed to follow, Robert and Simone continued up the path behind them. A sharp whistle brought them to a halt. Samaludin stood, pointing to the right. A narrow, barely visible trail that appeared to have been worn by sheep cut off from the main route. Sheep and goat droppings covered the path. They followed the Afghan, breathing hard as they tried to maintain his pace. They passed a graveyard and heard Samaludin utter the word *shaheed*, martyrs. Simone caught Robert's eye and he knew they were thinking the same thing, hoping that passing the world of the dead was not an omen. Dusk was settling quickly. Would the Russians really attempt an attack at nightfall? Robert asked himself.

Within five minutes he had his answer. They heard the planes before they saw them in the darkening sky. Samaludin said something in Pashto, trying to urge them to move faster. Robert looked back toward the village just as the first bombs hit. The ground beneath them shuddered with the explosions. Smoke and flames rose into the air as the jets pulled out of their dives and roared above them. Blast after blast followed them on their ascent. So Abdur had been right. The Russians were bombing the village and soon it would be as if it never had existed. Robert thought of the muezzin, wondering if the man was still in the mosque, and if it, too, had been destroyed. It couldn't have been a big mosque like those in Peshawar where tape recordings of the call to prayer were played. For the first time he knew with absolute certainty that no amount of bombing would destroy the faith of the people, that eventually that faith would drive the invaders from their land. Still, he couldn't help thinking of Shalah and Jamakhar and the other villagers, now up in the mountains, looking back to follow the diving jets as they released their loads, obliterating their village and their homes, turning their lives into dust.

34

The trail wound serpentine-like through the hills. By the time the moon rose, Samaludin had led them up and down so many winding paths Robert had no idea in which direction they were heading. When the trail finally straightened, Robert sensed they were heading south but it was too dark to confirm that. If he could see the mountains of Pakistan on his left when first light came, he would know for sure where they were. The moon was waxing gibbous, which made their progress easier but also increased their apprehension. If they were able to see where they were going, they would also be visible to any Russian troops in the area. Their forms cast long shadows on the rock faces they passed, making it seem as if specters were accompanying them on their march.

Robert licked his dry lips. As if reading his mind, Samaludin halted abruptly and hissed softly. He inched his way forward, peering to his right as if looking for something in the darkness. Then they all heard it, the sound of running water. They followed Samaludin to a stream about a foot wide, moonlight glinting off its surface. Samuludin knelt, cupped his hands, and drank. Robert removed the plastic bottle from his backpack, filled it, and added iodine. He swirled it around, then passed it to Simone. Robert finished off the rest of the bottle, refilled it, added iodine, and drank. Since they had no way of knowing when they might come to water again, he and Simone drank until their stomachs could hold no more. Robert felt the stream bed. It was no more than three or four inches deep. As summer progressed, he was certain these smaller water sources would dry up completely. That would certainly be the case once they descended into the valley below. He was frustrated at his inability to speak to

Samaludin. He and Simone had no choice but to follow where he led them, trusting that he knew what he was doing.

They continued marching until daylight. Mountains were silhouetted against the pale light in the east. Robert knew they were looking at Pakistan, so close, yet so far. Their path gradually wound down, then leveled out until they were on a narrow plateau above a broad valley. A hundred meters ahead were the shattered remains of a mud-brick house, its wooden door ajar. There was no sign of life. They approached cautiously. In the blackened remains of a campfire, tin cans with Russian labels were strewn. Samaludin pushed against the door of the house and immediately recoiled. Two skeletons, fragments of flesh still attached to the bones, were hanging from an overhead beam.

Robert and Simone backed away from the door. Samaludin had already turned away from the house and gestured to them to follow. The edge of the plateau lay directly ahead of them and Samaludin motioned for them to get down on the ground. They crept forward and looked down into the valley that spread out before them. It was planted with wheat. In several clearings yoked oxen were being driven in circles to pound the newly harvested stalks beneath their hooves. Clouds of dust enveloped the bullocks and the men driving them. Further to the south colorfully clad women collected water from a stream, possibly the lower reaches of the same one they had drunk from earlier.

Robert called their attention to a line of trees to the north alongside an irrigation ditch. Screened by the trees but visible in the gaps between them a fenced area with neat rows of houses appeared. Artillery muzzles poked out from camouflage nets and half a dozen tanks rumbled along the perimeter of the compound.

They crawled away from the edge and Samaludin headed back toward the tree line on the slopes rising from the plateau. They were no more than fifty meters from the first trees when the distinct throb of a helicopter's rotors reached them. In a matter of seconds it rose above the slopes, apparently heading toward the Russian base they had seen from the plateau's edge.

Samaludin raced for the cover of the trees, gesturing to them to run. Robert's heart pounded. He and Simone kept up with Samaludin. They probably would have passed him if they had known where they were going. Fifteen minutes later, when they were about a mile from where the helicopter had passed over,

Samaludin stopped, turned toward them, threw his head back and laughed. Simone and Robert stared at one another in amazement.

"How does he know the Russians aren't sending out troops to look for us?" Robert wondered aloud.

"These Afghans are—are—" She groped for a word in English, then came out with *incroyable*.

Instead of finding a place to hide during the daylight hours, Samaludin kept them on the move. They continued heading south, using rocks or trees as cover, following sheep trails through the shattered ruins of mud-walled Afghan villages and skirting what was left of orchards and gardens after Russian bombardments. Fruit trees had been blown apart, their stumps and twisted branches splintered on the ground. It was strangely quiet for a part of the country so close to the border. Since their encounter that morning, they hadn't seen any Russian helicopters or MIGs, and no tank or artillery fire broke the silence. They were hungry and hot, the afternoon sun beating down on them. At last, Samaludin called a halt. They sat in the shade of a rocky overhang and watched the shifting colors of the mountains on the other side of the valley as the sun set behind them. They were almost too tired to eat, but they nibbled on flatbread, untouched that day until now. Robert passed his water bottle to Simone, who in turn gave it to Samaludin. None of them took more than two swallows. Robert and Simone would have liked nothing better than to nap for several hours, but Samaludin soon had them back on their feet. It was almost dark when he pointed to the purple mountains to the east. "Pakistan," he said. Robert nodded. He already knew that. Then they heard the faint roar of a truck engine from the south, the direction in which they were headed. Robert came up alongside Samaludin and pointed toward where the sound was coming from.

"Torkham," Samaludin said.

Robert, stunned, turned to Simone. "He says we're approaching Torkham."

"I don't understand," Simone said. "We can't cross there. We're in the country illegally. The Afghans at the border will turn us over to the Russians."

Samaludin picked up on their concern and made a calming gesture with his hand. "Okay, okay," he said.

The path they'd been following ended abruptly. Ahead and to the right rock-covered hills rose, as bleak and parched a landscape as any they'd crossed. To their left, the ground dropped off sharply into dense woods. Barely able to see Samaludin in the gathering darkness, Robert and Simone groped their way through the trees and brush, hanging on to whatever handhold they could find but slipping nonetheless. As abruptly as the thick underbrush had enveloped them, it disappeared. They sensed, more than saw, a swathe of greenery ahead of them. Samaludin spread his partouk on the ground and indicated that this was where they would spend the night.

The mosquitoes at these lower elevations bit ferociously and Robert found himself wishing they were back in the high country, even if it meant enduring the cold. He and Simone sprawled on their blankets and covered their heads with their jackets. They were fatigued enough to fall into a dead sleep, awakening to the morning light with mosquitoes swarming around them. Their hands, which had been exposed to the insects, were swollen with bites and itching, but their faces for the most part had been spared.

They each took a few swallows of the water remaining in Robert's bottle and finished the remains of their naan. They were still hungry and thirsty.

Samaludin stood and motioned for them to follow him along an irrigation ditch which ran the length of a fertile valley. Robert and Simone trudged along behind their guide, sweat running down their faces as the sun rose. The last wisps of mist hovering over the valley disappeared and the ground ahead of them became a smudge of unbroken green. The few Afghans they saw in the fields were intent upon their work and ignored them.

"I'm so hungry," Simone said, after they'd been walking for several hours.

Samaludin, Robert saw, had understood. He pointed at his stomach, then directly ahead of them. What Robert had thought was a mound of earth in the distance was a mud-walled hut. A wooden door, the last vestiges of its blue paint peeling away, faced to the south. Robert hadn't noticed it as they approached. Goats browsed along the boundary between the house's dirt yard and a neighboring fruit orchard. On one side of the hovel, a small fire burned beneath a blackened kettle. Along the eastern wall of the house a *chapakat*, a simple frame bed covered with thin cushions, was set up. Samaludin held up his hand, signaling for them to wait, then rapped on the door. A white-bearded, turbaned Afghan leaning on a gnarled walking stick opened the door. Without dropping his stick, he took the young man's hands in his, murmuring greetings in Pashto. The exposed skin of the old man's face, wrinkled and tanned the color of saddle leather, was blotched with dark age spots. Robert thought he was the oldest Afghan he'd seen during their travels, eighty at least, perhaps older. The two men spoke for several minutes, and the old man looked at them with his watery blue eyes. The only word Robert understood was *feringhi,* foreigners. Samaludin turned and gestured for them to approach. "Grandfather," he said, in halting, heavily accented English.

The old man shook Robert's hand but drew back startled when Simone offered her hand.

"I should have known better," she said softly, taking upon herself the blame for the Afghan's seeming rudeness.

Samaludin pointed inside the hut. Relieved to get out of the midday sun, Robert and Simone entered the dark, mud-walled room. The old man lit a kerosene lamp. He peered at the foreigners in the murky light and pointed to the cushions along the wall.

Samaludin left the house, returning with a brass tray bearing bowls of a fatty stew and metal cups filled with sweetened black tea. The old man offered them naan he'd wrapped in an old faded cloth. To Robert and Simone, it was a feast. After they'd eaten, Salamudin explained to them with gestures that he was leaving, but that they should remain with his grandfather.

"What do you think is happening?" Simone asked.

"Maybe he's trying to work something out to get us across."

"It will be very dangerous."

"Everything in this country is dangerous."

She nodded.

The old man picked up his walking stick and hobbled outside. Robert and Simone waited a few minutes, then stepped through the door, blinking in the bright sunlight. The old man was lying on his primitive bed, oblivious to the bees crawling on his long shirt. Simone headed off into a patch of tall grass and Robert went in the opposite direction, looking for some cover to relieve himself.

Afterward, they sat in the darkened interior of the hut, dozing on and off, lost in thought. The old man brought them tea again, then disappeared outside.

Robert leaned against a cushion, his fingers playing with the pouch around his neck.

"I have Jean's passport," he said, suddenly remembering.

Simone looked at him, her confusion apparent even in the dim light.

"I took his neck pouch when we had to leave him. I didn't want the Russians to know he was a foreigner and I thought if they caught us, I might be able to pretend I was French."

"Your French is good, but . . . ."

"But not good enough?" He smiled.

"To fool the Russians, yes. But you don't look like Jean. You are much older."

"I thought that with the beard . . ." His hand went instinctively to his face. After weeks without shaving, his beard felt rough and thick.

"Your beard is all gray, Robert."

"Oh." He hadn't seen himself in a mirror since leaving Pakistan. Again he ran his fingers over his beard, as if by touch he could discern the color. His fingertips touched the gouge on his right cheek, still tender.

"But I'm glad you have his passport. I will give it to Jean's parents."

"I have his traveler's checks, too, and this." He opened his pouch and handed her the photograph of Jean and his parents.

Simone began to cry as she moved closer to the lamp to study the photo. "I will see that they get this, too."

"I'll hold on to everything until we get across the border." If we make it across, he thought, keeping his doubts to himself.

"We will make it across," Simone said, as if reading his mind.

"I wish we knew when Samaludin was coming back."

"I think now of all those months in Peshawar," said Simone. "I thought of studying Pashto, but I was always too busy."

Robert laughed. "In the hospital where I worked, I gave lectures to the staff, and twice a week I gave them an English class. I should have asked them for a class in Pashto."

The afternoon dragged on. Robert knew by Simone's slow, steady breathing that she'd fallen asleep. He stepped outside and looked around, wondering where the old man had gone. And then he saw him off to one side of the house, his partouk spread on the ground. He was on his knees, his forehead touching the ground as he prayed.

Robert contemplated the timeless scene. He envied the old man his faith. It was one of the strengths of the Afghans. Since everything was preordained, determined by Allah, one could be philosophical. Like Alexander and Genghis Khan and the British, the Russians were just one in a line of invaders, and like the others, they, too, would be repulsed, *inshallah*.

Robert sat in the old man's orchard, his back against a fruit tree, its branches not yet weighted down by the unripe apples, and watched the Afghan push himself to his feet, fold his partouk, and head back to his chapakat.
He wished he could ask him whether Samaludin was going to return or if someone else was going to lead them to the border. Maybe I should begin thinking more like a Muslim, he said to himself. Whatever happens is already written in the book of a man's life.

He leaned his head back against the tree and stared at the mountains of the Hindu Kush to the north. The setting sun glinted off the snow near their summits. The mountains changed color as the sun went down. For the first time in a long while he allowed his thoughts to drift back to America, a land now so distant in his memory that it seemed he had lived there in another lifetime. He thought of Davey, who'd probably been told that his father was never coming back. Alyssa, caught up in her relationship with Mike Finkel, was no doubt insinuating Mike into Davey's life, wanting the boy to accept Mike as his surrogate father. That thought would have made him furious a few months ago. Now he examined it objectively. If Alyssa believed he was dead, wasn't it a rational response? He wondered if, deep down, Alyssa would resent him if he were to return. It would disrupt the new reality she was creating. And if the shoe were on the other foot, if Davey lived with Robert and he was in a new relationship, say with Lynn, and Alyssa was suddenly reported to have been killed, wouldn't he be upset if she were to suddenly reappear?

Strange, he thought, how I can calmly sit here and think about all this. He wondered, too, how Lynn was reacting to the reports of his death. Was she close enough to him to truly mourn his passing? Or would she simply get on with her life, thinking of him occasionally when she looked at Josh and remembered the resemblance to his natural father?

His parents, in a way, concerned him the most. They were old people and he was sure they'd been devastated when they were contacted. He'd never in his life wished for a sibling—until now. If only there were another child to comfort them in their grief. Robert seldom examined his relationship with them. They'd always been there as a part of his life, but they were also something apart, a unit unto themselves, closer to each other than they'd ever been to him. They had never been overt in their affection for him, but there had never been anything cold or hostile either. Not even in his teenaged years. No matter how much time passed without his seeing them, when he did visit it was always comfortable. And, he believed, they really did look forward to his visits, when he brought Davey to see them. The overt demonstrations of love they'd never been able to show Robert as a child came easier to them when they were with their grandson. Another of life's mysteries. He wished there was some way he could let them know that he was alive. Perhaps they sensed it. It was all he could hope for in his present situation.

He was surprised to find Simone standing next to him. "I was daydreaming," he said. "Have you been here long?"

"No. I must have fallen asleep." She, too, stared at the distant mountains, mesmerized by their beauty.

"Well, no sign of Samaludin," he said.

Simone shrugged her shoulders. "He will come tonight, or he won't."

Was she also adopting the Afghans' resignation? he wondered.

"May I sit next to you?" she asked.

"Of course. I was just thinking that you and I are becoming very philosophical about things."

She glanced at him, almost coyly, and smiled. "We don't have much choice, *n'cest pas?*"

"I guess not."

"I dreamed of Jean again."

"Yes?"

"It is so strange. I loved him always as I would a brother, not in a romantic way. You understand, yes? But in my dream, I saw him coming toward me and I had my arms open to receive him, as I would a lover, not a brother. It was very confusing. And then I woke up before I could take him in my arms."

For a few moments Robert said nothing. He was aware that Simone was watching him.

"Maybe," he said, trying to put his thoughts into words, "maybe the relationship, being a brother or a lover, is not what the dream was about. Perhaps, it was just trying to embrace something that's been lost, a part of your life that's gone now. Do you understand what I'm trying to say?"

She nodded. "Yes. I believe you may be right."

"Have you thought much of home since you've been in Pakistan and Afghanistan?"

"No. Have you?"

"No, I haven't. I thought it was just me. It's as if this part of the world has suddenly become my only reality."

"I think perhaps it is because we are living so intensely." She looked at him earnestly. "Every morning now I wake up with the same thought. This may be my last day on earth. A Russian helicopter or a bomber may come and poof, *finis.*" She laughed. "Then I say to myself, you don't really believe that. There will be a tomorrow. And some day you will be across the border."

They sat together until the old man began puttering around his ancient grill and the mosquitoes, whining around their heads, drove them back inside.

"It's been such a quiet day," Simone said.

"You sound regretful. Maybe you'd liked to be strafed by a Russian gunship?"

"Strafed?"

"You know, shot at?"

"No, I much prefer this peaceful quiet. I think it must be unusual in this country."

The door opened, letting in the fading light of dusk, and they were surprised to see Samaludin peering in at them. He carried a tray with rice and chunks of mutton. His grandfather followed him with flatbread and tea.

Simone and Robert watched Samaludin expectantly. Robert sensed the Afghan was as frustrated as they were by his inability to communicate with them.

They ate in silence, Samaludin exchanging a few words with the old man, who nodded.

After dinner, Samaludin got abruptly to his feet and gestured to them to follow him. They stepped outside into the darkness and by the light of the moon, Robert and Simone saw Samaludin smile at them. They heard him whisper the word they'd been waiting for.

"Pakistan," he said.

They followed him along the same irrigation ditch that had led them to the old man's house, now lost in the darkness behind them. After an hour's walking, the sound of truck engines grew louder and the soft glow of lights appeared ahead. They left the irrigation canal and followed a dirt road that led them to a large warehouse with crates stacked outside. Three trucks, their low beams on and engines running, were parked at the rear of the building. The choking smell of diesel fumes filled the air. Turbaned figures were loading boxes of fruit and produce onto a truck. A ferocious-looking, black-bearded Afghan approached them. He nodded at Samaludin and studied the two foreigners appraisingly. He handed Simone a folded burqa of pale blue rayon. Samaludin gestured for her to put it on. "Wife," he said, pointing to the black-bearded Afghan.

"I think that would be an experience," Simone said, looking at Robert. She slipped the burqa over her head and was immediately transformed into an Afghan woman.

"At least you'll be safe in that," Robert said.

"Unless they talk to me."

"I'm sure your new husband will do the talking for you," Robert smiled.

"What about you? Are they going to put you in a burqa, too?"

Samaludin took his arm and pointed into the back of a truck. Half of the available space was already loaded with melons. A rectangular opening in the center of the cargo area floor concealed a double floor with a space that Robert estimated to be no more than fourteen inches high. With the amount of opium smuggled across the Afghan-Pakistan border, he had no doubt what the space was used for. A thick wooden cover had been pushed to one side of the opening. Samaludin pointed at the opening, then at him.

"Jesus!"

"What is it, Robert?" Simone asked, stepping next to him.

"They want me to hide in that space."

She turned and looked at the crates of melons and lemons piled up behind them, waiting to be loaded.

"You'll be covered with those. No one will find you."

"But what if the wood can't sustain the weight of those crates. That's a hell of a way to go. Crushed by melons."

Samaludin pushed at him, gesturing for him to hurry. He indicated Simone should climb up on the passenger side of the cab.

"See you in Pakistan," she said, her voice muffled by the tentlike garment.

"I hope so," he said, hoisting himself into the truck and maneuvering his body into the cramped space beneath the cargo floor. He tilted his head to one side, fearful that the cover would compress his face. He was relieved to discover he could move his arms and legs. As he did so, his fingers touched small slots in the floor upon which he lay. Air vents, he thought, as the odor of diesel fumes filled his narrow compartment. The cover was fitted into place with a thud, leaving him in total darkness. Thank God I'm not claustrophobic, he thought. More pounding noises came from above, and the wooden floor on top of him shook as the remaining crates were loaded. Before he had too much time to worry about asphyxiating on diesel fumes beneath tons of Afghan produce, the truck began to move, lurching its way over rough ground before picking up a little speed as they reached the paved road. The floor beneath him vibrated and the diesel odor began to dissipate, replaced now by the strong smell of lemons. He thought of Simone sitting in the cab next to the driver and wondered if she was frightened. Tough though she was, how could she not be? All he had to worry about was being crushed to death, but Simone would actually have to confront the enemy. The Russians only posted Afghans sympathetic to their cause at the border, and that was where, he assumed, they were headed. Ironically, beneath that hideous garment that represented the suppression of Afghan women, she was safer than she'd be in a suit of armor.

The truck slowed and the vibrations increased as it sat idling. It moved again, then stopped, repeating the process several times. We must be in line at the border, he thought.

He heard noise from the rear of the truck, then muffled voices, and knew they were inspecting the cargo.

The voices grew louder, then subsided. The diesel odor almost gagged him as the truck idled. Robert's anxiety increased. What if he coughed? Or panicked because he couldn't breathe? He tried not to think, to disassociate himself from the reality of his situation. He suddenly visualized Samaludin's grandfather kneeling on the ground as he prayed. The old man's total commitment to his god, a god more real to him than his life on earth, was strangely comforting to Robert.

Finally, they were moving again, the truck laboring on an uphill grade. The roar of the engine grew louder. He remembered looking down from the Khyber Rifles fort onto this same steep grade, watching the trucks from Afghanistan entering Pakistan. They must be across the border. They were safe. We must be passing the fort, he thought, and longed to be having a cup of tea with Major Tuma. He knew there was no way for him to escape his prison until the truck reached its destination, probably a market terminal in Peshawar. Only then, when the truck's cargo had been unloaded, would they release him. He tried not to think of the miles they'd still have to cover as they descended from the Khyber Pass. Perhaps he wasn't as safe as he thought. Anything could happen—an accident on the road, Afridi brigands attempting to rob the truck, or a mechanical breakdown before reaching Peshawar. The thought of the truck baking in the broiling sun was too hideous to contemplate.

Everything, he decided, was out of his hands. Like Samaludin's grandfather, he would have to place his trust in a greater power.

35

Robert and Simone were indistinguishable from any other Afghans as they walked through the bazaars of Peshawar shortly before dawn, Robert, bearded, wearing a Chitrali cap and a shalwar kameez that was filthy enough to be embarrassing, and Simone, swathed in her blue burqa. Merchants opening their stalls didn't raise their eyes to look at them.

Their truck driver had stopped at a large warehouse near the central market to unload the crates. Simone had waited in the truck's cab until the cargo had been removed, then climbed out to join the driver as he lifted the floor cover. Robert had sat up and the driver extended his hand to pull him upright.

"How are you?" Simone asked.

"Stiff," he said, rolling his head around. "Hell of a way to travel. We're in Peshawar?"

"By the central market."

They turned to thank the driver but he'd already walked away, disappearing into the warehouse.

"We never get to thank anybody," Robert said. "Abdur, Jamakhar, Samaludin, the old man, the truck driver—they saved our lives and we're never able to express our gratitude."

"What was the word Abdur used? *Melmestia?* These Pathans do not expect gratitude, Robert. It is their way, remember?"

A garishly painted Pakistani bus blew its horn at them as they stepped off a curb.

"Home sweet home," Robert said, as they entered the mayhem of a new day in Peshawar.

They threaded their way between trucks, buses, and donkeys, becoming a part of the throng in the bazaar until they were able to make their way back to a main street. The municipal hospital loomed up in the early morning light as they arrived at a major intersection.

"There were times I thought I'd never see all this again," Simone said. "The Medicins sans Frontieres office is down this street."

They stood there looking at one another, not knowing what to say.

"Here, let me give you this," Robert said. He removed his neck pouch and fished out Jean's passport, traveler's checks, and photograph.

Simone's hand was trembling as she took them from him.

"Will you stay on in Peshawar?"

"I can't, not after what happened to Jean. I must try to comfort his parents. I'm going to request a transfer back to France. And you?"

"I have to go back to the States. I should have been back weeks ago."

"Then this is goodbye, isn't it?"

"Maybe we'll meet one day in Carpentras." Robert felt they should embrace or at least shake hands, but the burqa remained a wall between them.

"Adieu, Robert. I will never forget you," she said.

He watched her as she walked away, a shapeless tent swallowed up almost immediately in a crowd of burqa-clad women. Strange, Robert thought. They'd been together for weeks, often in imminent danger of death, yet he felt as if he barely knew her. What he did know was that she was the bravest woman he'd ever met.

Robert turned into Sean and Samantha's street, wondering if it was too early to go to their house. What he really wanted to do was head to his old room, shower, and change out of his filthy clothes, but he no longer had his key. He stopped in front of the gated entrance at Sean's and stared into the courtyard, deserted except for sparrows hopping on the pavement. The chowkidar, whom Robert recognized, came around the side of the building and headed toward him.

He spoke to Robert in Urdu.

"I don't understand," Robert said. "I'm Doctor Morgen."

The chowkidar stared at him, suspiciously at first, then in amazement as he recognized the American doctor behind the beard. He opened the gate and walked with Robert toward the front door, turning frequently to look at him as if trying to reassure himself that it truly was the American.

He rapped gently on the door and Samantha, in her robe, opened it. She looked at the chowkidar, who was speechless, then at Robert. As she recognized Robert, her hand flew up to her mouth.

"Robert!" she said.

Sean appeared behind her in a tee shirt and running shorts, his hair tousled. He, too, stared at Robert as if seeing an apparition.

"Robert? Is it you?"

"I'm back," Robert said, feeling foolish at the banality of his words and embarrassed by their scrutiny.

Sean stepped past Samantha and embraced him. "We thought you were dead. Look at you. You're skin and bones, man. And you look like an Afghan."

Samantha, too, put her arms around him and began to cry. "Robert, you're alive," she said. She ran her finger along the gouge in his cheek and shook her head. "What happened to you?"

"Come inside," Sean said.

"I'm so dirty," Robert said. "I need a shower and a change of clothes. I thought I'd go back to my room if it's still available."

"I'll get you the key. And as soon as you're done, come back. We'll have a good breakfast for you. You look like you can use some food."

His suitcase was sitting on the floor, exactly where he'd left it. He set the bag on the bed and pulled out clean clothes. He peeled off his grimy Afghan garments, dropping them on the floor as he headed for the bathroom. The person staring back at him in the bathroom mirror was a stranger, a gray-bearded man, his face bronzed by the sun, who looked ten years older than Robert remembered himself. The furrow made by the bullet in his cheek was deeper than he'd imagined it, the scar tissue an angry red color. He had no idea how much weight he'd lost, but every one of his ribs was visible.

Robert closed his eyes in ecstasy as he stood under the shower. The water running off his body was gray. He toweled himself dry and stared at his face in the mirror. He debated shaving his full beard. It was too much of a chore. Sean had mentioned breakfast and he was starving.

"You're beginning to look human," Sean said as he opened the door.

"God, it smells so good in here," Robert said as he entered the dining room and took a seat at the table.

Samantha placed a plate of scrambled eggs and toast in front of him. "Juice and coffee are on the table," she said.

"I'd forgotten what breakfast was. It's wonderful to be home. That's what this feels like to me."

"Dig in," Sean said, as Samantha set their plates on the table. "There's plenty more."

Robert needed no invitation. He cleaned his plate and sheepishly asked for seconds. "You heard about the ambush then?" he said.

"A few days after it happened," Sean said. "A mujahideen from the village where you were headed made it across the border and said everyone in the convoy, including the foreigners, had been killed."

"Simone and I were the only survivors. Jean, the French doctor, was killed."

"Terrible. And you lost all your supplies?"

"Everything. The Russians must have been tipped off. They were waiting for us on the trail at night."

"You got that during the ambush?" Sean asked, pointing at his cheek. Robert nodded.

"You were very lucky, Robert," Samantha said.

"And you made it back to Pakistan by yourselves?" Sean said.

"So many people helped us. Mujahideen and ordinary Afghans. We were so fortunate. I'll never forget any of them."

"You must have gone through hell," Samantha said.

"I wouldn't want to do it again. Did you really think I was dead?"

"The American consul put in a request to the Russians for your body," Sean said. "And since it happened, the Pakistanis are cracking down on foreigners trying to cross into Afghanistan."

"I wonder if anyone back home thinks—"

"The consul asked me who you'd listed as next of kin. I gave him your parents' names and address."

"Jesus!"

"I'm sorry, Robert. We really believed you were dead."

"I'll have to try to get a call through to them."

"Give me the number. I'll place the call for you."

Emily Morgen shrieked and began to cry when she heard her son's voice. Robert's father quickly came on the phone, not knowing what had given his wife such a shock.

"Dad, I'm alive. Is Mom okay?"

"It's really you, Robert? We got a call from Washington telling us you'd been killed in Afghanistan."

"I'm all right. You didn't tell Davey I was dead, did you?"

"Your mother called Alyssa. We felt we had to."

Robert closed his eyes and shook his head. What a mess this had turned out to be.

"Dad, listen. Call them right away and tell Davey you spoke to me. Tell him I'm okay and I'll be back to see him soon. Let me talk to Mom again."

"Oh, Robert, Robert," she said, still crying.

Robert couldn't recall ever seeing or hearing his mother cry. It pained him to be the cause of it.

"When will you be home?" she asked.

"As soon as I can. I told dad to tell Davey I'm okay. The poor kid must have been so upset."

"Alyssa never called us back after I spoke to her. I tried to talk to her again but some man always answered."

She didn't waste any time moving Mike in, Robert thought.

"One more thing, Mom. Please write this number down. Call the doctor who's covering my practice in Vermont. His name is Doctor Jones. Tell him you've heard from me and that I hope to be back within a week or so, as soon as I can get my flight arranged."

"You must have given your parents a fright," Samantha said when he returned to the kitchen.

"I feel terrible for having put people through this."

"It's not your fault," Sean said. He laughed. "And I'm sure they forgive you."

"I haven't even asked about the hospital," Robert said. "Is everything going all right?"

"Yes, fine. Our volunteer will be with us for another week. Normally he'd be here for breakfast, but this is his week at the refugee camps. One of my associates took him down to Kohat."

"I'm sure you'd like to catch up on some rest today," Sean said. "Why don't you walk over to the office with me after breakfast and we'll get your flight to the States worked out. I imagine you're anxious to get back. Perhaps later, when you're up to it, you'll drop by the hospital. I'll let Doctor Mojarri know you're back with us, but I know all the doctors and nurses will want to see you. They were devastated when they received news of the ambush."

"At dinner this evening you can tell us more about your adventures," Samantha said.

"I will."

Rest was out of the question for Robert on that first day back. The staff at the Afghan Women's Hospital surrounded him, their customary reserve buried beneath their joyful relief at finding that he was alive. Anxious for news about their country, they bombarded him with questions about his experiences across the border, their patients in the clinic forgotten for the moment. Robert realized what a schizophrenic existence the Afghan doctors and nurses were living— they lived and worked in Pakistan, but their hearts and souls remained in Afghanistan. Doctor Mojarri ordered the hospital cooks to prepare a special lunch to celebrate Doctor Morgen's return. It was late in the afternoon when Robert left the hospital and returned to Sean's office to see what progress had been made on his tickets.

"We'll have you out of here in two days," Sean said. "PIA to Karachi, Lufthansa the rest of the way. You'll be in New York in four days."

Robert was on the verge of asking Sean if he could place a call to his son, but decided it would be too much of an imposition. He'd rely on his parents to tell Davey. What about Lynn? he asked himself. He wondered if Mike had passed along the news about his death. And if he had, would he also let her know that he was alive? He regretted not having asked his parents to call her. Perhaps he'd be able to reach her from Frankfort Airport.

By the time Robert returned to his room, it was almost time for dinner at Sean's. He sat down on his bed, suddenly overcome by fatigue. He knew if he put himself in a horizontal position, he'd be asleep in an instant.

So it's all coming to an end, he thought. He'd been away two and a half months, a time in which he felt so removed from America it might as well have been two and a half years. For six weeks he'd focused entirely on the health problems of Afghan women, problems that would never be solved without a cultural change. And then for another month he'd had to concentrate on his own survival in Afghanistan, something the Afghans who remained in the country had to do every day of their lives. Now, he'd be slipping out of the life that had become his reality, shedding it as easily as a snake sheds its skin. How many desperate Afghans wished they had that option?

But what am I returning to? he wondered. His son certainly. His parents. Lynn possibly. The people he loved were in America and he'd be going back to them. But the irony of the situation was unmistakable. Before Peshawar the practice of medicine had never fulfilled him. Here it was his life's work, his passion, and he'd be leaving it behind. He knew he couldn't recapture the intensity and fulfillment in an office in Vermont. That much was certain then. He'd had his fill of private practice. And what about Vermont? That, too, he knew was coming to an end. Davey lived with Alyssa, at least for the present, and he couldn't pretend otherwise. The only way to remain a major part of Davey's life was to be closer. Where that would be remained to be decided. And then there was the issue of money—he had to support himself and contribute to Davey's support. So not only would he have to figure out where, but how. The children's' books he was collaborating on with Lynn might provide an answer, at least initially. But he had to be honest and ask himself whether those initial sales had been a fluke. Did he really have what it takes to be an author?

"So many questions," he said aloud, pushing himself to his feet. Does everything get answered with time? he wondered. That was something he'd have to find out. If he'd learned anything in Afghanistan, perhaps it was to take life one day at a time. For who knows if there'll be a next day?

He hobbled with fatigue into the bathroom and splashed cold water on his face, the face that would take some getting used to.